Much Ado

About Russian

The Fair Hero Series

Book One

Kerry Rockwood White

Cover photograph ©iStockphoto.com/101 Dalmatians

KRW Designs Publishing
PO Box 850731
Braintree, MA 02185
Info@fairheroseries.com

ISBN-10 0-9835923-0-6

ISBN-13 9780983592303

Printed in the United States of America

First Edition

14 13 12 11 10 / 10 9 8 7 6 5 4 3 2 1

To Mom.

For all the things you taught me,

but especially for teaching me to love to read.

I love you and miss you dearly.

The Obligatory and Not-So-Obligatory Thanks

With every endeavor such as this, there are always so many people one must thank. Now, I don't mean that in a bad way, or that being obliged to thank someone is in any way negative. Not at all. If I didn't have these people to thank there would be no book at all. So, without further to-do; the Thanks.

Thank you to my wonderful husband Danny, for believing in me and supporting me and making me laugh. You're the best, baby! To Carol R. who was my first reader and critic. Without Carol there really wouldn't have been a book. You are such a great friend Carol! To my editor Cathy aka Bit. You're a doll and I don't know what I would have done without you. For all of my friends, on line and off line, who lent their support, their eyes, their criticisms, ideas, who helped promote and spread the word and kept me positive and laughing when I needed it. Shazzy, Kirsten, Nia, Lisa T, Gloria, Amy F., Nifer, Michele K, Michelle H., Susanne Z, Mia S, Tracey A, Jude K, Stacy L., Maria G., Pam, Tabz and so many others. For Simon S. and Trev and others for their feedback and inspiration during my cover art crisis. Forgive me for not naming everybody by name but that could fill up quite a few pages. I'm blessed with great friends and I'm very thankful for each and every one of them.

Also, thank you to my sister Julie for her support, for knowing just what I needed to hear when I needed to hear it and for having faith in my ability to succeed. And thank you to the rest of my family and friends for their support and assistance with the publication and promotion of this book. It is all greatly appreciated.

NOTE: Those who know me will note that Hero's friends all seem to share the same names as some of my dearest friends. That's no accident. I did this as a way of thanking these people for being my friends; for being there and being an important part of my life over the years. But other than the names, there is no similarity between the friends I have and the friends Hero has. In no way, shape or form are these depictions meant to actually represent my friends.

CHAPTER 1

If you are reading this page it's probably for one of three reasons. You love vampire stories and you bought my book. Someone you know shares your interest in vampires and has lent you this book. You've picked up this book in a book store and are browsing before buying.

If it's the first reason, thank you. If it's the second reason, please buy your own copy and give this back to your friend. They're sure to miss it. If it's reason three, don't hesitate, just bring this up to the register and buy it.

I'm not proud. I need the money. We aren't all Anne Rice with million dollar contracts. OK, so enough with the shameless begging. (By the way, this book makes a great gift! Buy one for all your friends and relatives).

On to what you're really here for, a vampire story and boy oh, boy, do I have a vampire story for you!

I am an expert in the field of dating vampires. All right, I'm a self-proclaimed expert, but really, it's not like you can look in the Yellow Pages for this kind of thing. If someone told me a year ago that I would be an expert in dating vampires I would have told them to check their medication! It's quite possible that you're thinking that about me right now. I wouldn't blame you. After all, we're told that vampires and werewolves and boogie men are all just make believe, right? They make great stories for the movies and novels and scary tales around the campfire, but they don't really exist.

Yeah, that's what I used to think, and I'll be honest with you, the jury's still out on whether I was happier before I knew the truth or now that I have been initiated in the 'dark side'. (Is it just me, or whenever anyone mentions the 'dark side', do you hear the raspy breathing of James Earl Jones in your mind?)

It all began just one year ago. The night before my 30th birthday. A bunch of my friends had taken me out to a club in Boston to celebrate my turning the big three-oh. Actually, it was the day before my birthday because it happened to fall on a Sunday that year, and who wants to go out and get drunk on a Sunday? That was a rhetorical question; but those of you who answered in the affirmative, you may want to check listings for local AA meetings. I'm just saying.

So, there I was with Susan, Amy, Debbie, Carol, Kelly and the rest of the faithful few who have been my friends for a large part of my life. This particular club had been chosen because some friend's brother's girlfriend's cousin or something or other of Carol's was the keyboard player in the band performing that night. It was a pretty good band too, though don't ask me their name. I never remember stuff like that. They played the usual assortment of favorites that drunken crowds love to dance to, and threw in a few unexpected gems. Any group of guys in their early twenties who have the guts to play The Partridge Family's "I Think I Love You" to a club full of people in various states of inebriation are just great, in my humble opinion. Plus, any song that invites the paying customers to join along at the top of their lungs in a cacophony of off-key singing is a good thing.

There we were, a group of women all around the dreaded age of 30, drunk, sweaty and silly, singing along as happy as clams. I was wearing a black leather skirt that came just above my knees, and I have to tell you that I was pretty pleased with myself that at 30 a black leather skirt still looked mighty good on me. I also wore matching black leather spiked heels, sheer black pantyhose and a bright red silk blouse. A silly choice to wear to a crowded bar, really, but after all, it was my birthday celebration. My dark brown hair was pulled back at the sides and the back hung loose. I'd considered cutting my hair now that I was entering my 30s, but I just haven't been able to take that plunge. All in all, I felt I was looking pretty hot, even if I did say so myself. Now all I needed was some attractive, single and not-too-drunk guy to ask me to dance, or offer to buy me a drink, and my night would be a total success. Ever the eternal optimist.

The night wore on and we were all having a great time. Kelly had generously volunteered to be our designated driver. She had stopped drinking rum and cokes and was sipping coffee in order to be sober by last call. Good old Kelly! The rest of us were noisily making toasts to God-only-knows-what as we prepared to down another round of shots. Each round of shots that night had been different. Probably not a good idea to be mixing all those different liquors, but, as I'm sure you know all too well, drunken women hell bent on celebrating something special with one of their own do not always exercise the best judgment. This round was a shot called a Sugar Baby, and it really did taste like the candy. Excellent call by Carol. Kelly raised her coffee mug with us and had a good laugh at our expense, no doubt savoring the inevitable stories of the world class hangovers we would all have the next morning. And then, it happened.

The band played "Sweet Caroline" and the crowd went nuts. Everyone was hooting and hollering (yes, we've been known to hoot and holler up North) and making quite a ruckus. It's amazing anyone could actually hear the band. Now, I have to admit, I have no idea why "Sweet Caroline" is associated with the Boston Red Sox or why it became such a big thing. All I know is that it did and like any good New Englander, I sing along, loud and proud, whenever the opportunity strikes. A word of warning for anyone visiting the Boston area, if you are in a club or a bar or even at a party where this song is played, don't worry, you are perfectly safe and the people around you are not going insane. We just like our rituals and get into them whole heartedly. Which reminds me, the same goes for "Charlie of the MTA," especially at St. Patrick's Day. I haven't any clue how that song became associated with St. Patrick's Day, but I don't question these things. I just adhere to the traditions.

While all the rest of the bar was gleefully participating in this Neil Diamond tradition, I noticed a dark haired man sitting at a table by himself who was looking at the crowd as though we were all some other species. As we chanted "So good, so good, so good," punctuated by thrusting our fists into the air, the man's eyes widened a bit and he looked as though he didn't know if he should laugh at us or check for the nearest exit. Obviously a tourist. He caught me watching him. He was handsome. I found myself wondering what color his eyes were and what he would look like when he smiled. Testing the waters, I ventured a little smile and, to my satisfaction, he smiled back. It was a nice smile too.

When the song ended, I boldly walked up to his table and sat down. Ah, the sheer raw nerve acquired by heavy drinking. "You're not from around here," I stated as I pulled my chair in.

He laughed a little. "That obvious, huh?" I raised my eyebrows in response. "What's the deal with that song?"

"It's sort of an anthem for the Boston Red Sox," I replied.

He looked puzzled. After a moment he asked, "What does that song have to do with baseball?"

"Nothing. It's just one of those things." He didn't look convinced. "Where are you from?" I asked.

"Lots of places," he replied cryptically. Not a good sign. I changed tactics.

"So, what's your name?"

"Kin," he said, emphasizing the 'I' and holding out his hand for me to shake. "You?"

The dreaded moment. "Hero," I said with a sigh, reaching to shake his hand.

"Hero?" he asked, just as surprised as everyone else in the world when they hear my name.

Feeling saucy, I thrust my hand on my hip and replied "Kin?" with raised eyebrows and a little jiggle of my head.

Kin laughed and looked down at his bottle of water. Funny, I hadn't noticed until just then that he was drinking a bottle of Poland Springs. "It's short for Kinley. Family name." He raised his head and met my gaze, waiting for my explanation.

"My dad's an English Lit professor. He loves Shakespeare and "Much Ado About Nothing" is his favorite play, so…," I let the sentence drift off. A good test to see if he was well educated.

"Ah, yes. Fair Hero. I bet you wish he'd named you Beatrice instead," he answered back with a smile. Bingo! The man knew his Shakespeare. Although I often used this test, I never could decide if it was a good thing or not that the guy was into Shakespeare. I mean, after all, my dad named me Hero!

"Yeah, it's come up." I found myself wishing I had a drink in front of me, but since his bottle was pretty full, I didn't know how to gracefully bring up the subject.

"It's a funny coincidence. Our names, I mean," Kin said.

"What do you mean?" I asked.

"Well, my name, Kinley. It means 'fair hero'."

"Get out! It does not!" I exclaimed. I can certainly say no one's ever tried a line like that before. Corny, but original at least.

"Seriously. Google it sometime. That's what my name means. Honest." He chuckled and held his hands up as though being sworn in.

I was definitely going to be Googling that. I just responded with a little chuckle. The conversation seemed like it was going to lapse. But then, "Do you have any siblings?" Kin asked.

That was unexpected. "Uh, yeah. I've got an older brother."

"What's his name?"

"William, of course," I answered.

"Ah. I was kind of hoping for your sake it was Hamlet or something."

Nice! Good sense of humor. The points were accumulating. "Unfortunately for me, no. Though I do call him 'Willie' sometimes, which really irritates him."

I noticed he was looking past me with a very amused expression. Glancing over my shoulder, I saw my friends all clustered together across their table and shamelessly watching Kin and me. Susan actually wiggled her fingers at him when she caught him looking back at them. I'd have to slap her later.

"Ah, perhaps we should dance?" Kin suggested with a smile.

And as the Fates also seemed to be smiling on me at the moment, the band began playing "Every Breath You Take." Kin stood and held out his hand for me. I took it and we walked to the dance floor, carefully avoiding looking at my friends along the way. He took me in his arms and I noticed for the first time that he was very broad shouldered and tall. Well, tall for me. I'm only five foot four inches tall. Kin had to be six two at least. Very glad I was wearing my spiked heels.

Now, I don't have to tell you ladies that when you meet a guy at a club and he asks you for a slow dance that it is usually awkward and weird, at least at first. All set for that awkward moment, I looked up at him, ready to give my typical "Gee, isn't this awkward" grin, but instead I looked up and was taken by surprise that his eyes were very, very green. Greener than I'd ever seen. And while I was at it, I also noticed how strong his jaw was, and how full his lips were, and how smooth his skin looked. Oh, damn! He noticed my unexpected inventory of his finer physical traits. I should have been annoyed at his expression, but the little lopsided smirk only made him look sexier. Just what I needed. A whole new embarrassing version of the awkward first dance. Lucky, lucky me!

Too embarrassed to do anything else, I rested my head on his shoulder, well, in the general vicinity of his shoulder, and prayed that I hadn't made as big a fool of myself as I feared. Kin tightened his hold slightly, but kept one hand at the small of my back and the other holding my hand against his chest. A gentleman! This guy was getting too good to be true. Boy, I must be really, really drunk, or else there was something fundamentally wrong that he was good at hiding. He was married. He was gay, but in denial. He was a commitment-phobe. He was a serial killer. I have a vivid imagination, but even I didn't imagine the bombshell that would eventually explode in my little universe.

The song ended and we parted slowly, that sexy little smirk still plastered on Kin's handsome face. I wanted to be offended, but I couldn't help myself. I laughed instead. He led me back to my friends. They were like sharks swarming at the scent of blood. It was comical the way they pushed each other, clamoring for the best position to get a good look at the guy who'd been occupying my attention for the last fifteen minutes or so. I actually found myself wishing we would walk right past them and out the door together. My luck had run out. He stopped right in front of them and introduced himself.

"Hi, I'm Kin," he said, addressing the blatantly curious group.

"Nice to meet you, Ken," said Debbie, trying to keep a straight face. I could just imagine all the cute little comments they had amused themselves with while I'd been with Kin and were just waiting to unleash on me the moment he was out of earshot. Hopefully, out of earshot.

"It's Kin, with an 'I'," I explained. Several pair of bloodshot eyes rimmed with smeared eyeliner tried to focus on me. "Kin," I said again. "K - I - N. It's short for Kinley."

"We get it," said Susan, giving me a push on the shoulder.

"Oh. Sorry." Debbie said.

"No problem. Happens all the time," Kin replied with a smile. "Well, umm...," he started, turning towards me. The moment of truth. Do I get the brush off or does he ask for my phone number? "Would it be ok if I called you sometime?" he asked, leaning towards me so he wouldn't have to say it too loudly. Not that it mattered. They knew.

"Um, sure. Ok," I said. Why is it at that moment, no matter how old we get, we suddenly feel fifteen again? Like it's the very first time a guy's ever asked you for a date. Feeling a little self-conscious, I reached for my purse and pulled out one of my business cards. I have my own business, so naturally, I always make sure I take them with me wherever I go.

"Give him one of your business cards," Susan suggested loudly. Right, like she didn't know full well that that was exactly what I was going to do. Note to self: Slap Sue really hard!

I handed Kin the card and explained, "I have my own business and my office is in my home, so you can reach me at that number." I pointed at the phone number on the bottom of the card.

Kin read the card. "A graphic artist. That sounds very interesting."

I shrugged. "I guess. What do you do?" I asked.

"I deal in antiques." Deal in? Hmmm. That could mean a lot of things.

I nodded my head and tried to look very interested. Well, I was interested. But, at the moment, I was more interested in getting him away from my friends who were practically bursting to find some way to interrupt the conversation. "Well, I guess I'll talk to you soon." I hoped that didn't sound as pathetic to him as it did to me.

"I look forward to it," he said, sounding very sincere. "Ladies," he said, addressing my friends with a nod.

"Bye Kin!" they all chirped. I was going to slap all of them. Every last one of them.

Then he walked toward the exit. Just before he walked through the door, he turned and looked back at me and smiled. I smiled too. Why is that romantic? I don't know why, but it is, isn't it? They always do that in movies. The guy has to turn and look back before he leaves. I don't know.

Then came the rapid fire questions. Blah, blah, blah. You know what they were, the standard fare. What did you talk about? Where is he from? What does he do? Does he have any brothers? I filled them all in on what little there was to tell. And it was just a little. We hadn't been together more than twenty minutes tops. Naturally, after being my good friends for so long, they eagerly awaited the news of how he reacted to my name, expecting yet another good laugh at my expense. When I told them what he said about his name meaning 'fair hero', Amy tore into her purse looking for her iPhone so she could pull up Google and have a look. I thought it had been funny watching them all clamor to get close to Kin, but it was nothing compared to watching a gaggle of intoxicated females all jockeying to read a tiny cell phone screen in a dark night club.

Sure enough, Kin had told the truth. A good sign. I found myself looking at my watch, wondering how soon we could leave. It wasn't that I particularly wanted to end my birthday celebration. It was just that now that I had a phone call from Kin to look forward to, I was anxious for it to be tomorrow. Do you ever outgrow that kind of thing? The excited expectancy? I hope not. If you do, please don't write and tell me. I don't want to know.

After a few more drinks and a few more dances, we decided to call it a night. Or at least call an end to the drinking portion of our night. Now it was time for an all-night diner and breakfast food. Ugh! Oh, no! It will be reasonably quiet there and they can ask me even more questions, and I can't pretend that I can't hear them, like I can at the club. Damn my love of home fries!

CHAPTER 2

The great thing about living alone is that there is no one around to tell you to get up, or to comment on how long you stay in bed. If you don't get up until noon, who's to know? Nobody! It's a beautiful thing. Not to mention you can hang out in your PJs or not bother putting on a bra, and there's no one there to mind. I might look forward to the day I'm married and have children of my own, but I'll tell you, right now, getting up early and being dressed and put together is highly over rated. I'll miss being a bum with no one to answer to when the mood strikes. Ah well, got to take the bad with the good I suppose.

Speaking of good and bad; no phone call from Kin yet. Ok, so it's only 2:30 and he probably doesn't want to look eager or whatever, but I can't help myself looking at the clock every two or three minutes and being frustrated at the way time has chosen to crawl at a snail's pace today. Of course, if I want to be a glass-half-full kind of gal, I could say it's a good thing to have the call to look forward to, but that's just a bit too Pollyanna for a 30 year-old woman with a hangover.

What a beautiful day in the neighborhood! Hung-over, looking a frightful mess in a ratty old t-shirt and sweats and hair that looks like I've stuck my finger in a light socket, probably reeking because I haven't managed to drag myself into the shower ('cause what if the phone rang while I was in the shower and I missed Kin's call?); flipping through every channel and all the On Demand guides repeatedly, hoping against hope that somehow the offerings will change and there'll be something worth watching that will help take my mind off of the excruciatingly slow passage of time. Not to mention eating Ring Dings for breakfast because my milk has turned and I forgot to get a new bottle the day before, and therefore can't eat my healthy, fibrous breakfast cereal. And on top of it all, despite it being a beautiful spring day, I've got all my windows closed because, naturally, every guy in the neighborhood feels compelled to mow his lawn, and cut grass gives me vicious sinus headaches. I suppose I should feel flattered that the entire universe is out to get me, but that would just take too much effort and I'm not up to it.

So, I give up and put on a DVD, and since I'm in a vertical position, I decide to get a bottle of Crystal Light and a couple more Advil before getting comfortable on my couch for a dose of Jane Austen. What is it about Jane Austen stories that makes us women feel better? It's not like the heroines don't triumph in just about all romantic stories; but somehow, Jane manages to do it better than most. There's probably a much better explanation than that, but you'll have to look elsewhere for it. Just not in me to be any more philosophical in my present state.

Though, I've got to say, and I hope you'll agree with me; Marianne Dashwood doesn't deserve Col. Brandon. I'm all for a happy ending, and I really love watching Sense and Sensibility, but after all the dozens of times I've watched the movie, and all the times I've read the book, I just can't help wishing that Brandon ended up with a woman who was as completely and passionately in love with him as he was with Marianne. I mean, come on, she settles for him because there's no one else for her. She "learns" to love him. What kind of crap is that? Do any of you want to marry a man you love desperately in the hope that he will eventually "learn" to love you? No way! Brandon is a great character, and I adore Alan Rickman's portrayal, but he's a dope. Still, it is a good movie.

While enjoying my visit with the Dashwoods, Middletons, Ferrars and others, I am finally able to forget the creeping pace of time. Before I know it, I find myself faced with decisions about dinner. TV dinner? Hot Pocket? Ramen noodles? Take out? A take-out that delivers, of course. I reluctantly accept that it's too late in the day to expect a call inviting me to dinner, and decide to order Chinese. As I reach for the phone, it suddenly rings. Oh, boy!

"Hello?" I answer, all too eagerly.

"Well, hello! You sound happy. Are you having a nice birthday?"

"Hi, Dad," I said trying not to sound too dejected. "I celebrated with the girls last night, so I'm just having a quiet day today."

"Oh, that's not right, Hero. You should be doing something to celebrate today. I wish I had known. I would have made arrangements to come down there today and take you out."

"That's ok, Dad. You don't have to worry. I had a really good time last night and I'm enjoying the peace and quiet," I said, hoping that that would be an end to it. No such luck.

"Nonsense!" he exclaimed. "I can be down there in about two and a half hours and take you to a nice dinner. How does that sound?"

Isn't it cute when parents try to be unnecessarily accommodating? "Really, Dad, it's ok. In fact, I just ordered some Chinese food for myself," I fibbed "so don't worry about it."

"Well, if you're sure?" he asked without waiting for a reply. "At least you had fun with your friends last night. Just the girls?" he asked. I knew he meant weren't there any men in the group. Any particularly special men.

"Yup," I replied, not taking the bait.

My father barely managed to contain a little sigh of disappointment. "Did you get my present?" he asked changing the subject.

"Yes, Dad, I did, thank you. Didn't you get the message I left on your voicemail?" As always, my dad sent me a book for my birthday. Every birthday, right from my first, a book. Never anything else but books. I suppose there's something to be said for consistency, but I don't know what it is. This year's entry was a hard cover edition of the works of Alfred Lord Tennyson.

"Oh, yes. Now that you mention it, I did. I must have forgotten." Also a birthday ritual.

As I rolled my eyes at the ceiling, the call waiting beeped. "Oh, Dad, I've got to go. That's probably Sue and I've been waiting for her to call me back."

"Oh, ok." he said. He sounded a little disappointed, but I knew it was only that I might feel Sue was more important than him, not that he was sad to end the call. Parents.

"Love you, Dad," I said.

"Love you too, honey."

I clicked over as soon as the words were out of his mouth. "Hello?" I said, even more eagerly than before, hoping I hadn't taken too long to answer.

"Hey, H, what's up?" It actually was Sue. Go figure.

"Not much. Just vegging. How's your head?"

Sue laughed. "Friggin' awful. How's yours?"

"Not so bad. The last dose of Advil seemed to help." I told her.

"How many doses was that?" she asked.

"Uh, three, I think," I said, laughing. "Of course the Ring Dings helped too."

"Oh, of course. Chocolate always helps." she laughed right along with me. "So..." she said, trailing off.

"So?" I replied, deliberately obtuse, knowing full well she wanted to know if I'd heard from Kin. "Sew buttons?"

"Ha ha," Sue said dryly. "Don't be coy, missy. You know I called to get the dirt."

"I regret to inform you that there is no dirt to be had, as of yet." I hoped I sounded confident and uncaring that the all-important call had not happened.

"Aw man! Why do men make us wait? We know they want to call, so just pick up the darned phone and call!" I appreciated her frustration for my sake. Maybe I wouldn't slap her too hard after all. In my preoccupation over the Inquisition that was to take place at the Main Street Diner, I'd forgotten to give her her much deserved slap.

I chuckled. "Probably for the same reason we pretend not to be waiting for the phone to ring."

"Yeah," she agreed. "Still. You're going to call me as soon as you talk to him, right?" Clearly this was not a real question and just a confirmation of the standard operating procedure.

"Oh, yeah, you know it." I agreed.

"That is really weird that his name means 'fair hero' though, isn't it? I mean, what are the odds? Do you think it's destiny!" she added dramatically.

"Goof! Oh, yeah, it's destiny! Please!" I laughed a little too hard and my head began to throb again. Damn those tasty little shots.

Sue laughed her very distinctive little giggle that she reserved for those moments when she was making fun, good naturedly, of those she loved. I couldn't resist a smile. Sue was my best friend and I loved her dearly. We both loved a laugh at the other's expense, though these days I was providing more than receiving. A best friend is a great thing, but a best friend who helps you laugh at yourself and enjoys laughing at her own self too is something very special. You know the saying "Don't sweat the small stuff, and nothing is big"? Friends like Sue are tailor-made to help you remember that.

"Ok, well I'll let you go. Be sure to call me as soon as you hear from Mr. Destiny, ok?"

"Yeah, yeah. Go bother someone else's hangover why don'tcha?" I asked playfully.

"He he he. Bye!" she cackled and then hung up.

Still smiling, I replaced the receiver. I was just about to start a fresh perusal of the cable menu when I remembered my Chinese food. Grabbing the phone, I dialed the number and placed my order. I ordered much more than I needed, but hey, it's not like the delivery guy knows it's just me in here, right?

So, while I salivated in anticipation of my Sesame Chicken, I began looking for something else to distract my attention from the ticking clock. It was going to be a long night.

Hours later, Sesame Chicken devoured, along with fried rice, chicken fingers, wings, ribs and some Crab Rangoon, I started to feel dejected. I tried to convince myself that he didn't want to appear too eager and was probably waiting until Monday to call so he wouldn't seem needy or anything. It didn't work. It was easier to believe he wasn't going to call at all. Why do we do that to ourselves, ladies? Like life doesn't trample us enough, we are always so ready to believe the worst and think ourselves undesirable. It sucks!

Feeling sad and sorry for myself, I resolved to at least end the day clean and dragged myself off to the shower. The hot water felt so good and the steam did wonders for the remaining dregs of my hangover. I did my best to just focus on the relaxing effects of the hot water and the calming scent of the cucumber melon body wash, but I couldn't help it. Instead I found myself remembering Kin's impossibly green eyes. I wondered if they're contacts. They're just way too green to be real. My mind wandered to the memory of his strong jaw and full lips. In spite of myself, I found myself wanting to know what it would be like to be kissed by those lips. Wondering what it would be like to be held tightly by those strong arms. Imagining my own arms wrapped tightly around him.

Ok, this was not good. Out of the shower before you do yourself any more harm, you stupid cow. I dried off and put on a clean nightgown. No sense in getting dressed now that it was after ten o'clock at night. I stopped by my office on the way back to the living room. I'd had my office phone forwarded to my home line, so I wouldn't have to keep an ear out for the phone ringing in there. I checked my schedule for the next day and my list of deadlines for the week. Nothing major due and no appointments. Cool. An easy week ahead.

Settling back down onto my comfy old couch, I flicked on the TV, and looked for something to watch. One of the newer channels was having a marathon of the 1990's revival of Dark Shadows. Excellent. I had liked that show and was disappointed when it had been cancelled. Though I have to admit, I'd never understood the attraction to vampires. Why would anyone want to be bitten and have their blood drank? Hello? Perfectly nonsensical to me. I wondered for the hundredth time if some guys with latent serial killer tendencies wrote these stories. Had to be, right? Only some sadistic guy with a penchant for wanting to harm or kill women could see the act of viciously biting a woman and drinking her blood as erotic. Oh, how wrong I was! Silly Hero.

Though I have to say, while Ben Cross made a great vampire, all the old world romantic mumbo jumbo was ridiculous. If some guy spoke to me like that, I would have had a hard time keeping a straight face. "Wouldn't it be deliciously romantic if we were the reincarnation of the original Barnabus and Josette?" Ugh, no - that would be creepy. And what kind of guy says things like 'deliciously romantic'? Ew! You wouldn't find me sighing dreamily. I'd be looking for the nearest exit and changing my phone number. Romance is great and all, don't get me wrong, but let's keep it within this century, please. Or even within the last century, but none of these overdone, flowery speeches from men. Something icky about them. Yeah, that's right, I said 'icky'.

And while the house he restored was pretty cool, keeping it the way it was when originally built in the 1700's, was so not cool, in my opinion. Sorry, I want indoor plumbing and electricity. I don't think that's too much to ask. Hardly qualifies me as high maintenance. If that makes me unromantic, so be it. I suppose talking about plumbing is unromantic, but I want a shower and a flushing toilet where ever I am, thank you very much. Those of you who read historical romances and such and like to fantasize about living in another era, let me tell you, you'd miss indoor plumbing and electricity mighty fast if you were deprived of it. You doubt it? Think the romance is worth it? I've got two words for you, ladies. Your period. Enough said.

I stayed up way too late watching the marathon. But seeing as I had slept half the day, I guess it wasn't too bad. I went to bed with thoughts of vampires, séances and time travel running through my head. The people in these shows that experience these things always take them way too much in stride, in my opinion (and yes, I have a lot of opinions). I can't imagine keeping cool when I discovered someone in the room had no reflection. Especially after several recent deaths where the victims had their throats ripped out. I'd go someplace to privately have a little freak out and then get the hell out of Dodge. Wouldn't you?

These were the thoughts that rambled through my mind as I drifted off to sleep. Silly isn't it, the way we imagine how we'd react in certain situations? We're always so sure of ourselves. People can be so dumb.

CHAPTER 3

Three years ago, I started my own business. I'd had a good job working for a public relations company and had no intention of leaving. Then my mom got sick. Cancer. She and my dad had split up several years before. She still lived in the house in which I'd grown up. My father had moved to New Hampshire to take a position at Dartmouth. His dream come true, a position at an Ivy League school.

At first, her treatments seemed to go well and we were hopeful. My employer was very generous and understanding about my needing time to drive my mom to and from medical appointments. Then things took a turn for the worse. Her treatments didn't seem to be working any more. More radical procedures were suggested and performed, but they only made her more sickly. Mom became very frail and needed round the clock help. I couldn't bear the thought of a stranger taking care of her and living in my childhood home, so, I quit my job and gave up my apartment and moved back home to take care of my mother. I started taking freelance jobs to help pay my bills.

I won't bore you with all the sad details. Suffice it to say, my mom passed, much too quickly. The freelance jobs led to starting my own company and working from the house I grew up in, which was now mine. The house had belonged solely to Mom after the divorce and she had left it to me in her will. William and his wife own their own home and live way out in Northern California. He has no interest in the house or anything back here. He's far too absorbed in his life to care. Like father, like son.

Aside from the eventuality of my father's passing, I doubt William will ever set foot in Massachusetts again. I love my brother, but I've got to tell you, it's no big loss.

I find I enjoy working for myself. I know it's not for everyone, but I am fortunate to have the drive and ambition to go out and find clients and promote myself. The field of graphic design is so open now-a-days with the internet and everything that there are plenty of jobs to go around. Plus, how great is it that I can go to work barefoot!

Yeah, I'm one of those people who hate to wear shoes if they don't have to. I'm like Gillian Holroyd in "Bell, Book and Candle". Well, except I don't look like Kim Novak, I'm not a witch and I don't have a cat with supernatural powers called Piwacket. Cool name for a cat though.

Oh, since we're into chapter three, you've probably already noticed I refer to pop culture kind of stuff a lot. Get used to it. That's me. An otherwise useless encyclopedia of pop culture references. We've all got to be good at something useless.

Well, here I am at Monday and doing a pretty darn good job of immersing myself in my work and not thinking about Kin. I'm designing a set of characters for a pair of college students who run online role playing games. Boy, times change. When I was a college student, a ninety-nine cent junior hamburger at Wendy's was a luxury. These kids have money to pay for websites with huge amounts of server space and bandwidth, advertising and hiring professionals to create their graphics for them. Even now, I couldn't afford to pay for a website like theirs. At least I'm the one getting their money for designing graphics. There we go; the bright side! I knew it was in there somewhere.

I was just settling down to a game of solitaire while having leftover Chinese for lunch, when the office phone rang. Trying to swallow a big bite of chicken finger without choking, I grabbed the phone and croaked "Good afternoon, Hero Images."

"Uh, hello. May I speak with Miss Fletcher, please?" asked a deep, sultry voice. It was him! At last! Took him long enough for crying out loud.

I gulped the last bit of chicken finger in my mouth as delicately as possible and cleared my throat, very ladylike. And yeah, that was sarcasm. "Hi, this is Miss Fletcher." Like I didn't know it was Kin on the other end.

"Oh, hi. This is Kin MacIntyre. We met the other night?"

"Kin, yes, I remember you. How are you?" My mouth now devoid of fried batter and chicken, I was able to sound reasonably classy. Or at least I hoped I did. Man, I hope we never get those video phones like they had in the Jetsons. A lot of romances will be over before they begin.

"I'm fine thanks. How are you?" He sounded very calm and sophisticated. Damn him. I found myself hoping he was wiping damp palms across his jeans and nervously playing with the phone cord. It was the least he could be doing.

"I'm just fine, thank you for asking." Ball back in his court.

"I was wondering if you might like to go out some night this week. Maybe a movie?" Ok, now there was a twinge of nervousness in his voice. The balance of power was shifting, as was only right.

"A movie sounds good. What night were you thinking of?" Calm as a cucumber.

"Um, I don't know, maybe Thursday or Friday? Which would be best for you?" he asked, deftly sending the ball back over to me.

Decisions! Damn, I hate to be the one to make the decisions the first time out. Too much pressure. Ok, Hero, time to look important and sought after. "Give me a second." I rustled some papers around my desk for effect. "Let's see. Thursday's ok. Oh, I have an important meeting first thing Friday morning. Perhaps Friday would be better? Would that be alright with you?" Smooth, very smooth. Good girl.

"Friday sounds great. I could pick you up around 7:30. Would that be ok?"

"Seven-thirty would be fine," I replied. I gave him directions to my house and after a moment of banal pleasantries, the call was ended.

I hung up and took a deep, steadying breath. Then, lifting the receiver, I kept my promise and called Sue.

"This is Susan."

"He called." I said simply. No need to identify myself or specify who 'he' was.

"Yes!" Sue said triumphantly. "So, what happened? When are you going to see him again?"

"Friday. We're going to the movies." I told her.

"Ugh, not until Friday? Well, at least that gives you all week to prepare."

"All week!" I said indignantly. "I know I'm no supermodel, but really! Am I in such rough shape that I need five days to prepare for sitting in a dark movie theater?"

Sue laughed at me. Of course. "Chill out, I'm just saying. You know I don't mean you need a week. It's just that it's good to have a few days. You can get stuff to and from the cleaners, get a manicure or pedicure. Or, um…"

"Um? What's 'um'? Do I even want to know what 'um' is?" I asked with a sneaking suspicion that I was going to find out exactly what 'um' was no matter what, and that I would be have been better off not knowing.

"Well, 'um' like, you'd have time for a waxing if you needed one."

Yup! I was right. Could have lived without knowing what 'um' was.

Seeing as it was Sue, I said "I don't know whether to be flattered or offended. Am I such a ho that you assume I'm going sleep with this guy on the first date, or is it that I am so incredibly sexy and desirable that he won't be able to keep from throwing himself at my feet? My freshly pedicured feet, of course."

Laughter. More laughter. I cleared my throat, rather expressively.

"Sorry," she choked. "Of course I don't think you're a ho. I wouldn't be best friends with a ho!"

"Oh, I'm sorry if I've offended your delicate sensibilities," I interrupted, dripping with sarcasm. I like sarcasm. I'm good at it. It's one of my many talents.

"I just thought, better safe than sorry. That's all." Sue answered, still laughing.

"Oh, yeah, I forgot you were a Girl Scout. But save any of your other 'be prepared' advice for if and when I have more than one date under my belt with Kin, ok?"

"Tch! Some people are so touchy."

I blew a raspberry at her through the phone. You're allowed such childish responses during phone calls of this nature with your best friend. It's a rule. Somewhere, it's a rule.

"Ok, ok. I'll give you a call when I get home from work."

"Ok," I said. "Love ya."

"Love you too!" she said as she hung up.

Well, I had done my duty. Naturally, there were other friends to be brought up to speed, but the obligatory immediate call to the best friend was out of the way.

Darn Sue! Now I couldn't help thinking about whether I should get a wax or not. I decided to leave nothing to chance. I called the salon and scheduled a full day's beauty. Manicure, pedicure and waxing. Not that I had any intention of hopping into bed with a total stranger, but there was an odd sense of security knowing you wouldn't have to worry about something as embarrassing as a stubbly bikini line if the unthinkable happened.

Then I got up and went to my bedroom and threw open the closet doors. I'm a bit of a pack rat. Well, a big pack rat, if truth be told. I hate to get rid of anything. I began wading through the overabundance of tops, blouses, skirts, slacks and dresses. In a matter of minutes my bed was covered with a pile of possible contenders for Friday night's trip to the movies. Now the hard part. Weeding them out.

First off: eliminate anything red or close to red. I wore a red blouse the night we met and I don't want him to think I have a thing with the color red. Second: eliminate black clothes. Same reason. Third: The crucial choice. Dress/skirt or pants? I didn't want to be too dressed up, but I didn't want to be too casual either. I decided upon a nice pair of pants. Not too dressy, but not completely casual. Pale gray. I had a pair of low gray boots that matched them very well. And finally, the top. I chose a soft lilac blouse with cutout collar. Feminine, but not too much.

Great! Wardrobe picked out and salon scheduled. And only four days to go. Sometimes I really hate dating.

The next four days passed more quickly than they had any right to. Oh, the irony. When you are waiting for a phone call, minutes seem like endless hours. When you are excited, and yet nervous, about a first date, time disappears in big clumps. I'd picked out my wardrobe days before. I'd gotten waxed, buffed, polished and plucked. I'd practically memorized each and every movie at all of my local theaters that started between the hours of eight pm and nine pm on Friday night. When the time came around, I'd done my hair, twice. Changed jewelry and accessories more times than a one man drag show. I'd brushed my teeth and flossed and gargled and chewed gum guaranteed to give you sweet breath. I wasn't taking any chances.

I'd done all of this and more, and I still had over half an hour to wait. Half an hour! I could bite all of my perfectly manicured nails off before half an hour was up. I didn't dare have a drink to calm my nerves. Not only would I have to go through all the brushing and flossing etc. again, but I recalled that Kin had been drinking water at the night club and I didn't want him thinking I was some kind of booze hound if he detected liquor on my breath. If there was an ounce of justice in the world, Kin would be at least half as nervous as me. It struck me funny just then and I had to laugh. What a place to be in. Where you half wish the guy you're going out with shows up sweating like some kind of farm animal and yet, you hope he doesn't because, well, let's face it - that's gross.

What's a girl to do? Call someone, of course. I knew Sue was out at a play with some friends, so she was no good. Carol was out with her boyfriend. Kelly bowled on Fridays. I'd give Debbie a call and see if she was in. Debbie was married, but she and her husband still had a pretty active social life. Success! She answered on the second ring.

"Hey, it's me," I said when she answered.

She gasped. "What happened? Did he cancel?"

"No, no. It's fine. I'm just ready early and,"

Debbie cut me off. "Gotcha," she said knowingly. "Do you know what you're going to see?"

"No. We'll probably decide when he gets here.   Any suggestions?"

"Well, you could see whatever the latest romantic movie is that's out."

"Is there one out?" I asked, sounding more curious than I was. Really, I was just wondering if I wanted to go in that direction on the first date.

"Isn't there always? I can't keep them straight." She was probably right.

"I don't know, but I don't think I want to start off with some girlie film full of dumb clichés and fluff." Yeah, after thinking about it, that was definitely not where I wanted to be on a first date. You have to be careful when choosing the first movie you see as a couple. If you start off with some silly puff piece of female drivel, you might give him the wrong idea that a relationship with you will require him to suffer through that crap on a regular basis. If you go to an action movie, you might give him the idea you're willing to sit through that kind of crap on a regular basis. Horror movies are ok when you're a teen or early twenties, because it's still acceptable to hide your head on his shoulder and squeal during the nasty gross parts. At my age though, it was just viewed as ridiculous. That didn't really leave a lot of choices.

"I don't know. Maybe you could let him pick?" Debbie suggested.

"Yeah, I guess," I said, unconvinced. "I'll just have to wait and see." The sound of a car pulling into my driveway surprised me. He was early. "Oh! I think he's here. I'll call you tomorrow." I said hurriedly.

"Ok, go! Have fun," Debbie said before hanging up.

I took one last look in the mirror in the front hall and waited for him to ring the bell. The bell rang, and like a total loser, I stood in the hall and counted the seconds until I could open the door without looking like the loser that I was. Sometimes I'm so pathetic, I annoy myself!

At last I opened the door. There he was. All six foot something of him, looking gorgeous in an oatmeal-colored Henley sweater, that hugged his broad shoulders, and a pair of navy cargo pants. My breath caught, so I just smiled.

"Hi," he said, returning my smile.

"Hi," I said. "Come on in." I stepped aside and gestured for him to come in. It was all so innocent.

His smile broadened as he crossed the threshold. "Thanks," Kin said as he started his perusal of my home.

I closed the door and followed him into my living room, enjoying the view from behind. "Would you like a drink or anything before we go?" I offered.

"No, thank you. You have a very nice home." Kin walked to the fireplace and looked at the family pictures that had been there for decades. He chuckled. "How old were you here?" he asked pointing at a picture of me from elementary school.

"Oh, um, nine or ten, I think." I muttered, making a mental note to remove that picture as soon as possible. In fact, I resolved to overhaul all the pictures that were out for others to see.

"You look mad," he noted, trying not laugh. Kin turned and looked at me, obviously expecting a story to go along with the picture.

I sighed. Might as well tell it. "My mom loved that photo of me because the photographer commented on my dimples and I got embarrassed and refused to smile," I explained.

He didn't bother trying not to laugh this time. "That's a great story. And you do have very cute dimples."

"Oh, my, look at the time! We'd better be going," I said a bit more curtly than I had meant. Not that it mattered. Kin just laughed louder. Gee, what a great start to the evening!

"What did you want to see?" I asked as I swung my pocket book over my shoulder and moved toward the door.

Kin was suddenly beside me. Damn, he moved fast! "Whatever you choose is fine with me," he said as he placed his hand at the small of my back and led me toward the front door. Oh, great! Now I'm going to have to choose.

"Why don't we just see what's playing in Randolph when we get there?" I suggested.

"Sure," he said, opening the door for me. I wasn't thrilled about the start of our evening, but that killer smile sure helped.

In the end, we settled for an historical drama that turned out to be really good. Unfortunately, he bought the large popcorn to share, which normally would be a good thing, but I noticed halfway through the movie that I was the only one eating it. I self-consciously slurped my Diet Sprite while he sipped his bottled water. For me, popcorn is right up there with chocolate. I feel very strongly that they both should have recommended daily allowances. In fact, I'm of the opinion that chocolate should be the fifth food group. We really ought to lobby for it. I wanted to keep eating the popcorn. I told myself that it was a crime to just let it go to waste, but my vanity won out and I refrained from making a pig of myself. Besides, I told myself, there was always popcorn waiting at home. Always.

The movie ended and Kin stood, holding out his hand to help me up. "Did you enjoy the movie?" he asked.

"Yes, did you?"

"Yes," he replied. Once again his hand was at the small of my back and he was leading me up the aisle. It was a nice feeling.

After we made our way through the throng of movie-goers, we headed for the parking lot. We'd been lucky to get a decent space, not too far from the doors. Not that I minded the walk, but I'm such a ditz about cars, I wouldn't have put it past me to walk up to the wrong one. Being close to the door made it easy. Thank goodness for that at least.

Once inside the car, Kin suggested we go for coffee. I agreed and we went in search of a nice place to relax and talk. Of course, I could have invited him back to my place for coffee, but I thought it was too soon.

Now, you'd think in this day and age, a place to go and have coffee would be easy to find, wouldn't you? Nope! At least not in the suburbs of Boston after 10:30 at night. All the Starbucks and trendy places are closed by nine or ten. There are restaurants, but they make you feel like a leper for ordering nothing but coffee. So, where did we end up? Dunkin Donuts. Not that I mind Dunkin Donuts. On the contrary, I love them. Especially their orange Coolattas. (Please Double D – don't ever stop making them!) But you've got to admit, it's not exactly a romantic place to bring a date.

So, there we are in a very brightly lit Dunkin Donuts that just reeks of coffee and sugar, and not in a good way. I wondered if Kin would just get water again. He did. The first date is not the time to question such things, but let me tell you, I was getting curious. I ordered a small tea and we sat down in a corner of the fairly deserted shop.

I didn't discover an awful lot about Kin that night. I can tell you that I did discover that he is very adept at getting people to talk about themselves while revealing precious little about himself.

I replayed the evening in my mind while lying in bed, I tried to decide if this meant he was good at being interested in other people or if it meant he was secretive about himself. I wanted to be positive, but there was something nagging at me. I didn't know what, but there was something there. Oh, damn! He probably was married or something. Just my luck. There I went again! Daisy Doom imagining the worst.

I didn't want to fall asleep thinking negative thoughts, so instead I focused on the good things. His smile, his soothing voice, the fact that I was going to see him again on Sunday, and most of all, the sweet way he walked me to my door and gave me a nervous peck on the cheek as he said goodnight. Very sweet. I was glad he wasn't one of those guys who gets all handsy or climbs all over you right off the bat, but that didn't stop me from imagining what other kisses might be like. Oh, yeah. That was the stuff to fall asleep thinking about. Kisses from a handsome man.

CHAPTER 4

As I settle into my 30th year, it occurs to me that my life is much more like the beer commercials I remember from my youth than I ever would have imagined. No, no. Stay with me on this. I'm not talking about people playing volleyball in the snow covered Rocky Mountains or having a psychotic penguin crank calling you. Though I must say, the Bud penguin was quite possibly the most brilliant ad campaign ever.

No. I'm talking about the ones way back. The ones that showed a group of friends just hanging out at a local bar and enjoying each other's company. Or at a cookout at a friend's house or things like that. Do you remember the jingle? "Here's to good friends, tonight is kind of special." Well, I'm pleasantly surprised to have the kind of friends who would have made an excellent beer commercial. A strange accolade, I grant you, but there's a certain happy satisfaction in the knowledge that your most intimate friends are a group of good natured, easy going people that always make you feel at ease and contented. I think if you can look around you and honestly say that, then you're doing pretty well.

As it happens, I can. And just to prove my point, my friends and I all gathered together at our local tavern for a night of drinking and fun. Now, don't go thinking that all my friends and I do is drink, drink, drink. Sometimes we eat too. Seriously though, it is a tradition with us that we all get together at TJ's on the last Saturday of the month. We all don't make it each and every month, but there are enough of us to make a decent sized group each time. We get what is now our regular table, or rather set of tables, and the first ones to arrive put in the order for pizzas and appetizers and a couple of pitchers of beer. They've got really good pizza too. Barroom pizza. If you have never tried it, it's great. Most barrooms that offer pizza make it the same. Small with a thin crust and just enough cheese. They always seem to know how much is just enough before it becomes too much. And yes, there can be too much cheese. Especially when you're drinking. Trust me.

I had decided not to invite Kin to our monthly meeting just yet. I felt it might be too much for him with a bunch of people who mostly know each other well. Plus, I saw him Friday and was going to see him again on Sunday. I needed a night off to be myself and let my guard down.

Debbie and Bob arrived early, along with a few guys that Bob worked with. Carol and her boyfriend, Lenny, had followed them right in. By the time I came in, the food was ordered and the waitress was just setting down the beer. Kelly and her fiancé Chris came in a few minutes later, followed by Amy and Tim. Susan had said she'd be late this time. Other members of the group straggled in over the course of the next hour. Soon we were a bona fide gang of locals, drinking beer, eating pizza and Buffalo wings and pumping money into the jukebox. A modern day Norman Rockwell image if ever there was one. Life in a small town on Saturday night. And it was A-OK with me.

"So, H," said Bob as he reached past me to grab a slice of Hawaiian pizza. "I hear you got a new guy on the line?"

A comical chorus of "Ooooooh," went around the table. Mostly the guys. I was suddenly the center of attention. Oh, joy!

"H! You cheating on me?" called Bill. Most of them all called me H. I didn't like it at first, but it grew on me. And I've actually become to appreciate it. It comes in handy in situations like a crowded bar where I'd rather not have strangers overhear my weird name.

"Oh, now, Bill. You know I'm as faithful to you as you are to me." That met with a roar of laughter. Not just because Bill is a notorious Romeo, but because I'm funny.

I fielded a couple more questions from the male sector of our group before the female faction took over and changed the subject. It was one thing for them to brow beat me into divulging every teeny tiny detail of my love life, but it was unacceptable for the men folk to pry. One of the best things about having guys in your circle of close friends though is this: The moment they discover there's a new guy in your life, all joking aside, they remind you that if the jerk does anything to hurt you that they're going to kick his ass. It's sweet really, in a stupid Neanderthal kind of way. Men, sometimes they're just so darned cute.

All cuteness aside, I was grateful for the change of subject. The last thing I wanted was to be shouting down a table the little scraps of information I'd managed to find out about my latest flame. And I didn't want a reminder of just how little I did know. Several of my lady friends had pointed that out to me earlier in the day during our ritualistic debriefing.

Like there wasn't enough salt in that wound already, they felt it necessary to caution me against monopolizing the conversation and to remind me to give him a chance to talk. What crust! I tell you, if I didn't love them so much they would have gotten a good dose of my cruder conversational skills. I tried to convince them that I had tried to get him to talk and I didn't monopolize the conversation. Kin is just really good at asking questions and getting you to talk. They didn't buy it.

One of the few drawbacks of close friends. They often presume to know you so well that they will not listen to what you have to say about your own thoughts or actions, but instead hold fast to their own notions of what you must have said or done. This was one of those times. And it was pandemic.

I was going to have to consider censoring future informational sessions. Trying to get to know someone new is stressful enough without your own friends making you even more self-conscious. I know they all meant well, but you know what they say about good intentions.

As always, I enjoyed myself with my gang, but I just couldn't keep my mind from wandering back to Kin and our date the next day. He had asked me to accompany him to an antique auction. I've never been to one and was a bit nervous. I know it's not really like they show in TV and movies where you can accidentally bid on something by scratching your nose or something, but I had a terrible fear I'd do something to embarrass myself. Though, in fairness to myself, I'd probably worry about that no matter where we were going. Second date jitters.

Sunday morning began with a call at quarter past eight. Who the hell calls someone at quarter past eight in the morning on a Sunday? I fumbled for the phone and answered it ungraciously.

"Well, good morning Sunshine," came a much too happy voice.

"William, are you on crack? It's got to be the middle of the night for you." I said, just as unpleasant as when I answered.

"Actually, Marissa and I are in Morocco at the moment." he said in a snotty, superior way. How did we ever come from the same gene pool?

"What are you doing in Morocco?" I asked, in spite of myself, because I really didn't care.

"Well, it's interesting that you should ask, because there's this," he began, sounding a bit excited at the opportunity to bore me with crap I couldn't care less about.

"Never mind, Willie. What are you calling me at the crack of dawn on a Sunday for?" I was still grumpy.

He sighed. "Please don't call me that. As it happens, I am calling to wish you a happy birthday." William made it sound like some immense honor that he should humble himself to call me for my birthday. Jerk.

"Thanks Will, but my birthday was last week."

"No, that can't be. Your birthday is the twenty-eighth." Just like my brother to inform me of the correct date of my own birthday.

"Ah, no, actually, my birthday is the twenty-first. It says so on my driver's license. But thanks just the same."

"Well, then whose birthday is the twenty eighth?" he asked, frustrated.

"Gee, I don't know. Why don't you ask Marissa? Maybe it's someone in her family." I just loved conversations like this with my brother. What a great way to start the day.

"Don't be silly. You know Marissa's mother stopped celebrating birthday's years ago. Oh, well, happy birthday anyway."

"Thanks." This had gone on long enough. "Well, I don't want to run up your phone bill,"

William laughed. "Oh, Hero! I have unlimited International calling on my cell phone. You know that. With all the traveling Marissa and I do, it's a necessity. Why, I can't imagine what we'd do if,"

"Yeah, I forgot," I interrupted rudely. William and Marissa were anthropologists, but don't ask me what the heck they actually did. They were a perfectly matched pair of intellectual bores. Guaranteed to put you to sleep, or make you want to blow your brains out.

He took the hint. "Well, we've got to run. There's an exhibit and we're meeting some people there."

"Sounds great," I said with fake enthusiasm, hoping I would be spared any more details or, God forbid, name dropping of allegedly famous people I'd never heard of. William was very fond of doing that. "I hope you two have a great time."

"I'm sure we will. Good-bye, Hero." I'd ticked him off. Oh, well.

"Bye, Willie. Take care," I said, hanging up before he could complain about me calling him 'Willie' again.

Well, isn't this just a fabulous way to start my day? I suppose I should be glad he even thought about my birthday. I loved William, he was my only sibling, but we were just so different. We didn't have much in common except that we came from the same family. And Marissa! Ugh! She was about as warm and friendly as a tarantula on ice.

I snuggled back down into my bed, hoping to catch another hour's sleep. But now my mind was full of thoughts about family and old frustrations and annoyances. Great, thanks a lot, William. How could a cold, pompous jerk like my brother manage to find someone to marry, and I was still single at 30? Ok, granted, there probably was a specific market for people like William and Marissa, and it obviously made things easier finding a match. At least that's what I decided to tell myself.

Thirty. There it was. I'd been waiting for it to hit. Thirty. I was 30. Why does society have to put stigmas on certain ages? It's not fair. I don't feel any different than I did at 29, or 28, or 27 even. All these outside influences making me feel inferior because I was unwed and my biological clock was ticking. Funny, I couldn't hear it.

Women are starting their families much later now than in past generations. So, why are we still made to feel like we've failed if we haven't at least gotten the ring by 30? I suspect the diaper companies, the baby food companies and the toy companies have some kind of conspiracy going. I'm not usually one to consider conspiracy theories, but in my present state of mind, this one made sense.

Conceding that further attempts to sleep would be futile, I decided to get up and take a shower. Feeling refreshed and slightly more optimistic after my shower, I made myself some tea and toast and sat down in front of my laptop.

After checking my email, I figured I'd do a little research about antiques before I had to get ready for my date with Kin. Easier said than done. It might have helped if I knew what kind of antiques he dealt with or what type of auction we were going to, but I had no idea. Note to self: Ask more questions and don't get sidetracked.

Abandoning my fairly useless attempt at reconnaissance, I opted instead for a few hands of solitaire. Toast eaten, tea drunk and computer card game beaten, I turned my attention to preparing for my date with Kin.

It was a little after ten and he wasn't picking up until one o'clock. That gave me time to do some things around the house and make it look nice. I put my dishes into the dishwasher and wiped down all the counters and surfaces in my kitchen. Living on my own, it doesn't have much chance to get dirty.

Then I went into the bathroom and wiped down the vanity and cleaned the mirror. After cleaning the toilet bowl, I took the dirty towels out of the hamper and headed for the basement. I hate basements. I'd always wished we'd had one of those nice finished basements with a family room, but instead we had a cold, dank stone basement, full of dark corners and spider webs. Now this is when you really needed a man. Real men do laundry. Especially when the washer and dryer are in a creepy basement.

Once that nasty job was out of the way, I went back upstairs and dusted and vacuumed the living room and front hallway. I ran a dust cloth over the dining room table, but didn't bother much with that room. I hardly ever used it and you can only access it through the kitchen, which has a door between them. No sense in wasting time and effort. Don't judge me.

I was just about to go upstairs and pick out something to wear when I remembered the pictures on the mantel. I'd dusted them, but was so used to them, I'd forgotten that I meant to replace them. There was that horrible picture of me as a kid. Another picture was of me and William on some long ago Christmas. We were both holding new books. Go figure. An old picture of my parents from one of their anniversaries. Graduation pictures of me and William. One of William and Marissa's wedding pictures, and a photo of my mother's parents. I left the picture of my parents, grandparents and William's wedding. The other pictures I gathered up and carried upstairs.

I went straight to my closet and opened the doors. I placed the discarded photos on the upper shelf. Then I tried to decide what one wears to an antique auction. I settled for a pair of khakis and an olive green jersey. A gold pin and earrings added a little sparkle to keep the outfit from being too plain, but it was still understated. I hoped I had struck the right balance.

I ran a brush through my hair and tried to decide if I should pull it back. Looking at the clock, I decided I had enough time for trial and error in the hair department. After a few different styles, I settled on a slim tortoise shell headband. I grabbed a pair of beige flats from my closet and headed back downstairs to the living room. I dropped my shoes on the floor in front of the couch and sat down. Now what? It was five minutes till 12. I had an hour to go. Great.

Why did I get ready so early? Beats me. Guess it was better than trying to find something else to keep me busy. While I tried to think of some way to pass the time, I accidentally rested my head on the back of the couch and fell asleep. Classic.

Kin rang the doorbell at exactly one o'clock. My head snapped up, and for a moment I didn't know where I was or what was going on. I heard the bell ring again and realized what had happened. I cursed under my breath and ran for the front door, pausing for the briefest of moments to check my hair and makeup. Kin was just about to ring again when I pulled the door open. "Hi," he said with a smile. "Did I catch you at a bad time?" he asked.

"Uh, no," I stammered, trying to think of some excuse. "I was just getting off the phone with my brother." It was as good a lie as any.

"Oh, I'm sorry." Kin said sincerely as I motioned for him to come inside.

"It's ok, really. I was just getting ready to hang up when you rang the bell." Isn't it amazing how easily we can tell these little lies? Come on, you know you do it. We all do.

"Good," he said, turning to face me. "You look nice. That color suits you."

"Thanks," I said, blushing.

"Are you ready to go?"

"Sure thing," I said, grabbing my purse from the peg on the wall.

"Uh, I think you forgot something," Kin said.

I turned to look at him, a puzzled expression on my face. What could I have forgotten? In answer to my questioning look, Kin pointed at my bare feet.

"Oh," I said, blushing even more brightly. "Um, sorry." Sheepishly, I went over to the couch and slipped my feet into my shoes. "Ok, now, I'm all set," I said with a weak grin. Kin smiled at me and reached to take my hand as we walked to the door.

As we buckled ourselves into Kin's shiny black Infinity SUV, I was frantically hoping he'd start some conversation and ease my embarrassment. Speak! Say something! I thought at him. Strange, isn't it? Most of us don't believe in telepathy and ESP and all that, but it doesn't stop you trying at moments like this.

Finally I couldn't take it anymore. "So, where is this auction?" I asked as we headed toward Route 3.

"It's on the Cape. In Falmouth." he replied.

'The Cape?' I thought. Well, he's been around here long enough to say 'the Cape' and not just Cape Cod or Falmouth. That was something at least. But there was no other info forthcoming.

We drove south on Route 3 in silence for several minutes. It was unbearable. "Uh, you've never said. What exactly do you do in antiques?" Please, God, don't let him give some short simple answer.

"A little of this, a little of that."

Yeah, ok. That wasn't going to fly. "Gee, how interesting," I said, dripping with sarcasm. I gave him a pointed look, clearly stating that his answer was insufficient.

Kin laughed. Not good. "I don't want to bore you," he said.

Ding, ding, ding! Warning, Will Robinson, Danger! Danger! This did not bode well. Why was he so secretive about his work? Was he an art thief? A smuggler? A forger of priceless antiquities? My imagination was about to run rampant, but I exercised control and reeled it in. "You wouldn't bore me at all. I'd like to know more about what you do," I said. After a pause, I added, "After all, I've told you all about my business." Bingo! That did it. He'd have to talk now.

He smiled, a bit ruefully I thought. "I guess you could say I'm mainly a consultant. I appraise antiques, but I also advise collectors and auction houses which items to sell and which item to hold on to."

"Why would an auction house want to hold on to something? Isn't it their business to sell things?"

"Well, yes, but that doesn't mean the market is always right for every type of product. I let them know if the market is flooded, or if something is coming up that might increase interest in a particular type of item. Sometimes it's worth it to hold on to a piece or a particular collection until the demand is at its peak."

"So, how do you know what to advise them? How can you tell what the market is going to do?" I asked, genuinely interested.

"Well, there are a lot of factors. I have to keep up to date on what's selling at the major auction houses in the region. What type of items sell above the expected price, what items sell for less, or don't sell at all. Which items entice multiple bidders. What items collectors are calling about. Lots of things."

"Wow. It must be hard to get all that information."

"No," he said with a little shake of his head. "Not really. It was a bit tough when I first started out, but now that I have relationships with the major auction houses, and a lot of dealers, it's pretty easy."

"It doesn't sound easy." It didn't. I couldn't imagine having to try and keep track of countless types of products and how to identify them and value them, in addition to calculating the market for them.

"Did you go to school for this?" I asked.

Kin blushed. He seemed uncomfortable. "No," he said faintly. "I don't have a college degree."

I felt bad. I hadn't meant to embarrass him. It was no big deal to me if he went to college or not. He was obviously really smart without it. "Geez, you learned all of this without going to school for it? You're really smart." I hoped that didn't sound too sappy.

Kin smiled a little lopsided smile that made my heart beat faster. "I don't know about that. I guess I just have a gift for this sort of thing."

"Yeah," I agreed. "And you're smart." We both laughed.

We talked about nonsense the rest of the way. Traffic, the types of cars we saw, the weather, songs on the radio. It was a pleasant ride and the time passed quickly. Before I knew it, we were pulling into a huge dirt parking lot. There were tons of cars already here. Kin found a space on the end of a row. Before I could even get my seatbelt off he was beside me opening the door. It startled the hell out of me. I stared at him for a second. He turned his face from me and pretended to be watching an elderly couple who had walked past. Ok, now if I thought it was weird that he got to my door so quickly, that was one thing. But to see his reaction to my reaction, that was something else altogether. Something was definitely weird.

Kin helped me out of the SUV and put his hand at the small of my back as he led me toward the old barn that had been converted to an antique dealer's showroom. We were just about to go inside when a voice called out "Well, well. Imagine running into you here Kinley!"

Kin went rigid, just for a instant, but I noticed it. The robot in my head was warning me of danger again. We turned and saw an absolutely gorgeous woman approaching us, with a dazzling smile plastered on her face. Oh, yay! She was tall, close to six feet. She had long, thick honey blonde hair. She had a perfect heart shaped face with porcelain skin. Her brown eyes were so dark they were almost black. She had a full mouth, perfectly painted crimson, and her long fingernails matched. She was wearing black slacks and a maroon sweater with a bright patterned scarf over her left shoulder. I hated her instantly.

"Leontine. Small world." Kin said coldly. That was good. Cold was good.

Leontine was standing right in front of us now. She smiled a Cheshire cat kind of smile. "Smaller than you know, darling," she purred.

Darling?!? Oh, man, if she wasn't an Amazon, I'm telling you. She looked at me, making no secret of the fact that she was looking me up and down and judging me. Bitch. "So, this is the flavor of the month. What do you call it?" she said in a snotty tone, addressing just Kin, clearly signifying I was not worthy of her attention.

Worthy or not, she'd gotten my attention and now she was going to get a piece of my mind. "IT!" I said loudly, not caring who heard me. "Did you just call me 'IT', you,"

Kin moved his hand from the small of my back to my waist and pulled me against him tightly. "Don't bother," he said, interrupting me. "Leontine, this is Hero. She's with me." He said this rather sternly and gave her what should have been a withering look, but the Amazon just looked amused.

"Hero? Oh, my! That's good, Kin." She saw that he was about to say something and she put her hand up to stop him. "Ok, ok. I'll let you two get on with whatever it is you're doing. Hope you're not wasting your time." Still looking highly amused, she turned and walked toward the side of the building. Over her shoulder, Leontine made her parting shot. "Bye, Kin. Bye, Lunch.

CHAPTER 5

Lunch! Lunch? Did the bitch actually call me 'Lunch'?! I couldn't believe it. I never thought I'd find myself in the position to decide which was more offensive: being called 'It' or being called 'Lunch'?

"She called me 'Lunch'!" I yelled at Kin, pointing in the direction the Amazon had gone. I couldn't help the yelling. "What the hell was that?"

"Calm down," he said foolishly, taking the arm that wasn't pointing and pulling me into the auction house. I was about to burst out with a response when he turned his head and placed his finger against his lips, signaling for me to be quiet. The nerve! I had every right to be noisy. I'd just been called 'It' and 'Lunch' by a snooty Sasquatch. Kin pulled me along after him down the crowded aisle. By the time he stopped and thrust me into the farthest corner of the room I was ready to explode.

"How dare you! It's not enough to be humiliated by that, that, that woman, but you have the nerve to tell me to calm down, and then drag me through here like so much baggage, and shove me in a dark corner! What's the matter? Afraid someone else you know might see us together? And what the hell is 'Lunch' supposed to mean?" As that all came out in one breath, I was forced to stop for a second and inhale. Stupid bodily functions. That brief second gave Kin a chance to jump in.

"Hero, you have every right to be pissed off. Leontine is horrible and her behavior was inexcusable. But, surely you didn't want her to hear you being so upset over what she said? Surely you didn't want to give her that satisfaction?"

Damn him. Reason. This was no time for reason. This was a time for yelling and stamping my feet and being loud and obnoxious and unreasonable. So, in keeping with my unreasonable mood, I folded my arms across my chest and scowled at him.

"I'm sorry about what she said. I really am. But Leontine loves to get a rise out of people. Waiting until you were out of earshot to let you blow off steam was the best way to deal with things." He seemed to look apologetic. I was too pissed to be gracious.

"And?" I snapped, tapping my foot impatiently.

"And? And what?" Kin asked. This was not one of those adorable clueless moments that men have. It just fueled my fire.

"And," I stressed loudly, "And what about being called 'It' and 'Lunch'? I mean who the hell calls somebody 'Lunch'"?

Kin ran his hands through his dark hair. "I told you, she likes to get a rise out of people."

"That's it? That's all?" I paused, waiting for him to elaborate. Wasn't happening. "Ok, maybe 'It' was to get a rise out of me, but 'Lunch'? Come on, Kin. That meant something, I know it did." I wasn't letting him off the hook.

He sighed. "It was just a stupid comment. A lame joke. She called you the flavor of the month, remember? It was just a poor attempt at a play on that."

"Yeah, what about that flavor of the month thing? And the thing about wasting your time? Something you feel you should tell me about that? I mean, I know this is only our second date, but if you change girlfriends as often as you change your underwear, there's no point in us seeing each other again." I was in a ripe mood now. God help the poor guy if he misstepped.

"Hero, I am not like that! I don't appreciate your saying things like that about me. I've already told you. Leontine is a horrible woman who likes to get a rise out of people and cause trouble. Don't pay any attention to anything she says."

Ok, I felt a little bad. But only a little. "I'm sorry, but try and imagine how you'd feel in my place," I explained, feeling the need to justify my cranky behavior.

Kin reached out and took both of my hands in his. "I'm sure I'd feel awful. I'd be angry and hurt and I don't blame you for feeling that way at all."

"I'm not hurt," I said peevishly, looking down at my shoes.

"Come on," he said softly. "Let's not let this ruin our day."

I breathed a deep sigh and resolved to shake it off and enjoy the day. "Ok," I said, looking up and trying to smile. Kin smiled back and led me towards the main part of the room.

"The auction will be starting pretty soon. Let's save a couple of seats and then we can look around. Ok?"

"Sounds good."

We saved a couple of seats in an area that Kin felt was advantageous. I have no idea why it was advantageous, and I didn't ask. Then we went to look at the items up for auction. Kin had marked off several items in his sale book. He had some interest in a set of old dining chairs and he also spent several minutes carefully looking over some old china plates and figures. When he looked at some silver match cases and snuff boxes, he tried to show me about the hallmark that shows the maker, but it all looked like little squiggles to me.

Kin asked me if I saw anything that interested me. I had, but I didn't want to say anything. What if he bid on it for me? What if he bid a lot of money? Nope. Too soon. So, I just said "It's all so interesting," and hoped he'd let it go.

The auctioneer announced that the auction would begin in five minutes, so everyone went to their seats. It took us a few minutes to wend our way back through all the displays and groups of people, to the seats we had reserved. I wondered if our seats would still be saved. There were so very many people and there was no way there were going to be enough seats for everyone. A large amount of the people weren't even bothering to look for seats. They were making themselves comfortable leaning against the walls and doorways. Some brave souls were actually leaning against some of the display tables.

Our seats were waiting for us when we finally managed to get to them, and not a moment too soon. I'd no sooner got my butt in the chair then the gavel began pounding.

"Ladies and gentlemen. If I could please have your attention, we would like to begin the auction." A man with a pencil thin mustache, slicked back hair and an expensive navy blue suit announced. He looked like something from a different era. It would have suited him better if the suit jacket had had broader shoulders and pinstripes, and if he'd had a big fedora and Tommy gun at his side. When he gestured towards the first item up for bid, I noticed a very large gold pinky ring on his hand. That only confirmed the stereotype in my head. Not at all what I expected an auctioneer to look like.

The first few items didn't generate too much interest. There were a couple of bids, but not more than one or two per item. One of the sets of china that Kin had looked at came up for bid.

"Up next is lot 634. The Ginori Dinnerware. This is a beautiful set; white with gilt rims, comprising; 24 dinner plates, 24 dessert plates, 12 soup plates, 6 pudding plates. There are printed factory marks."

The auctioneer opened the bidding at $300. I thought that was a bit steep for a set of dishes that was incomplete. Someone jumped right in at $300 and there was an immediate influx of bids.

"Three-fifty, three-seventy-five, four hundred, four-twenty-five, four-fifty, four-seventy-five," called the auctioneer as he tried to look everywhere at once to make sure he caught all the bids.

"Aren't you bidding on this?" I whispered to Kin.

"Not yet," he whispered back without taking his eyes off the auctioneer.

The bids kept coming. I didn't get it. A bunch of white plates with gold edges and not even enough to make a full service. Obviously, I had no idea about antiques. The bids started to slow. There were definitely a couple of diehards who wanted this set.

"Six-seventy-five from a new bidder," said the auctioneer, pointing at Kin. I hadn't even seen him move. I tried to watch the other bidders and Kin at the same time. It was worse than a tennis match. Every time someone else bid, Kin would nod his head, holding his gaze steady with the auctioneer.

"Seven-twenty-five, I have seven-twenty-five over here. Any other bids? Do I have seven-fifty anywhere, seven-fifty? No? Seven-forty, anyone give me seven-forty? Seven-forty from the man at the back, thank you, sir. Seven-sixty, do I have seven-sixty anywhere?"

Kin nodded. The auctioneer tried again to up the bid, but the man at the back had had enough. Sold! I was starting to enjoy myself now. Auctions can be kind of exciting even when you're not the one buying anything. Who knew?

The afternoon flew by as lot after lot was sold. Kin managed to win a couple of other items in the course of the day. Some of the crowd was beginning to trickle out as the amount of remaining lots dwindled. Then the auctioneer announced lot 974 and there was somehow a change in the room. I didn't know why, but I sensed this was a big deal.

"Our next lot, lot 974, is a Russian silver and cloisonné enamel snuff box, circa 1730, with St. Petersburg mark. Most exquisite. Who'll start the bidding at $2,000?"

Cripes! Two thousand dollars for an old snuff box? People don't even use them anymore. Kin's expression was very intense as he stared at the auctioneer. I had no idea why he did that instead of watching the room, or instead of anything else, but whenever there was an item he wanted to bid on, he stared at the auctioneer. The bidding climbed hundreds of dollars at a time. I couldn't keep track of how many bidders there were for the box. The auctioneer looked ridiculous pointing here, there and everywhere as the bids were flying. Well, it looked ridiculous to me. The rest of the room probably didn't think anything of it.

Suddenly Kin sat forward in his seat. It was the most he'd moved since we first sat down. His jaw was clenched and I noticed he had taken his eyes off the auctioneer for a second. I followed his gaze and saw him looking at Leontine. She was standing up front right near the auctioneer. I hadn't seen her throughout the entire auction. Where had she been? I looked back at Kin. His eyes were darting between the auctioneer and Leontine. She didn't appear to be bidding, yet, but she was watching the auctioneer just as intently as Kin had been.

The bidding had slowed and I was waiting for Kin to jump in and make a bid, but he was too busy watching the two people up front.

"Nine-thousand-two-hundred and fifty, do I have nine-thousand-five-hundred? Nine-thousand-five-hundred? Nine-thousand-five-hundred for this beautiful Russian snuff box? Any other bids, any bids?" He looked searchingly around the room silently willing the bidders to keep going.

"Nine-thousand-five-hundred," said Leontine out loud, forgoing the traditional hand signal or raising of her bidder number. The auctioneer didn't seem put off by her verbal bid. He opened his mouth to confirm her bid, but before he could get it out Kin stood up and raised his bidder number.

"Nine-thousand-five-hundred, and nine-thousand-seven-hundred and fifty," he said pointing at Kin. "Two new bidders."

Leontine's head snapped around and she glared at Kin. Good. I hope he really pisses her off. I bet she can swivel her head all the way around too. Psycho bitch. She thrust her hand into the air. Kin nodded. They went back and forth in rapid succession. I don't know how the auctioneer kept track. He barely had time to acknowledge one bid when another was made.

The bid was up to twelve thousand. The auctioneer looked to see if Kin would up his bid over Leontine's. I clutched his hand and said in a stage whisper "Don't you let her have it." Pretty nervy of me considering I had no idea of the thing's worth or how much money Kin could afford to pay for it.

"Twelve thousand going once, going twice," said the auctioneer.

"Fifteen thousand!" called Kin, speaking his bid for the first time. He and Leontine glared at each other. She turned her back on the auctioneer and looked completely pissed off at Kin. Yes! You just have to love a guy who's willing to spend thousands of dollars to piss off a woman who's insulted you.

"Sixteen." Leontine said, over enunciating the two syllables. She was still giving Kin the death look.

"Seventeen," said Kin very calmly. He raised his eyebrow and smirked a little, as if to say, keep going, I'll out bid you no matter what.

She frowned and announced her bid of eighteen thousand.

"Twenty thousand," called Kin, skipping over nineteen. He didn't bother to conceal a satisfied grin. She got the message and stormed out of the auction house, actually pushing people out of her way. Kin was right. She was horrible. It was nice to realize I wasn't the only person there who was glad she was gone. She hadn't made any friends during her little tantrum on the way out.

I didn't know what to say. I didn't want to think he'd made that huge bid because of me. But if he had, I should thank him, right? Awkward.

Kin sat down on the edge of his chair. He was obviously upset over the encounter. "I'm going to go and settle up. I'll meet you back here in a few minutes, ok?" I hoped he meant settle up with the auction house and not Leontine. I just nodded.

While he was gone, I watched the remaining auctions. There were a few exciting ones, but nothing to compare to the battle between Kin and Leontine. I reflected on the clash between the two. It seemed awfully fierce for just a snuff box, even if it was Russian and over 275 years old. There was something in it that was personal, and I didn't think it had anything to do with me.

Were they rival dealers? No, Kin said he was more of a consultant than a dealer. Were they competing for the same customer? I couldn't come up with a reasonable explanation, or even a good unreasonable one. Had they been lovers? That had been bouncing around in the back of my head from the first moment I saw her. Maybe. But even if they had, it had to be more than that. If this auction had taken place in the animal kingdom, there'd be a bloody carcass on the floor right now. My thoughts were interrupted by Kin's return.

"Shall we go? Or was there something that you wanted to bid on?" he asked as he shuffled sideways in the aisle to his chair.

"Nope," I said cheerfully, hoping he was in a better mood. "Let's go." I stood up and started shuffling alongside of him. He reached out and took my hand as we walked through the remaining crowd.

Once outside I realized just how stuffy it had been in the barn. The fresh air felt good and I said so to Kin. He grunted. Not good.

"Are you ok?" I asked, almost dreading the answer.

"Sorry," he said with a sigh. "I can't explain it now. It's complicated."

Figures. Of course it's complicated. It involves a drop dead gorgeous blonde. Funny phrase, isn't it? Drop dead gorgeous. Except they never do drop dead do they? Very misleading phrase. "It's ok," I answered, hoping I didn't sound petulant.

Kin turned and smiled at me. I was becoming very fond of that smile. He opened his mouth to say something, but instead he stopped dead in his tracks and a terrible expression of anger came over his face. Fortunately, he was not looking at me. I would not want someone looking at me the way he was looking at whoever was standing behind me. And I had a sneaking suspicion I knew who it was.

"Hero, wait for me in the car, please," he said, handing me the keys. Great, just what I needed. To try and find someone else's car in a crowded parking lot.

"Of course," I said, taking the keys. I couldn't resist a peek over my shoulder. Leontine was standing just a couple of feet behind me, looking murderous. It was my time for a parting shot. "Be careful with Gargantua, she's not graceful under pressure."

A great line like that and no reaction at all, from either of them. What a waste. Instead, I heard Leontine demand, "I want that snuff box."

I couldn't hear Kin's reply because, like a good girl, I was finding my way back to his car. Hopefully. Ok, a black Infinity SUV. I could find that, couldn't I? I remember it was parked on the end of a row. That helped. I went to the end of the row I was in and started walking down along the side of the rows. I found a black SUV and when I clicked the security button on the keychain, the car beeped and the lights flashed. Woo hoo! I did it! And on the first try. It was a shame Sue or someone wasn't here to witness it. They'd never believe me.

I let myself in on the passenger side and sat down. I debated switching to the driver's seat and going and getting Kin. I decided against it. He might not appreciate a woman coming to his rescue in front of Amazon woman. I swiveled around in my seat to see if I could catch a glimpse of them. No such luck. I had been hoping to see Leontine thoroughly pissed off and fuming uselessly. Perhaps that's petty of me, but don't act like you wouldn't have wanted to see the same thing if you were in my place.

After craning my neck as much as I could without satisfaction, I decided it was probably better if when Kin did appear he didn't find me searching for him. I put the keys into the ignition and turned on the radio. I settled back into the seat and tried not to imagine what might be taking place between Kin and Leontine. Easier said than done.

Why was that snuff box so important? Was it just her pride that was hurt? Was her reputation at stake, or her job? Surely not everyone who deals in antiques wins every auction they want to. And what was between her and Kin? Were they just business rivals? My Spidey senses told me 'no'. There was definitely more there, and it wasn't strictly professional. I reminded myself that this was only our second date and I didn't have a right to question him about his past relationships. As it was, I'd be lucky if he wanted to see me again after the way I blew up at him after she called me 'lunch'. I still wasn't convinced that there wasn't more to her comment than Kin had said. There was part of me that wanted to believe Leontine wasn't clever enough to come up with a better put down than a stupid attempt at a play on words over 'flavor of the month'. Unfortunately, I had to admit it was pretty unlikely that she was that dim, and that she had had a specific meaning in mind. The question now was, do I pursue it or do I just let it drop? Sighing, I realized that I wouldn't get anywhere trying to force Kin to give me a better explanation and that it was probably best just to let it go. Damn it.

Submerged in my own little world, I hadn't noticed Kin walk up to the car. When he knocked on the window for me to unlock his door I screamed. Yippee, another embarrassing incident. I was beginning to lose count. I flipped the switch to open his door and laughed at myself. What else could I do? Kin got in and slammed the door. He quickly pulled on his seatbelt and turned the engine over. As he put the car into gear he looked across at me and said "I'm sorry about that."

"Don't worry about it. It's not your fault," I said, hoping that I was right. We drove in silence as we made our way back toward the Bourne Bridge.

I hated the silence, but I didn't know what to do. If Kin had felt like talking, he would have been. I had figured that much out about him in the short time we'd been acquainted. Luckily, a song I liked came on the radio. I started singing along with Cat Steven's "Peace Train". I'm not a great singer, but I can carry a tune, and as a general rule, people don't run screaming from the room when I sing. After a few bars I was getting into it and enjoying myself, much to Kin's amusement. Good. If laughing at me brought him out of his dark mood that was ok with me. To my surprise, Kin started singing too. He had a deep, rich voice. Of course. He would have a nice singing voice. But the ice was broken and we enjoyed the rest of our ride, singing along with the radio all the way.

When we pulled on to my street, I worried about whether or not I should invite him in for a drink. "I'm sorry," Kin said as we approached my house. "I didn't even think to ask if you wanted to stop for something to eat."

"That's ok," I said, realizing for the first time how late it was and that I hadn't had any dinner. "I'm not hungry," I fibbed. "But, I could make some coffee or something if you'd like?" Oh! Hmm. That decision just sort of made itself for me.

"No, thank you," Kin said as he put the car in park. "I'd appreciate a rain check though, if that's ok?" He turned to face me and I could see that he meant it. "Hero, I am so very sorry for the way things turned out today."

I put my hand up and waved his comment off. "Please, Kin, it's ok. Really. You're not responsible for Leontine. I'm just sorry I went off on you."

He gave a little, self-deprecating laugh. "You had every right to be upset. I don't blame you a bit for being angry with me."

"I wasn't really angry with you. I was angry with her and frustrated." He gave me a very disbelieving look. "Ok, I was a little mad at you for shushing me, but you were right. It was better not to let her hear how upset she'd made me."

"Thank you. That's more than I deserve."

"You're being too hard on yourself. Come on, come in and let me make you a cup of coffee or something," I asked, opening my door in the hopes that the action would cause him to go along with me.

Kin opened his door and stepped out. He came around my side and took my hand as he walked me to the front door. "No, Hero. I think it would be better if I said goodnight now."

"Oh, ok" I said. I tried to smile but I know my disappointment showed.

We reached my doorstep and Kin took my keys from me and unlocked the door. He pushed it open and then handed me my keys back. "Would it be ok if I called you tomorrow?" he asked.

"Of course. Why wouldn't it be?" Relief!

He just smiled in reply. It was a genuine smile this time. My heart beat just a little faster. "Uh, there's one other thing," Kin said, the smile disappearing from his face. He looked down at his shoes. "I have no right to ask you, but, I could use a small favor, if you don't mind."

Curious. "Sure," I replied, wondering what kind of favor he could possibly want.

"I'd like you to keep this for me for a while, please. Keep it somewhere safe." He took my hand and pressed the Russian snuff box into it.

"Oh!" This was certainly unexpected. Why would he want me to keep it someplace safe? Was Leontine going to try and steal it? "Um, I guess I could do that."

Kin sensed my nervousness. "It's ok. No one's going to bother you about it, Hero."

"But they might bother you?" I said, more of a statement than a question. It was the only reason that made sense, and I wasn't letting him off the hook on this one. "Tell me the truth, Kin," I demanded after he didn't answer.

"Yes. It's unlikely, but not impossible," he admitted reluctantly.

"Don't you have a safe or something if you deal with this stuff all the time?" A reasonable question I thought.

"I have a safe deposit box, but I can't get into it tonight." Damn, a reasonable reply.

"So, you just want me to hold it until tomorrow then?" That didn't seem so bad.

Kin hesitated. Uh oh. This wasn't a good sign. "I'm not sure."

"Kin, are you in some kind of trouble?" I was getting nervous.

"No, no. It's nothing like that." He looked around at the neighborhood as though trying to find something.

"What is it? Do you hear something?" I was liking this less and less.

"I'm just trying to think." He ran his hands through his hair. "Hero, I need you to keep this for me for a few days, please. I'm not sure exactly how many, but no longer than the end of the week, ok? Can you do that for me, please?"

What was I supposed to say? I knew he had obtained it legally and it was rightfully his, so I had no fear of the law. But I felt there was something to be worried about. Kin was scanning the neighborhood again. I whispered to him "You're afraid we're being watched. Don't deny it," I added when I saw he meant to protest. "I will hide this for you," I said, as I slipped the box into my pocket, "but I want you to pretend I didn't take it. If someone is watching us, I want them to think I didn't take it. Ok?"

He didn't miss a beat. "Well, I guess I understand, Hero. You're right, I shouldn't put you in that position, I'm sorry." Fine time to think of that. "Besides, you're right. The best place for it is in a safe deposit box. I guess I was being unreasonable." He leaned forward and kissed my cheek. "Get inside," he whispered in my ear.

Oh, crap! "Thank you for understanding, Kin. I'll talk to you soon. Good night," I said as I walked into my front hall and turned around.

"Good night," Kin said, and he turned and went to his car.

I watched out the window next to the front door as he got in, started the engine and drove off. I was worried. Worried for him and for me. What the hell had I gotten myself into? I was just about to let go of the curtain and head for my bedroom when something caught my eye. A movement in the bushes on the left side of my front yard. Someone was out there. I couldn't move. I wanted to run to the phone and call 911, but I couldn't move. A man came towards the window. He wasn't very tall, but he was broad built. He appeared to have long hair, though it was hard to tell in the dark. I knew my front door was locked, but I didn't know just how safe that made me. Still frozen, I watched him come closer and closer; deliberately walking right towards me. There was a rhododendron in front of the window, so I knew he couldn't come right up to the window itself. He stopped at the hedge. Oh, God, I wanted to run. Please God, make my legs move. Then something happened that did make them move. Move faster than I could have imagined. The stranger outside my window snarled at me like a wild animal. And he had fangs.

CHAPTER 6

I don't know if this counts as some kind of out-of-body experience or what, but as I was barricading myself in my bedroom (a pretty stupid thing to do, upon reflection), I heard this horrible, blood-curdling scream. It was awful. The kind of thing to make your blood turn to ice in your veins. And it wouldn't stop. I couldn't think for all the screaming. My head was pounding and I was panicking and trying to think what to do, but I couldn't because of the terrible screaming. So finally I yelled "Stop the screaming!" And guess what? It stopped, instantly. And why did it stop instantly? Because it was me. How idiotic is that, that I didn't even realize that I was the one who was screaming?

So, obviously, I was barricading myself in my bedroom after having fled up the stairs faster than Jackie Joyner-Kersee. Once I managed to stop myself from screaming, I sat on the floor on the far side of my bed and grabbed the phone off the night stand. "Nine-one-one, Emergency Services. What is the nature of your emergency?" said the woman.

"Please send someone right away. Eleven Georgia Road. There's a man outside, he's probably trying to get in, or already in. Oh, my God! Help me! Send someone quick!" I yelled at her.

"There's someone outside your home miss?"

"Yes, yes! He walked right up to my window. He looked right at me and," I paused. I couldn't tell her about the fangs. Instead of the police protecting me, I'd get a police escort to the funny farm. "And he sort of snarled at me."

"He snarled at you?" she asked.

"I guess so. I don't know what to call it. But it doesn't matter! He's out there, or he may be in here. I don't know. Please send someone now!"

"What is your name?" the woman asked.

"My name? My God! It'll be the deceased Miss Fletcher if you don't get someone over here right now!" I was starting to lose control. "Holy fucking shit! Stop asking me stupid questions and get someone here to help me!" I screamed.

"I've already dispatched a unit to your location. They should be there any moment. Where are you right now Miss Fletcher?" she responded calmly.

"I'm in my bedroom. On the second floor." I told her. "Tell them to use their sirens, ok? I want to hear them coming. I need to know they're coming."

"It's alright Miss Fletcher. They're nearly there." She paused and in a far off sounding voice I heard her say "Unit seventeen, this is Dispatch. Caller requests use of sirens on route to eleven Georgia Road."

"Thank you, thank you," I said loudly to make sure she could hear.

"That's ok. Miss Fletcher, my name is Officer Norris. I'm going to stay on the line here with you while you wait for the officers. Is that alright?"

Was she kidding? "Yes, yes. Thank you." Where were they? Why couldn't I hear them? "Oh, God! He could be right outside my door waiting for me to hang up! What if he's waiting for me?" I was becoming hysterical. Give me some credit though. I would have thought hysteria would have set in automatically after being snarled at by a strange man on my dark front lawn bearing fangs.

"Hang on, Miss Fletcher. Everything's going to be fine. You should be hearing the sirens now," Officer Norris said.

I got up on my knees and leaned toward the window. Yes, there was definitely a siren in the distance. Oh, thank you God! "I can hear them!" I announced to the officer. "They're coming." Like she didn't already know that. Boy, people in hysterical panic say some pretty dumb things.

"Ok, that's good. You just hang in there a few more seconds and everything is going to be alright."

The sirens grew louder and before I knew it, they were right in front of my house. "They're here," I told Officer Norris.

"Ok, good. You need to go and let them in now," she instructed.

"No!" I said unreasonably. "What if he's in the house? I can't go out there, he's probably waiting for me!" I started to become hysterical again, imagining that hideous face waiting for me right outside my door.

"Miss Fletcher, the officers need to come inside to help you. You need to let them in," she explained calmly.

"I can't! He could be right there! Oh, my God! What if he kills me before I can reach the front door?"

"Have you heard any sounds that would lead you to believe he is inside your home?"

"I don't know," I answered truthfully. "I was making so much noise myself."

"Ok Miss Fletcher, this is what I want you to do. Are you on a cordless phone?"

"No."

"That's ok. I want you to stretch your phone as close to your bedroom door as you can, and leave the receiver off, so I can still hear you. Then I want you to carefully open your door. If everything is clear, go downstairs and let the officers in. If you see or hear anything, just shout as loud as you can and I will instruct the officers to break down your front door. Do you understand?"

"Yes, I understand," I replied. Not a perfect solution, but I didn't have much choice. I pulled the phone toward the door and placed it on the floor. Then I stretched out the squiggly cord between the phone base and the receiver. Holding the receiver in my left hand, I pulled a chair out of the barricade pile with my right hand, and then hung the phone receiver over the back of the chair. I removed the chest I had pushed up in front of the door. Taking a deep, shaky breath, I put my hand on the doorknob. Oh, God, please don't let him be out there! I turned the knob and called out to Officer Norris, hoping she could hear me, "I'm opening the bedroom door now." Slowly, I turned the knob and pulled the door open. My heart was hammering hard against my chest. Little by little I opened the door. No one there. Thank you, God! I could hear the officers outside. One of them was knocking on the front door and calling my name. Summoning all my courage, I kicked off my shoes and leapt out of my room and onto the stairs. How I didn't fall down the stairs and break my neck I'll never know. I flew down the stairs like a bolt of lightning and threw myself at the front door. I undid the lock and pulled it open.

"Oh, my God, thank you, thank you," I babbled at the young officer.

"Are you ok, miss? Are you hurt?" he asked as he came inside.

"No, no. I'm not hurt. Just terrified." Well, I was. "Did you see anyone, or anything?" Anything was probably closer the truth.

"I'm afraid not," he said. Ironic isn't it? The cops are 'afraid' they didn't find anything and I was 'afraid' they would. "Why don't you sit down and you can tell me what happened."

We went into the living room together and I sat on the couch. "Oh!" I gasped, remembering nice Officer Norris. "The dispatcher. She's still on the phone. She was listening for me."

"Don't worry. I'll take care of it." The officer pushed the button on the side of the microphone or whatever the hell you call those things clipped to their shoulders. "Dispatch, this is Unit Seventeen."

"Seventeen, this is Dispatch. Go ahead," came a female voice.

"All set, Brenda. You don't need to hang on the line for eleven Georgia."

"Copy that Seventeen."

"All set," he said as he crouched down next to me. "What's your name?" he asked.

For one of the very few times in my life, I didn't think twice about saying my name or wonder what the reaction would be. "Hero. Hero Fletcher."

God love him, he didn't even raise an eyebrow. "Ok, Hero. Can you tell me what happened?"

I described the event for him, providing as much detail as I could, except for the part about the fangs. Had I ever seen this man before? I said I hadn't. He asked if I would be able to identify the man if I saw him again. I told him I could. The officer wanted to know if I participated in any on-line chat rooms, dating services, or had a website where I would have a picture of myself posted. No. None of that. I did have a website for my business, but there was no photo or mention of the fact that I was female.

The officer told me that his partner was looking around outside. Did I want him to search the inside of the house, or would I prefer he stay with me. I wanted him to stay with me. He asked if I had anyone I could stay with or who could come and stay with me. I hadn't thought of that. There was no way I could stay here tonight. But where could I go? Or more to the point, where should I go? I knew several of my friends would take me in after such an ordeal, but where would I feel the safest? "Yes," I said. "I have friends I could stay with."

"Would you like to call them now?" he asked as he took my cordless phone off its base and handed it to me.

I didn't mind. I did want to call now. I nodded and took the phone from him. When I pushed the button, I got a fast busy signal. The officer heard it and said he'd be right back. He ran up the stairs and into my bedroom. I could hear his footsteps on the ceiling as he hung up the phone in my bedroom. As soon as I heard his footsteps on the stairs, I hurriedly dialed Debbie's number. I wanted to stay with Debbie and Bob because I'd feel better staying somewhere where there was a man present, and also because I knew Bob had a gun. "Hello?" she said as she answered.

"Deb, it's me. I need a favor. Can I stay with you guys tonight?"

"What's wrong?" she asked in a panicky voice. She could tell something bad had happened.

"I'm ok. It's just some weirdo was outside my house tonight and he scared the hell out of me, and I don't want to stay here tonight. Can I stay with you guys, please?"

"Of course you can!" she took the phone away from her ear and called out "Bob, go pick up Hero. She's going to stay with us."

"No," I interrupted. "That's ok. I'll drive myself over. Besides, it's quicker that way."

"Ok, if you're sure?" Debbie said, full of concern. I hated making her worry.

"I am. I just need a few minutes to pack a bag and finish up with the police," I said.

"Police! The police are there? My God, Hero, what happened?" She was really worried now.

"Don't worry, Deb it's ok. I called the police so they could make sure he was gone and stuff, ok?" And stuff. Very technical police activity. Dumb ass.

"Ok," she answered, unconvinced. "We'll see you soon."

"Ok, thanks," I said as I hung up.

While I had been on the phone, the other officer had come inside. He talked briefly with the first officer and then went to look around the house. When I hung up the phone, the first officer came back over and updated me on what they had discovered.

"We didn't find any evidence of anyone trying to force your doors or windows. There were several partial footprints in the dirt at the edge of the driveway, but we didn't find any usable impressions in the grass near the window."

"What about over by the bushes where he had been hiding?" I asked.

"No footprints. However, we're going to have someone stop by in the morning for a better look. See if they can find any trace fibers or anything like that. Ok?" He sensed my concern that there was no evidence of this creep and all they had to go on was my account of the evening.

"He was there. I did see him," I insisted.

"I don't doubt it one bit, Hero. I'm certain you did see someone. That's why we're going to have someone come back for a better look in the daylight." He reached out and patted my hand reassuringly. Funny. At another time I might have found that patronizing, but at the moment I was glad of it. "My partner is checking the rest of the house for you now. Would you like me to go upstairs with you while you pack a bag?"

He was so nice. I know it's his job, but he was good at it. "I think I'll be ok," I said, not anxious to have a stranger watching me pack my unmentionables. He nodded and I stood and went upstairs. My shoes were in the doorway where I'd discarded them. I slipped them back on and went to my closet. I took an overnight bag from the floor of the closet and put it on my bed. I noticed the phone had been put back on the night stand by the nice, young officer.

I hurried around the room, grabbing underwear, bra, jeans and a shirt. I stuffed them all into the bag. Then I went into the bathroom and got my toothbrush and my nightgown off the back of the door. As I put these into the bag with my clothes, I remembered the snuff box in my pocket. I took it out and looked at it. The enamel design on the lid was full of colorful butterflies done in bright jewel tones. The bottom was silver with embossed butterflies. It was a beautiful box and in excellent condition. Had the freak outside my window been after the box? Had he followed us here? Was he working with Leontine, or was this another interested party? It was all too much to think about. I shoved it into the bag and zipped the bag closed.

When I got to the bottom of the stairs the two police men were waiting for me. "Would it be too much to ask for you to follow me to my friend's house? She just lives a few minutes away on the other side of town."

"Sure, we can do that," said the second officer. "Let me carry that for you," he added as he reached to take my bag. I thanked him and bent down to get my pocket book where I had dropped it on the floor beneath the window. I rummaged around for my keys, thankfully finding them quicker than usual, and went to the front door.

Both officers walked me to my car. When I opened the driver's side door, the first officer, who had stayed in the house with me, put his hand on my shoulder. He flipped the locks and opened up the back door of my little Camry. The second officer bent his head inside to check that no one was hiding in the back, then placed my bag on the seat. Very thorough, these two. I got in and reached for my seatbelt. "We'll follow you," the young officer said as he closed my door for me.

I backed out of my driveway and waited in the middle of the street while the two police officers started their squad car and pulled up behind me. It was a short ride to Debbie and Bob's, but I felt better knowing the cops were following behind and would be watching while I got out of my car and went into my friend's house. Debbie had been waiting for me and came out her front door and on to her porch before I could even get my car in park. I got out quickly, reaching over the seat for my bag. Locking the doors with my remote, I waved with the other hand to my escort and called "Thank you!"

I ran over to the steps and up the porch, hugging Debbie when I got there. "Are you ok?" she asked.

"Yeah, I'm fine. Just a little shaky, that's all." I gave her a weak smile. We went inside and Debbie dead bolted the door and drew the chain lock across. I wondered if things like that would stop a guy with fangs.

Naturally, she and Bob wanted to hear the whole story, and I told it to them. All of it. Even the fangs. I wasn't worried about them wanting to ship me off to a psycho ward. "Are you shitting me?" asked Bob incredulously. "Fangs? Are you sure?"

"Abso-fucking-lutely. The bastard had fangs. And I don't just mean his canines were unusually long. They were fangs!" I said emphatically.

Debbie and Bob looked at each other, neither of them knowing what to say. "I can't believe that," Debbie said. "Oh! I don't mean I don't believe you, honey," she added quickly. "I just mean, well, it's so unbelievable! A guy with fangs! Do you think he's one of those gothic people who like to dress up?"

"I have no idea," I said. They asked why someone would be hiding in my bushes. Why would anyone hide in anyone's bushes? I told them to ask Ted Bundy. Bob reminded me that he was dead. Smart ass.

We talked and talked and talked. We exhausted every avenue of speculation as to why this freak had been outside my house. Well, almost every avenue. I hadn't told them about the snuff box. I saw no reason to involve them with whatever was going on any more than I already had.

Around one in the morning, Bob declared that he had to go to bed, as he needed to be up in just a few hours for work. I felt bad. It was bad enough I had put them out, but I kept them up late too. "Don't worry," Bob said, "you're safe here, H." He came and gave me a little peck on the forehead. "Try and get some sleep."

Oh, sure! Sleep. No problem. I was going to sleep knowing some freaky goth, vampire wannabe, and a bitchy Amazon were out there somewhere, maybe even watching this house. Oh, yeah. I was sure to have sweet dreams with fang boy's ugly face revisiting me every time I closed my eyes. Right. Sleep was not going to happen.

Debbie and I sat up and talked for another hour. Then I got ready for bed and she helped me pull out their sleeper sofa and make it up. I didn't have the heart to tell her I'd be up all night, and I saw no reason to make her feel like she should sit up with me. We hugged and said goodnight, and I climbed under the covers.

What the hell had I gotten myself into? Could it possibly be a coincidence that that freakazoid was lurking in my bushes at the exact same time that Kin was asking me to hide the snuff box? Something told me it was no coincidence. I didn't like that. Not one bit. I know I didn't know much about Kin, but what I did know, I liked. Sure our second date had been rocky, but it wasn't his fault. It was Leontine's fault. I silently cursed her again. Once more I wondered what could possibly be so important about an old snuff box. If it was important enough to have someone sneaking around my house and scaring the crap out of me, then we were dealing with something more than your typical antique.

As quietly as I could, I peeled back the covers and swung my legs over the side of the bed. I grabbed my overnight bag and clicked on the lamp on the end table. I hoped Debbie wouldn't notice the light. I knew Bob was fast asleep, but Debbie might not be. I dug around in my bag and pulled out the curious object. I scooted up to the top of the sofa bed and held the box under the light. Examining it as closely as possible, I turned it over slowly again and again. Stamped on the bottom of the box was the manufacturer's hallmark, like Kin had shown me on other silver items before the auction. Just like those other items, it looked like nothing more than a series of squiggles to me. Once I was sure that there was nothing unusual on the outside, I opened it up to inspect the inside. It was as smooth as glass. I ran my fingers over the surface just to be sure I hadn't missed anything. I closed the box and ran the tip of my index finger over the butterfly pattern, hoping to discover some inconsistency, or loose piece, or secret compartment or something, but I found nothing.

Sighing in defeat, I wriggled my feet back under the blankets and slunk back down, resting my head on the pillow. I kept turning the box over and over in my hands. It was driving me batty that I had no idea what was so special about this one Russian snuff box. The auctioneer hadn't mentioned anything special. He hadn't noted that it had belonged to anyone famous, or made by any noteworthy silversmith. Certainly an auctioneer would know such things and would make use of them to drive the price up. Though this had fetched a pretty hefty price. I wondered what price it had been expected to fetch?

The sky was starting to lighten when I finally drifted into a restless sleep. Disjointed images fluttered through my head. Kin's face. Leontine's face. Fang Boy's face. The auctioneer's face. The young policeman's face. They came in and out in random order, like pieces of a puzzle that you can't fit together. They overlapped and blurred, becoming barely recognizable. A jagged procession of eyes and mouths jumbled together. I awoke with a start, feeling more anxious than I had when I went to bed.

It was a little after six thirty. Bob was already gone to work and I could hear Debbie in the shower. I stood and stretched, rotating my head slowly to work out the kinks in my neck. I rubbed the gunk out of my eyes and stepped over my bag to head out to the kitchen and get something to drink.

A movement somewhere to the right caught my attention. Someone was outside. Oh, God! Had he followed me? I ran to the big picture window, bumping one of the wingback chairs out of my way as I went. I was in time to see an early model Oldsmobile parked across the bottom of the driveway; a hairy, muscular arm closing the passenger side door. The door slammed and the car sped away. I was at a bad angle to get a license plate number, but I could see that it was a Massachusetts plate and that it only had a few digits. The last might have been a six or the letter 'G'.

What should I do? Should I call the police? I didn't want the police to come to Debbie's house. Debbie was still in the shower. Thankfully, she liked to take long showers, so I figured I had a couple of minutes at least. I grabbed my pocket book and sat on the edge of the sofa bed. I fished out the card one of the officers had given me and picked up the phone. After a couple of rings my call was rerouted. I shouldn't have been surprised. I'm sure the officers who had responded to my call last night were off duty now. When the call was answered by an officer, I explained who I was and why I was calling. I was transferred to a detective on duty.

"Detective Joyce," came a loud, blustery voice on the other end of the phone.

"Good morning Detective Joyce. My name is Hero Fletcher."

"Hero?" he interrupted in a slightly snide tone. Clearly not the same class of guy I dealt with the night before.

"Yes, Hero. And yes, it is my real name. I'm calling about the man who was outside my home at eleven Georgia Road last night. Are you familiar with that?" I was not going to take crap from anyone, detective or not.

"Yes, Miss Fletcher. Officer Salucci left something for me about your complaint. I was planning on going out there later this morning to have a better look."

"Well, I stayed at a friend's house last night and I believe the same man was just here." That made him interested.

"You saw the same man at your friend's house?" he said in much more serious tone.

"I'm not completely certain," I admitted. "Let me tell you what just happened." And I did. I described the car for him as best as I could, though I wasn't very good at the names of older cars.

"But you didn't get a look at him. It might not be him at all," he pointed out.

"No, it might not be. But don't you think it would be far too much of a coincidence if someone was trying to see me through my friend's living room window the morning after someone was looking at me through my own window?" I asked in a tone that made it clear that no matter what he said, I did not think it was just a coincidence.

"Yes, I agree. I just wanted to be clear on the details. What is your friend's address?"

"Why?" I didn't want the police there.

"Well, Miss Fletcher, we need to check out the premises to see if any evidence was left. What's the address?"

I hesitated. I felt sick to my stomach. Debbie had finished her shower and would be out any second. "Do we have to do this right now?" I asked.

"Miss Fletcher," Detective Joyce said, getting impatient with me, "did you or did you not see someone looking in your friend's window?"

"Yes, I did. But my friend doesn't know and I don't want to upset her."

"Don't you think she'd be a lot more upset if she was to find someone looking in at her and reported it to us, only to discover you had experienced the same thing and not told her?" he said rationally.

Oh, damn. Don't you hate when other people are right? I gave in and gave him the address. I wasn't looking forward to telling Debbie.

It was just as awful as I had feared. She freaked. I couldn't remember feeling so rotten. Now, thanks to me, she wouldn't feel safe in her own home. I tried to convince her that once I left, they would just follow me and leave her alone, but that didn't help matters. Go figure.

She insisted on calling in to work and spending the day with me. When the Detective arrived we both went outside to greet him. He wasn't any more pleasant in person than he was over the phone.

"Which one of you is Fletcher?" Nice.

"I am," I said. (Isn't that a song?) I didn't give him a chance to piss me off. I walked right out onto the lawn and showed him approximately where the person had been when looking through the window. Then, without missing a beat, I briskly walked over to the driveway and repeated what I had told him over the phone about the car. "Do you want to see where I was inside?" I asked him.

The Detective just stood and looked at me, trying to figure out if I was a loon looking for attention or if I was trying to bust his balls. He walked up to me slowly. When we were nearly toe to toe he asked, "Do you want our help or not Miss Fletcher?"

"If I didn't, I wouldn't have called. Haven't I shown you and told you all I can?"

"I don't know about that yet. But I know you could do it without the attitude."

"So could you," I shot back. "I've got someone stalking me and you show up looking for 'Fletcher'. Not Miss Fletcher, or which one of you ladies made the call or anything like that."

He rolled his eyes. "I'm sorry if I offended you by not calling you 'Miss', but I am out here to help you. So how about you stop treating me like the enemy?" I guessed he had a pretty short fuse and wondered how glad the force must have been to get him off a beat. Then again, maybe I just watch too much TV.

"Fine," I said. "What else do you need?" All this time Debbie had been standing on her porch. She took turns watching us and looking up and down the street. It reminded me of Kin looking around my neighborhood the night before.

Detective Joyce said he'd like to go inside, so I brought him up to the porch and introduced him to Debbie. The three of us went inside. I showed him where I had been standing and where I had been when I watched the car speed away. He asked Debbie if she had seen a car like I described around the neighborhood. She hadn't. Debbie was even worse with cars than I was, but I didn't volunteer that information.

There really hadn't been anything to see outside Debbie's so we decided to all drive over to my house. I wasn't thrilled about spending more time with the Detective, but I figured it was best to get it all over with as soon as possible.

Debbie rode with me in my car. "What are you going to do? You can't stay at your place until they find the guy? Where are you going to work?"

Oh, crap. I hadn't thought about all of that. She was right. What was I going to do?

CHAPTER 7

We stood by my car as Detective Joyce began searching for evidence in the bushes on the left hand side of my yard. Pulling on a pair of rubber gloves, he started running his hands gently over the grass.

"Do we have to stay out here?" Debbie asked. "I could really use a cup of coffee."

"Sure," I said as took my keys out of my pocket. "I could use a cup myself."

Debbie followed me to the front door. I turned the key, pushed the door open, and we walked into the front hall. As I began closing the door, I called to Detective Joyce to let him know we were going inside and to offer him some coffee. Suddenly, Debbie screamed.

I jumped a mile and ran to the other room. The Detective sprinted for the house and was beside me in a matter of seconds. Debbie was standing in the middle of my living room, at least I thought it was my living room. It had been completely torn apart. Literally. Lamps and knick-knacks lay in ruins on the floor. Every picture in the room from the mantle, the walls, the tables, were all smashed. Fluff from the couch pillows lay in clumps over half the room. They had even ripped open the upholstery on the couch and chairs. They'd done everything but tear up the carpet and punch holes in the walls.

"Oh my God, oh my God!" I cried. "My house, my home," I thought I was going to be sick. "My childhood home. Oh! Mom's favorite chair. Oh, Mom!" It was too much. It was more than I could bear. I sunk to the floor and starting crying loudly.

Debbie came over and put her arms around me. "It's okay, Hero. It'll be alright." she cooed.

"Alright?! How? How? How is this ever going to be alright? They've destroyed my home. Oh, God! God! They've ruined everything. They've," I couldn't talk anymore. My throat was constricted and I gulped for air. I sobbed uncontrollably, unable to hold it in.

"I'm sorry, Miss Fletcher," said the Detective. I had a feeling he really was sorry, but I didn't care. "I'm going to go have a look at the rest of the house, if that's ok?" I nodded. I heard his heavy footsteps go down the front hall. Then I heard the beeping of his cell phone. "This is Joyce. I need a forensics team out here at eleven Georgia right away."

How could this happen? It didn't seem possible. Somehow I knew in my heart that my whole house was in the same state as the living room. I didn't need to see it to know. I could just feel it. I knew then what it was to be utterly heartbroken. Everything that mattered to me had either been destroyed or desecrated. "Debbie!" I cried, snapping up my head to look at her. "Mom's figurines," I said before lapsing into a fresh wave of sobs. "Oh, no, no. Mom!" Debbie cried silent tears and held me tighter.

I could hear Detective Joyce walking around upstairs. Déjà vu. It was only a matter of hours since I listened to that nice young office walking upstairs when he went to hang up the phone.

I wailed pitifully, rocking back and forth. "Please, please God, no." I was in pain, real pain. It hurt so badly: my head throbbed violently, and my stomach was in knots, and I felt like I was never going to be able to take a good breath again. I wished that God would just strike me dead there and then so I wouldn't have to deal with any more. It was too much. More than anyone should have to bear. How could I ever possibly recover? I couldn't imagine.

Detective Joyce came back in the room. "I'm sorry Miss Fletcher, but I'm going to have to ask you to tell me if you notice anything missing."

"What?" said Debbie incredulously. "Are you kidding me? How in the world is she supposed to tell if anything is missing among all this mess?"

"I don't expect her to know for certain. I only want her first impressions. Anything she can tell me now will help us get the investigation moving more quickly." he explained. I sniffled in an undignified manner and nodded my head at him. At least I would be doing something productive, I told myself.

Debbie helped me up and I clung to her arm as we walked out to the hallway. He asked if I had noticed anything missing from the living room. I told him I hadn't. We went down the hall and into my office.

Well, at least my computers weren't broken. That was unexpected. My two hard drives were still tucked safely underneath the desk. The monitors had been tipped over, but they were in one piece. My laptop was on the floor under a pile of papers. Hopefully, they all still worked. But everything else, all my files, my office supplies, CDs and disks; they were all over the floor. Every drawer pulled out and emptied. The one painting in the room pulled off the wall and the back torn open. I couldn't tell for certain if my backup drives were damaged or if they were all there. I wasn't sure of the number and I told this to the Detective.

We moved on to the kitchen. It was even worse than I had imagined. It wasn't bad enough that they had tossed every pot, pan, bowl and dish onto the floor. But they had emptied all the cabinets, the refrigerator and freezer as well. Every box and package ripped open and poured on the floor. "Holy crap," declared Debbie, under her breath. My thoughts exactly. Why had they dumped all the food out? It was crazy.

I stifled a sob and shook my head at Detective Joyce and he nodded back. Then he began picking his way carefully across the kitchen to the dining room. Debbie and I followed on tip-toe, careful not to slip on any of the messy blobs of food. I stopped at the door. I couldn't go in, and tried to step back. "It's ok, H. You can do this," Debbie said softly. I wish I had as much confidence in myself.

I closed my eyes, took a deep breath and stepped into the room. When I opened my eyes, I was looking at my feet. There were shards of broken glass and china all around me. I spun around and buried my face in Debbie's shoulder. "Oh, God! Nana's wedding china!" I cried miserably. "Oh, God, no, no. Why? Why is this happening?" Debbie patted my back.

"It's not all gone, honey. There are a few pieces left," she said pitifully.

I peeked over her shoulder. She was right, there were a few pieces in tact here and there, though it didn't help my sorrow much. Why break the plates? I couldn't have hidden a snuff box in the plates or saucers, and the tea cups were too small to hide anything in. The senselessness of it only made it worse.

I shook my head again and picked my way back through the kitchen and out to the hallway. Debbie and Detective Joyce were right behind me. I could hear the forensic people outside. "Just a minute," Joyce said as he pushed past us and went to the front door. He opened it just as one of the analysts was about to knock. They spoke to each other quietly for a couple of minutes, both looking over at me from time to time. The Detective instructed them to start in the living room and came back over to me and Debbie. "Ok, let's look upstairs." He held out his arm, gesturing for me to go first.

The first room at the top of the stairs was mine. I stood in the doorway, recalling that just a few hours ago the only things out of place were the chest and the chair I had used to barricade the door. Now it was totally destroyed. The bed was moved and the mattress and box spring were both cut completely open. All of my clothes were on the floor; the closet emptied and the drawers of my dresser upturned. My hope chest was open and the contest strewn about. I went over and knelt beside it, gathering up a puffy cloud of white and clutching it to my chest. "Mom's wedding veil. I wore it for First Communion, remember?" I asked, looking at Debbie over my shoulder. She nodded and smiled weakly.

"I'm afraid I'm going to have to ask you not to touch anything," said Joyce.

"I've already touched everything here. It's my house!" I snapped.

"Yes," he sighed, "but you could be rubbing off evidence."

Gently, I put the veil back in my hope chest and stood up. "I don't know if anything's missing here," I told him and I walked to the hallway and straight into the bathroom. I figured that would be the easiest room to deal with.

All of the towels and linens were on the floor. The closet was completely empty. They had even dumped out all my Q-Tips. The medicine cabinet had hardly been touched, but I kept very little in there. After the kitchen, I found myself surprised they hadn't emptied out all my shampoo and conditioner and shower gel. Thank goodness for small favors, I guess. I shook my head and went back into the hall.

There were two rooms left. One was William's old room, which had been turned into a guest room years ago, and the other was my mother's room, which I hardly ever went in. After my mom had passed, Debbie and Sue had helped me pack up her clothes for Goodwill. Since then, I rarely entered her room. I couldn't do it now. That was where the bulk of her collection of Royal Doulton figurines were kept. There was no way I could face going in there. "Debbie, could you?" I asked cryptically, jerking my head towards my mother's door. She knew exactly what I meant. Debbie told the Detective that she felt confident she would know if something obvious was missing from the room and went in.

"Fine," he said. "I'm going to check on things down stairs. I'll be back in just a minute." Joyce ran down the stairs and I continued down the hall to William's old room.

No surprises here. Mattress and box spring cut open, the closet and all drawers emptied, and the one photograph (a picture of William's graduation from college) was smashed. No reaction. Maybe because there really wasn't anything personal left in this room or maybe I was just numb. There was way too much to cope with, and now I was numb.

Could all of this be because of an old Russian snuff box? It seemed crazy. I needed to talk to Kin. He owed me an explanation. Plus, I wanted to talk to him before I had to answer any questions from Detective Joyce. He was sure to ask me what the culprits were looking for. In fact, I was surprised he hadn't already. Did I tell him about the snuff box? Should I hand it over to him and let him deal with ugly guys with fangs stalking him? Kin had entrusted it to me, but how much loyalty did I owe a guy I barely knew? Not to mention a guy who put me in a position to be stalked and have my home destroyed. Still, I felt I should talk to him first.

Oddly, the phone was still on top of the table next to the bed. Or sort of next to the bed. Probably because the table had no drawers so there was no way to hide something there. I hoped I'd have enough time to talk to him before the Detective came looking for me. I picked up the receiver and heard a rapid busy signal. Great. It was off the hook somewhere, probably a lot of somehweres actually. So much for that. As I headed toward the door, I saw Debbie coming towards me with something in her hands.

She held out one of my mother's figures and pushed it into my hands. "There are a few that are fine, hun. And I think a couple of them can be repaired." Her eyes were filled with tears and her jaw was trembling with the effort to not cry. "I remember you told me that that one was her favorite," she added, pointing to the figure in my hands.

I hadn't even looked at it when she gave it to me. Now I looked down and saw that it was her favorite one. Thank you, God! At least there was that. One tiny little fleck of silver in an otherwise enormous, jet black cloud.

My mother's figurines had been her pride and joy. She had worked so hard to collect them. Her 'fancy ladies', as she used to say. From a dollar or two left over from the week's grocery shopping, to loose change under the cushions, to a few extra dollars made from knitting sweaters for friends at work and church; she managed to scrimp and save enough so that once a year she could go up to the outlets in Kittery, Maine and buy herself a fancy lady. Mom had been so proud of them. She had made special mention of leaving them to me in her will. I was very glad she hadn't lived to see this. It would have killed her.

I smiled down at the pretty brunette figure. She had flowers and ribbons at her crown and big, dark curls cascading down her back. She wore a pretty blue ball gown with a pink sash and a delicate pink ribbon at her throat. One hand held up the skirt slightly and a tiny foot clad in a matching blue slipper poked out, as though she were walking. The other hand clutched a bouquet of violets. This had been her favorite because it was named Valerie. Valerie was her mother's name and it was the name she had wanted to give me. Obviously, she had lost that battle.

I smiled in spite of myself. I remembered the time when I was twelve and I'd had a huge argument with my mother for letting Dad name me Hero. I felt she'd had a duty to protect me from going through life with such a stupid name and had failed in her duty miserably. Dad might be to blame for the odious name, but she was the Mother. She was supposed to keep things like this from happening. Poor Mom made the mistake of letting it slip that she had wanted to name me Valerie, after my grandmother. I became livid. I stormed out of the room, vowing never to talk to her again. I kept it up for a week, giving her the cold shoulder. Finally, Mom had enough. But she didn't scold me, or punish me, or demand that I stop. No, not my mom. Mrs. Fletcher came into my room early one morning and sat down on my bed. She began singing "Good Morning Starshine" at the top of her lungs. I loved my mom, but she couldn't sing worth a damn. In fact, it was painful. I got up and went to the bathroom. She followed me and stood outside the door, still singing. When I went back to my room, she managed to get in before I could slam the door on her. No matter what I did she just kept singing that silly song over and over, gleefully. In the end, I couldn't help myself. I started to laugh at her. And once we started laughing together, all was forgiven.

I started laughing now. Laughing while tears ran down my face. Detective Joyce had come back upstairs and he and Debbie looked at me as though I was losing my mind. Maybe I was.

The laughter turned back to tears. "Can I take this?" I asked the Detective. "Please?" I must have looked really pathetic because he said I could.

We walked back toward the stairs. I could hear the forensic people going through my rooms, doing whatever it is they do. I felt like shouting for them to stop, for everyone to leave, go away. My home and my possessions had been violated enough for one day, thank you. But I knew they had to do it if they were going to catch the guy, so I bit my tongue.

Once we were back downstairs, Detective Joyce asked "Is there somewhere we could sit down and go over some questions?"

My first impulse was to ask him if he was high, but it was one of those rare moments when my brain worked faster than my tongue. Instead I just raised my eyebrows at him.

"There are some chairs in the back yard," Debbie suggested. We all agreed not to attempt to reach the back yard via the kitchen and went out the front door and walked around.

There were several weathered Adirondack chairs and a table in the back. We sat down and I waited for the big question.

"Now, Miss Fletcher, can you tell me what the person or persons were looking for?" he asked as he adjusted his jacket.

"I have no idea," I lied. "What makes you so sure he was looking for anything at all?"

"Oh, come on now!" he cried in frustration. "You know damn well this was done by someone looking for something!" The pleasantries were over.

"I know nothing of the kind! I have no idea at all why the hell this was done to me!" I continued to lie. Well, sort of. I didn't really know for sure. "How do you know that freakazoid didn't just do this because he was angry that I called the cops, or to scare me, or just because he's a psycho? I mean, after all, look at some of the stuff he broke? What could I hide in dinner plates, or in the solid figures he broke in the living room? Or why smash all the picture frames but not look in the back?" I tried to reason. Until I spoke to Kin I couldn't tell the cops about the snuff box. After all, there was a chance that this wasn't related to it, though I doubted it. And if it did turn out to be about the snuff box, I could always claim I had no idea anyone would want to steal it.

"You have to admit, some of the stuff they broke doesn't make sense," Debbie piped in.

"For crying out loud! You're telling me you think the suspects tore open your couch,"

"Suspects! How about criminals?" I cut him off. "Violators! How about scum, or bastards! They completely ruined my home, everything I own!" I was past trying to hold my temper.

"H, he has to call them that, honey," Debbie said soothingly.

Detective Joyce sighed and pinched the bridge of his nose. "Look, your place was tossed in a way that clearly shows the 'violators'," he said snidely, "were looking for something."

But I wasn't done with my alternative theory. "Then tell me, Detective, why did the guy walk right up to the window and let me see him? Why didn't he wait until I was in bed, or not home, and then break in and search for it? Or for that matter, why didn't he take me by surprise instead of letting me see him? He could have broken in and sacred me into giving him whatever it was he wanted."

He just sat there staring at me. I felt I had a good point. In fact, the more I thought about it, the more I legitimately wondered about these things. Why did he allow me to see him? Why not break in when I wasn't suspecting anything?

"If there's nothing else right now, perhaps we could go back to my house. I'm sure Hero could use a nap," asked Debbie.

"No, I can't go back to your place Deb. I've involved you enough," I protested uselessly.

"You're coming back with me and that's that. We'll go as soon as Detective Joyce arranges to have someone watch you."

"Excuse me?" he asked, genuinely surprised. "I never said anything about police protection."

"Well, certainly you agree this person or persons are violent. They could be dangerous."

"Well," he started, but Debbie kept on going.

"And surely after he's already been following her around, you're not going to leave her unprotected." Debbie badgered the Detective for a few more minutes and wore him down. He called for a squad car to keep watch outside her house. I have the best friends.

"Can I take some clothes and things with me?" I asked.

"I'll have one of the forensics people go with you to get a few necessary items."

"I'm going to need some information from my office." It looked like he was going to protest that one, so I added "I have my own business and I'm going to need to call my clients and tell them about what's happened. I could just copy their numbers down from my Rolodex."

He agreed to that. As we walked back around to the front of the house I asked for one more thing. "They didn't touch my computers. Can I take them so I can keep up with my work?"

"I don't know about that. I'll have to check and see with the forensics team. If they don't find anything, then you can probably have them later today or tomorrow. Otherwise, if they do find some evidence, you probably won't have them back for a while."

"Oh, no! You can't do that! I'm a graphic artist. I need those computers. They have all my programs and images and account information. I can't earn a living without those!" This was too much.

He put his hand up to silence me. "Let's wait and see if they even find any evidence on them. If they do, I'm sure they will work something out with you, ok?"

I didn't have any choice. We went back into the house. Joyce talked to the same forensics person I saw him speak with earlier. He called to a female member of his team, spoke softly to her for a moment, and then pointed her toward us.

"Hi, I'm Angela. I understand you want to get some things from your room?" I nodded and she lead the way to me room. It was surreal. Getting permission from other people to go into my own bedroom and take my own clothing. And then, I get led there by one of these strangers, as though it's not even my own home.

She pulled a plastic bag out of God only knows where and handed it to me. "We'd rather you not take any of your luggage. You understand, so you are actually removing and coming in contact with as little as possible." Yeah, sure. I understood. I didn't like it, but I understood.

I got what I absolutely needed in my bedroom and office and got the hell out of there. I couldn't bear being there with that crowd of cops taking over everything. It was a relief to get into my car and drive to Debbie's.

We finally got to have our coffee, but neither of us was hungry. While Debbie went to the kitchen to pour us each a second cup, I sat on the end of the couch and looked at my mother's figurine.

What the hell had I gotten myself into? My home was destroyed and I was being stalked by a fanged freak! When we had been pulling up to Debbie's house a little while ago, I had been afraid that we would find her house had been trashed too, but fortunately, everything was fine. I felt so guilty for getting her and Bob mixed up in whatever this was.

"Here we go," said Debbie, placing a steaming hot mug of coffee on the table in front of me.

"Debbie, I'm so sorry about all of this. I should never have come here last night."

"Don't be silly! If you'd have stayed in your own house that weirdo might have killed you!"

"Well, I wouldn't have stayed at home. I should have gone to a hotel instead though."

"No," Debbie said emphatically. "You should have done exactly what you did." She took my hand and squeezed it. We sat there side by side holding hands for a few minutes.

I had to talk to Kin. No, I needed to see him. I needed to see his face when he explained why all this was happening. And he needed to see mine when I told him about my mother's figurines and my grandmother's china and putting my friends in danger. I asked Debbie if I could use the phone in her room to make some calls, as my cell phone needed charging. Of course she had no objection.

I took the numbers I'd written down in my office and went to her bedroom. I decided I had to call my clients first. I owed it to them to let them know about my circumstances, and to assure them that their privacy had not be compromised, and that I would still meet my deadlines. This was not going to be easy. How to put a spin on this so it doesn't sound as bad as it was? I dreaded making the calls. By the third call, I was getting my story down and soon the calls were done. Thankfully, all my clients had been sympathetic and supportive. I was more grateful for that then they could have imagined.

Next I called Kin. The phone rang and rang. Just as I was about to give up, he answered, all out of breath. Good. I hope I'd made him run. He deserved a little inconvenience after all I'd been through.

"It's me, Hero. I need to see you right away," I said in my best no nonsense voice.

"What's happened? Are you ok?"

"I'm fine. Well, no I'm not, really. But I'm not hurt. I need to see you, Kin. Immediately." He said he'd be right over. I told him I was not at home and gave him directions to Debbie's.

When he asked why I wasn't at home, I said "Because I can't be there now. I don't know when I'll be able to go back there again. Just get here as fast as you can." I hung up without waiting for a reply.

I stayed alone in the bedroom for a few minutes more, thinking things over. Kin would have to take back the snuff box. There was no question. And it had to be done where it might be seen. Whoever was after this box, Leontine, Fang Boy, and anyone else; they needed to know I no longer had it.

I went back out to the living room and told Debbie that Kin would be coming over. She just said "Oh, ok." I was thankful that she didn't ask why or act like it was weird. My coffee was cold now, but I drank it anyway. Coffee was coffee and I needed the caffeine.

Before I knew it, Kin was pulling up to the house. He must have had the pedal to the floor. That was ok with me. Maybe it was mean or spiteful, but the thought of him being nervous or upset over what might be going on gave me satisfaction. Since I figured he and his Russian snuff box were the cause of all my problems, he deserved to be sharing in some of the anxiety and stress that had been heaped on me.

"Kin's here. I'm going to talk to him outside," I told Debbie. Of course she said it was ok to ask him in, but I wanted to talk to him in private. I assured her that I would be fine and gave a little wave as I walked out onto the porch.

I hurried down the stairs to meet Kin. "Hero, what are the police," I didn't give him time to finish. Grabbing his arm, I turned him around and dragged him away from the house.

"The police are here to make sure that Debbie and I are safe. A lot has happened since I saw you last night, Kin. Now, I'm going to tell you what happened, and then you are going to tell me what I need to know. The truth." I declared forcefully.

"Can we go inside?" he asked.

"No. Debbie's already more involved than I would like. We're staying out here."

"Then can we at least sit in my car?" asked Kin.

"We'll sit in my car," I said curtly, stalking off toward the driveway. After all I'd gone through I needed to feel that I had some control over something, no matter how small. I waved to the cop to signal I was alright. Then I opened the driver side door and got in. After a momentary pause, Kin followed and got in the passenger side.

"What's happened, Hero?" he asked me, genuinely concerned.

I turned in my seat to face him and began my tale, beginning with the fanged freak that was hiding in my bushes. "And he had fangs, Kin. Fangs!"

"Are you sure? Perhaps the light on the window played tricks,"

"No!" I cried, stopping him in his tracks. "I know what I saw and I saw fangs!" Then I told him about the police coming to my house and staying here with Debbie and Bob. I told him about seeing someone looking in the window, and the mysterious Oldsmobile peeling out from in front of the house.

"What did the car look like?" Kin asked. I described it as best I could, but there was no reaction from him.

"Then we went back to my house. And when I went inside, my house... my home," I got choked up and couldn't speak. Tears threatened to flow. I swallowed a few times and tried to continue. "It's been destroyed. Completely and totally destroyed. They broke, smashed, dumped and tore up almost every single thing in my home." Silent tears were falling as I told him about my mother's favorite chair, my grandmother's wedding china, my mother's figurines, and all the rest of my ruined possessions.

"Oh, God," he whispered in a husky voice several times throughout my story. When I finished, he said "Hero, I am so very, very sorry. I can't tell you just how sorry I am."

"Try." I demanded. I wasn't going to cut him any slack. He just looked down at his hands in his lap. "Why, Kin? Why did this happen? Was this all because of the snuff box you forced me to take for you?"

He nodded. "I think so."

"God damn it! How could you do this to me?" I raged, pounding my fists against his hard shoulder and upper arm. "How could you put me in this position? That freak might have killed me. As it is, he's stalking me, and God only knows what he might do. Not to mention that now Debbie and Bob are involved in all of this. Plus, what about my house? All my things, Kin? I've got homeowner's insurance, but that won't make me whole again. They can't replace the memories or the sentimental value of my family heirlooms."

"I know that. Don't you think I know that? I'm sorry. I didn't know this would happen." He closed his eyes and leaned his head against the dashboard.

I reached into the back seat and pulled out my overnight bag, then I rummaged around for the box. "You owe me an explanation, Kin. I want the truth. What's so important about this stupid snuff box?" I took his hand and thrust the snuff box into it.

Kin turned his head to look at the box. "Hero, there's a lot I need to tell you. It's very complicated and some of it won't make sense to you. You might even think," he paused. "Before I can explain about the snuff box, I've got to tell you, tell you about some, um, uh" he stammered. "There are things in this world that are not what we think. There are people, beings, in this world that are not what we think." He paused again, still hanging his head.

"For crying out loud Kin, just spit it out!" I cried impatiently.

"Ok. That man outside your window was, is a, a, he's a vampire," he blurted out quickly. "And so am I."

CHAPTER 8

"Excuse me?!" Oh, no. He didn't just say that. He couldn't have. "Did you just say that you are a vampire?" My voice had raised several octaves.

Kin still hung his head. "Hero, I know it's hard to believe, but,"

"No! No, no, no, no, no. No 'but'. How the hell can you be a vampire? They aren't real. They're just not! Are you one of those people who likes to pretend they're vampires or thinks they suck the energy out of people or whatever? 'Cause I'm telling ya, Kin, I am not in the mood for any goofy shit. You cannot imagine what I've been through, and it's all your fault, and now you give me this bullshit about being," I stopped short and gasped. "Oh, Holy Christ!" I cried.

Kin had finally raised his head to look at me. When he did, I could see had two big fangs protruding from his mouth, and his beautiful green eyes were jet black. He was a vampire. No! I'd fallen asleep in Debbie's bedroom while making phone calls. This was a bad dream. It was all a dream. It had to be. I wanted to get out of the car, but I felt too weak to move. I didn't even have the strength to cry. It was all too much. How much more could I stand? God! I'd already asked myself that several times today, but more and more crap kept getting heaped on me!

He reached out to touch my arm. "Don't touch me," I said in a whisper as I recoiled against the door. Kin pulled back his hand, looking wounded.

"Hero, I did plan to tell you eventually, but I hadn't meant for it to happen like this."

"Oh? How had you imagined it would happen? Tell me, Kin, how did you think you could tell me that I'm dating a vampire and put a good spin on it?"

He sighed. "I don't know. I hadn't really planned it out. I just figured the right time would present itself."

"Well, lucky us! Here it is!" I said sarcastically. I was trapped in a small enclosed space with a vampire, and I was being sarcastic. Probably not a bright thing to do, but that surge of sarcasm seemed to give me a bit of strength back.

"Look," Kin snapped, losing his patience, "I never asked to be a vampire, you know? This was done to me against my will, and now I have to keep starting myy life over and over and over again, until the end of time. I have to keep reinventing myself and making new friends, new relationships, knowing I will have to end them unhappily some day because of this curse."

"Yeah, I bet they end a lot more unhappily for the people whose throats you rip out!" Sarcasm again. I told you I like sarcasm, didn't I?

"I don't kill people. Well, I did kill a few when I was first turned, but that was because it was hard to stop and not drain them. But since then, I only drink from willing donors and animals," he said defensively.

Ew! I can honestly say that this was not a conversation I ever imagined myself having. "Willing donors? Yeah, I bet people are very willing to 'donate' blood when faced with the alternative. 'Gee, let me think? Do I willingly let this scary vampire drink my blood, or do I foolishly put up a fight and end up dead? Hmmm? Decisions, decisions!'"

"I'm not like that," he growled. "I would never hurt you or anyone else. But that doesn't mean I can help that I need to have blood to survive. Do you think I want to be like this?"

Suddenly there was a sharp rap on the window. I started. It was the police officer who had been watching the house. I didn't have my keys with me, so I had to open the door. "Is everything ok, Miss?" he asked.

"Yes," I said, unsure whether or not it really was ok. "We're fine, just a bit of a, a, um, lover's spat. You know?" He might have known about lover's spats, but I doubted he knew about this kind.

He bent and looked into the car. Kin looked straight out the front windshield, keeping his mouth closed over his fangs. "Ok," said the officer. "I'm just over there if you need me," he whispered as he closed the car door for me. What would that be like? 'Excuse me officer, I've just discovered that my boyfriend is a vampire and I'd like him to leave. Can you take care of that for me?' Yeah, that would go over well. With my luck, he'd have one of those cop cars with the camera in them and I'd end up on TV, where they'd show me being carted away to the nut house.

'Tonight on Disorderly Conduct, Video on Patrol, a crazy woman claims her boyfriend is a vampire and asks an officer for help. Watch as it takes two officers and a crew of EMT's to get her into the straight jacket.' I would have laughed if I wasn't sitting next to a guy with fangs.

I smiled at the officer and gave a little wave. We sat in silence for a moment. "So, are you telling me that my house was trashed by a vampire?" I asked without looking at Kin.

"No," he said.

"No? Then who?"

He sighed. "I'm fairly certain that it was Leontine that wrecked your house."

"Leontine?" I had thought it was the freak from my front lawn, and said so.

"No, she probably had Nigel watching you while she went through all of your things."

"Nigel?" He hadn't looked like a Nigel to me, but what do I know about vampires? "But why did she destroy everything? She ruined so many things that couldn't possibly have been concealing the snuff box."

"She has a very nasty temper. The more her search was unsuccessful, the angrier she would have gotten. And she probably resented that a human had possession of the box." Kin explained.

I was confused. "Wait a minute. You said my house wasn't ransacked by a vampire?"

"It wasn't."

"Well then isn't Leontine human?" I wasn't sure I wanted to know the answer to this.

"No. She's a shape shifter." Kin answered matter of fact.

"A wh-, a what?"

"Leontine is a shape shifter. She can take the shape of an animal," he explained.

"Are you kidding me? First vampires, now shape shifters! This can't be happening," I said, burying my head in my hands.

"Shape shifters are like werewolves, except they turn into other animals rather than wolves."

"There are werewolves too!" Oh, God, this couldn't be happening. Please let me wake up. I pinched myself. It hurt. What a dummy.

"What does she change into?" Curiosity got the better of me. I hoped she turned into a germ infested rat.

"A cat. She shifts into an orange cat." Well that was a letdown.

"Ok, so, let's sum up. You and the freak on my lawn, excuse me, Nigel, are vampires, and Leontine is a shape shifting cat who completely destroyed my home, not just because she wants that snuff box, but because I'm human?"

"Well, um, yeah," he answered inadequately.

"Well that's just great! I'll be sure to note that on my homeowners' insurance claim. 'Reason for destruction: Because I am a human.' I'm going to either end up dead or committed to the funny farm before this is over, I just know it."

"You will not die! I won't let that happen. I won't allow you to be hurt. Do you hear me, Hero? I won't allow it."

I couldn't help it, I laughed. "Don't waste your time telling me. Talk to your blood sucking friends and the cat woman. In fact, talk to them right away and let them know I don't have the damned thing and I'm not part of whatever this is."

"But you are now," he said quietly.

"The hell I am! This has nothing to do with me!"

He sighed again. I was beginning to hate that sigh. "Unfortunately, it does. If they feel they have to, they will use you to get to me."

I was struck dumb. How much more could I really and truly take? Was there no end to this nightmare? No limit to what I would be forced to endure and suffer? "Give it to them," I said in a husky voice. I cleared my throat and repeated, "Give it to them, Kin. Give them the damned box. It's not worth all of this."

"I can't do that, Hero. You don't understand."

"You're right, I don't understand. I don't understand how that stupid snuff box is worth more than my life! You paid twenty thousand dollars for it. Does that mean my life is worth less than twenty thousand dollars? Is that damned thing worth more to you than an innocent person's life?"

"I'm not going to let anything happen to you. It's complicated. There's so much more to this than just the box," he started.

"Then tell me, Kin. If my life is in danger, I deserve to know. Tell me everything and don't leave a damned thing out," I demanded.

I was exhausted, more tired than I had ever been in my life, but I couldn't sleep. My mind was too full of disturbing images. Kin and I had talked for hours. Well, he talked mostly. I sat and listened, taking turns between disbelief, anger and fear.

When Kin left, I made a point of saying out loud, before he got into his car, "And I never want to see that damn snuff box again!" After I said it, I realized it was probably not a good thing for the cop to hear me say that. He'll tell Detective Joyce and there'll be some uncomfortable questions. Fortunately, I don't think he really heard what I said. Or at least, that's what I told myself. Kin did hear me though and he didn't look happy. Like I cared at this point.

I knew Debbie had come to her window several times to check on me, but God love her, when I came in, all she said was "Everything ok?" I told her it was, because what else was I supposed to tell her? 'Oh, yeah, great. By the way, Kin's a vampire. And the freaky guy outside my house, he's one too. Oh, and my house was probably trashed by a shape shifter, who was looking for a priceless relic that unlocks some kind of puzzle for all the vampires, shape shifters, werewolves and other creatures we always thought were make believe.' Hmm. Yeah, that would have gone over really well.

Debbie just nodded and said, "Can I get you anything?" I said no and asked if it would be ok if I took a nap in her room. Naturally, she said yes and I went to lie down.

Now I was lying here in the semi-dark that the shades provided, trying to digest all the fantastical crap that Kin had just laid on me. I took inventory of what I had learned.

1. Kin was a vampire, and so was the freak from my front yard, whose name was Nigel.

2. Leontine was a shape shifter, who apparently liked to turn into an orange cat. I decided I was going to buy a really big dog as soon as I could get back into my house. Really big. Like a Mastiff or something.

3. The Russian snuff box had been made by a vampire named Sereysky sometime around 1730, and it contained clues to some puzzle that would reveal the location of some secret text that the members of the supernatural world had been searching for for centuries. Kin wouldn't tell me what this ancient text was about, or why it was so important, but I was kind of glad really, because I was already on information overload.

4. There were several groups all trying to find the items that would unlock the puzzle. The group Kin was working with had possession of most of the found items, and knew about the items they did not have. At least I was part of the winning team. Sort of.

5. I no longer had the damned snuff box, but that didn't mean I was safe. Any vampire, shape shifter, werewolf, or whatever that was looking for this ancient book might decide to try and use me to get to Kin.

Conclusion: No more talking to strange men in bars and clubs. The next time I talked to Kin I would tell him to hand over the box to someone else that he was in league with, so hopefully, I would no longer be of value to anyone. In league with. Now that's a phrase I never thought that I would use with a straight face.

A vampire. I was dating a vampire. Hello, have you met my boyfriend, the vampire? I absolutely never, ever would have believed anyone if they had told me vampires were real. But it was hard to dispute the fact with one sitting about six inches away from you with his fangs hanging out.

My mind started cataloging all the things I knew about vampires. Strike that. All the things I thought I knew about vampires. I'd seen Kin twice during the daytime, so there was some key info there that I was missing. I had specifically invited Kin into my home the other day, but obviously, I wasn't going to invite Nigel in, which may explain why he didn't break into my house. I'd never seen Kin eat, though I had seen him drink water, so that was another myth to be explored.

What else? There had been a couple of silver crosses at the auction and he had no reaction to them. He picked up silver and held it with no problem. Wait. Was that just for werewolves? I was going to have to make a list of questions to ask Kin the next time I saw him. The mean, spiteful part of me considered having a large helping of shrimp scampi and garlic bread before I saw him again. Just in case that one was true. Hey, he had made me plenty uncomfortable today, I just thought he should get a little back.

I could hear Debbie talking in the next room. She must have called Bob. What would he have to say? Would I still be welcome here when she finished filling him in? Not like I could blame him if he asked me to leave. If he did, I'd just go check in to the local Marriot. I wondered if the having to invite the vampire in thing worked at hotels? With a little luck, I'd never need to find out. Of course, luck was in very short supply these days.

Mom. Oh, Mom! What would you say if you could talk to me now? Would you forgive me? Silly question. This was the woman who sang to me mercilessly instead of getting mad at me for giving her the cold shoulder for a week. Still, I was overwhelmed with grief. The past three years had been so hard.

First her illness and then her passing. I had thought at the time that I'd never get over it. But as the months wore on, it didn't hurt quite so much. Now the pain was back and it was compounded by tremendous guilt. Part of me felt like I had lost her all over again.

Tears began rolling down the sides of my face and on to the pillow. I would have thought I was all out of tears the way I'd cried today. I closed my eyes and in my head I talked to my mom. I apologized for her fancy ladies being ruined and Nana's china and the crystal. I told her how much I missed her and how much I needed her now. As I lay there having a silent conversation, sleep finally came and put me out of my misery for a time.

But not for long enough.

CHAPTER 9

"Hero. Hero, wake up," Debbie said as she gently shook me. "Hero, please."

I felt as though I was under water and could hear someone calling my name from above. But the water felt heavy and I couldn't seem to rise to the surface. Subconsciously, I knew it was Debbie trying to wake me, but that didn't make it any easier to wake up.

"What's up?" I asked, without opening my eyes.

"I think there's someone outside," she whispered.

I don't know why she whispered if they were outside, but then again, I don't know why that was my first thought. I propped myself up on my elbow and looked at her. She looked scared. "Isn't the cop out there?"

"Well, the car is there, but I can't see inside it. I was looking out the window and I thought I saw someone crouching down beside the Forsythe's fence. They're the ones diagonally across from here," she said, pointing in the general direction of her neighbor's fence.

I swung my legs over the side of the bed and rubbed my eyes. "Let's go tell the officer outside and he'll look into it."

"Wait. Do you think that's the best way?"

"What do you mean?" I asked, confused. "That's what he's there for."

"Yeah, but if we go out and talk to him, whoever is watching us might take off and the police officer won't see him," she explained.

Interesting take on the situation. "Ok, then what should we do?"

We both looked at each other, both hoping the other would think of something. "Should we call the police station and ask if they can radio him?" I suggested at last.

Debbie nodded. "I think that might be the best way." She handed me the phone. Why I had to be the one to call. I don't know, but I wasn't going to argue.

"Not here," I said. "I'll call from the living room and you can peek out to see if he's still there or not."

A plan of action agreed upon, we went to the living room. I walked by the big picture window without looking out. I didn't want to raise any suspicion if there was someone there. As I sat on the couch and picked up the phone, Debbie crept to the far edge of the window and carefully peeked out. "He's still there," she whispered. I don't know who she thought was going to hear her.

"Step back," I instructed as I dialed the phone. It was answered on the first ring and I quickly explained who I was and our situation. The officer who answered sounded slightly annoyed, but I really didn't care. My taxes paid his salary and he was going to have to do his job, no matter how irritating I might be.

"Thank you very much, Officer," I said as I hung up. "They're radioing him now," I told Debbie. She took another peek out the window. "Is he still there?" I asked.

"I think so. It's starting to get dark, so it's hard to tell. The cop just started his car. Where's he going?" Debbie looked panicked.

"Maybe he's just going to pull up a bit so he can see better," I suggested.

I carefully crept to the edge of the window opposite Debbie. Getting down on my knees, I slowly raised my head until I could just see the street in front of the house. The officer did pull his car up a few feet. He seemed to be looking for something in his cruiser. I tried to see to the house diagonally across, but the cop car was blocking the area next to the fence.

Debbie and I briefly exchanged curious looks before turning our attentions back to the goings on outside. The squad car slowly inched up the street and then suddenly cut to the left, making a U turn. Pulling up by the fence, the Officer shone his flashlight on the area next to the fence. There was no one there. The policeman put his car in park and got out. He checked the area next to the fence and walked around a bit, looking up and down the street.

Debbie and I returned to the couch and sighed in unison. "He probably took off as soon as the car began moving," I said.

"Probably," Debbie agreed.

The clock chimed in the dining room. "Shouldn't Bob be home by now?" I asked.

"He was stopping to pick up dinner. I didn't feel like cooking."

"Don't blame you there," I said. I realized I was hungry. When I thought about it, I realized I hadn't eaten since early yesterday. Just to emphasize the point, my stomach growled loudly. We laughed.

A knock came on the front door and we both jumped, and then laughed again. We could see the policeman's hat through the little window in the top of the door. "You ladies ok?" he asked when Debbie opened the door.

"We're fine," she told him. "Did you see anything across the street?"

"No. I didn't see anyone and the ground is too hard there for any impressions."

"Thanks for looking," I said.

"Not a problem. You let me know if you see anything else." He smiled at us and walked back to his car. As he was about to get in, Bob came down the street.

Debbie called out "It's ok. That's my husband." The officer waved to her and got into his squad car.

Bob parked and got out of his truck. He reached into the back seat and pulled out a large white bag full of take-out food. I could smell it before he even got inside. Boy, I was hungry. He came in and gave his wife a peck on the cheek. "Hey H, you hanging in there?"

"As best I can," I said with a smile. The prospect of food had made me almost cheerful. "Thanks for stopping to get dinner, Bob. I appreciate it."

"No sweat." We followed Bob out to the kitchen where he unpacked three prime rib dinners with baked potatoes. I was salivating. I helped Debbie gather silverware and condiments and napkins. We each grabbed a Styrofoam container of food and headed for the dining room table.

I could hardly wait to dig in. Scooping out a big wad of butter from the tub, I quickly mashed the inside of my potato and added some salt and pepper. I shoveled a big forkful of potato into my mouth and started to cut up my steak. Red drops ran down and puddled beneath the meat, reminding me that somewhere out there, there were vampires watching me. Maybe even plotting to kidnap me, or God only knows what in order to get that stupid snuff box.

Suddenly, I didn't feel very hungry. "Are you ok? You look funny. Are you sick?" Debbie asked, very concerned.

"Yeah, I'm fine," I fibbed. "Just went down the wrong way. I need a drink." I pushed my chair back to get up but Bob stopped me.

"I'll get it. I think we could all use a drink." He came back in a minute with three cold Rolling Rocks and placed one in front of me.

"Thanks," I said as I picked up the chilly bottle and took a long swig. It tasted good. I hadn't realized how thirsty I was either. I took another long pull. The beer seemed to renew my hunger, because the bloody puddle around my prime rib no longer mattered. I dug into my steak like a true carnivore, savoring every delicious bite.

We ate mostly in silence, except for the obligatory, "How's your steak?" and "Do you want another beer?" type of questions. It was an excellent meal and I was grateful to my friends for it. And grateful that I hadn't been asked to rehash my day. I figured Debbie had relayed all earlier events to Bob, so he didn't feel the need to ask. We'd have to tell him about the person Debbie had seen by the fence though. That could wait, I decided.

"How much do I owe you?" I asked, intending to pay for the food, since it was my fault Debbie wasn't up to cooking.

"Put your money away," Bob said. I explained that I felt I should pay and he said, "Never be sorry for an excuse to order prime rib." He rubbed his belly and let out a very loud belch.

"Nice," said Debbie.

"Jealous," he retorted. They were cute.

"Well, at least let me clear all this away. You two relax." There was no opposition to that suggestion.

I scraped all the leftovers, such as they were, into one container and stacked the other two beneath it. Then I grabbed the salt and pepper shakers, butter and the bottle of ketchup. Yup, ketchup. Bob used it with almost everything. I carried it all into the kitchen, then returned for the empty beer bottles.

There were just the two coffee cups Deb and I had used earlier in the sink, along with two spoons and the silverware we'd used at supper. I decided to wash them up quickly by hand. As I stood rinsing a cup under the hot running water, I noticed a little spiral of smoke through the window over the sink.

My first thought was that the dryer was on and this was from the vent, but then I realized the tiny spiral was too small for that. I turned off the water and picked up the dish towel to dry my hands. Slowly, I carefully tip toed towards the back door that lead to the deck. It was pitch dark out now and I didn't know if I'd be able to see anything. I had mixed feelings about that.

The back door had a large pane of glass in the top half of the door and a glass screen door in front of it, so I had a fairly clear view of the back deck and part of the yard. As I stepped directly in front of the door, a tiny orange glow appeared. It blossomed, becoming more intense and giving off an eerie light. In that eerie light I saw Nigel's face. He was sitting, as relaxed as if he were at home, in one of the chairs on the deck. He blew out his cigarette smoke and I could see it rising in the moonlight.

I didn't know what to do. I stood there like a deer in the headlights. It wouldn't do any good to get the policeman from out front. Nigel would be gone before he could get back there, and he was no match for a vampire any way. I didn't think Nigel could come inside without an invitation from Debbie or Bob and I didn't see that happening. Worrying them with the knowledge that there was a vampire on their back deck was not on my list of options either.

There was a small marker board hanging on the wall next to the phone. I took it down and wrote on it. Going back to the door, I help up my sign for Nigel to read. 'I gave the box back to Kin' it said.

Nigel stood up and took another drag off of his cigarette, the bright orange reflecting off the glass of the screen door. He came up to the door and smiled at me. A big cruel smile with his fangs bared. He held his cigarette between the thumb and middle finger of his right hand and pointed at me with the index finger of the same hand, so it was illuminated in the light of the cigarette. He jabbed his finger right at me. I expected to hear it touch the glass. Then he flicked the cigarette away and was gone.

I hadn't realized that I'd been holding my breath. "H, you okay in there?" Debbie called, bringing me back to animation.

"Yeah, fine. I'll be right in. You guys want anything?" I asked as I erased the marker board and hung it back up next to the telephone.

I had to get out of there. I couldn't put Debbie and Bob at risk any more than I already had. Where could I go? Where would I be safe from a vampire? The answer was obvious. With another vampire.

I went back to the dining room and thanked them again for dinner. "I just realized I haven't checked my cell phone all day. I've probably got a ton of messages. Will you guys excuse me for a bit?" I asked. Of course they didn't mind.

I unplugged my cell phone from the wall outlet, and sure enough I had seven missed calls and three messages. One was from one of my clients, which I had known to expect because I talked to her earlier. One was from Sue, calling to see how things had gone with my date yesterday, and the third was a call from Kin, calling to check on me.

While I did want to talk to Sue, I needed to call Kin first. I dialed his number and was glad to hear him pick up right away. "It's me," I said. Funny isn't it, the way you expect people to recognize your voice though you've only ever spoken on the phone a couple of times?

"Are you ok? I tried to call you a while ago, but I got your voice mail."

"I know, I just listened to your message. I had my phone off. Listen, Kin, Nigel was here."

"What! Did he try anything? Did the cop see him? What happened?" A lot of questions all at once.

"He just looked at me. No, the cop didn't see him. He was at the back of the house. I don't know how he got there without being seen."

"Well, we can run faster than you can see," Kin explained.

"Huh? Do you mean to tell me that vam-" Oops! Didn't want to say that out loud. "That you guys can move so fast that you can't be seen?" That was a bit of information that would have been helpful to have earlier. Made having a police officer out front sort of useless.

"Basically."

"I let him know I didn't have to box any more, but he didn't seem to care." I told him.

"You talked to him!" Kin said angrily.

"Not really. I held up a sign, sort of. It doesn't really matter now." I looked to see if Debbie and Bob were coming into the living room, but they were still seated at the table and having what looked like a serious discussion. I could guess what it was about. "Kin, I want you to come and get me. I don't want to stay here anymore. I'm putting Debbie in Bob in danger."

"Ok, I was going to ask you that earlier, but I was afraid after all we talked about," he let his sentence trail off. "I'll be right there. Stay inside, Hero. Don't go outside without me."

"I wasn't planning on it," I told him. I hung up and called Sue.

"Hey, it's me," I said when I answered. "I'm sorry, I had my phone off. Listen, Sue, a lot has gone on since last night and I don't have time to go into it now. I'm sorry."

"My God, H! What's going on?" I'd worried her. I didn't mean to, but I guess I didn't have much choice. She was my best friend and if she didn't hear from me she'd start to worry and call Debbie anyway.

"Look, wait a little while and give Deb a call, ok? I got her and Bob messed up in all this, so she can fill you in. I'll call you as soon as I can. Love you."

"Ok, H, if you say so. Are you ok, though? Tell me you're ok."

"Yeah, Sue. I'm ok. Really." I wasn't, but how could I say anything else?

We hung up and I put my cell phone away. I got up and went to talk to Debbie and Bob. They stopped talking as soon as they saw me coming toward them. Don't need three guesses to figure out what they were talking about. I told them that Kin was coming and that I was going with him. That upset Debbie.

"You have to stay here! There's a cop outside to make sure you're safe, and besides, you hardly know Kin," she argued.

I sat down and ran a hand through my hair. How was I supposed to explain this? "Kin lives in a security building," I lied. "No one can get in unless they live there or the concierge has to call to get permission." In truth, I had no idea where Kin lived. "I just can't bear to put you guys out any more than I have and Kin said he has a spare room I can stay in."

Debbie continued to protest, but at last Bob said, "You've got to let her do what she wants. H knows she can stay here as long as she likes. If things don't work out with Kin, you come back here, ok?" I agreed, and gave Bob a hug and Debbie a kiss on the cheek.

"Don't worry, Deb. I'll call you in the morning." I went and collected my things and came back to the dining room. "I'll tell the police officer where I'm going." Debbie was still brooding over my decision to leave. "Oh! Susan is going to be calling you. I hope you don't mind. She had left a message for me and I called her back, but I just can't bear to have to go through telling anyone what's been happening right now. Sorry." I put on my best pitiful face in the hopes of soliciting as much sympathy as possible.

"Of course," she said, a bit tight lipped.

"Oh, Deb, please don't be angry with me," I begged. She didn't have a chance to answer because the doorbell rang.

"I'll get it," Bob said, and he got up quickly to let Kin in. Deb and I followed him. "Hi, I'm Bob," he said, offering Kin his hand. Kin shook his hand, but remained on the other side of the threshold.

"I'm Debbie."

"Yes, we met at the club. It's nice to see you again." Kin said, still on the porch. There was brief moment of awkward silence while they all looked at me.

"Well, I'd better go let the cop know what's going on," I said to break the silence. I said good-bye to my friends and thanked them again for the dinner.

"Oh - that reminds me," said Debbie. "I'll walk out with you and ask if he wants anything to eat or drink. The poor guy's been out there all day."

"No he hasn't. There's a different guy out there now," Kin informed us.

My heart beat faster, and not in a good way. "Well, the other guy probably went off duty," I said hopefully.

Kin, Debbie and I walked outside. Bob stood on the porch. "Do you think it's ok?" I whispered to Kin. He reached and took my hand. I looked at him and he winked. I relaxed.

The officer rolled down the window as we approached. "Everything ok?" he asked.

"Yeah, fine. I just wanted to let you know I was leaving." He wanted to know where I was going. Kin handed him his driver's license and the officer called in to the Detective on duty. Debbie offered him something to eat and drink. He declined, but thanked her.

We walked together to Kin's SUV. "Call me in the morning," she reminded me before I closed the door. I assured her I would and smiled at her.

Kin started his truck and he pulled into their drive way to turn around. As we passed by the front of the house, he rolled down his window and called to my friends, "Don't you worry, she'll be fine."

"I'd better be," I told him. "It's a good thing you don't sleep at night because I've got an awful lot of questions and you're going to answer each and every one of them."

CHAPTER 10

WHAT I'VE LEARNED ABOUT VAMPIRES

Or, a Baker's Dozen of Vampire Facts

By Hero Fletcher

1. You do, in fact, need to invite a vampire into a private home in order for them to be able to enter. You can also revoke the invitation, but you must say so specifically. "Get out!" etc, will not work. You must tell them you are revoking their invitation.

NOTE: Vampires can enter any public place without an invitation, even if that public place is located in a house. So, I was right about thinking that was why Nigel hadn't come into my home after me. Yay me!

2. Vampires do have reflections. Apparently, a lot of the myths about vampires were started by the vampires themselves to help them 'prove' they weren't vampires and remain undetected. Many myths and half-truths abound, so I've discovered. More info about these to follow.

3. Vampires burst into flame or turn to dust in sunlight. This is false. Vampires do avoid the sun as it will burn their skin, but

they will not burst into flame. After just a short time in direct sunlight, a vampire's skin will burn and feel what we feel when we have a severe sunburn. If a vampire's skin is exposed to direct sunlight for an extended period of time, it will blister, like a 3rd degree burn. Most vampires will keep as much of their skin covered as possible, wearing long sleeves even in hot weather. And vampires' cars all have tinted windows. Sunblock will help them slightly and buy them more time out in the sunlight. Most very old vampires still avoid the day time all together out of habit for the old traditions.

Also, because of this, many vampires choose to live in places that are often cloudy, overcast and rainy. Alaska has more vampires than Louisiana, which is thought to be the vampire Mecca, thanks to Anne Rice (sorry Anne). But according to Kin, you can't throw a rock in the land of the Midnight Sun without hitting a vampire. Makes sense when you know the facts.

So, this is why I've been with Kin in the daytime, but we stayed in the car or indoors.

Oh - and also because of this, the myth that vampires must sleep all day is also untrue. Because most vampires are more comfortable being out at night, no sun and easier to hide their efforts to obtain blood, they will then sleep most of the day. This also applies to people who work night shifts, but it doesn't make them vampires.

4. Crosses and crucifixes. These generally have no effect on vampires, except in the following circumstances:

A. If a cross or crucifix is used against a vampire who, when they were alive, was brought up in the very strict doctrine of the church, fully believing that the symbol would guard them against evil. Thus, once made vampire, this symbol is abhorrent to them because they share the belief that it should drive them away. I'm sure Freud would have loved to dissect that.

B. The cross or crucifix is made of wood. Not that it has any religious significance. It just means you can use it as a stake if it's large enough.

I've been told that some vampires find humor in this myth and the crueler ones actually relish the act of advancing on someone with a cross who realizes that it will not help them. I have to keep reminding myself that there are vampires like Kin. Thankfully!

5. A stake through the heart will kill a vampire. This one is true. It needs to be wooden or pure silver. No silver plate, I guess. Only the best for the undead. If you try staking them with something else, you will momentarily incapacitate them and it may give you time to escape. Just remember if it isn't wood or pure silver, once they get that bad boy out, they're probably going to come after you. And a vampire in and of itself is bad enough, but a vampire that you've pissed off with a failed attempt at staking…. I wouldn't want to be that guy.

The only other way to kill a vampire is to take them to pieces, literally, and then burn the pieces separately. Since vampires are hard as rock, that's not an easy thing to do. Mostly, only other vampires can do this. I asked if you could just burn a vampire. Apparently, burning only affects them if they are dismembered. Kin didn't know why that was. I guess I shouldn't be too surprised. We humans don't know everything there is to know about being a human and why our bodies work the way I do, so why should a vampire know every possible thing there is to know about being a vampire?

6. Garlic. Apparently, all of a vampire's senses are heightened. Therefore, certain every day smells are offensive to them and ordinarily offensive smells are completely revolting. Since a lot of vampire lore and myths originated in areas of Europe where garlic was in heavy use and often found hanging in kitchens, it was one of the most commonly witnessed reactions in

potential vampire victims. Humans would observe a vampire draw back, or even cover their noses because of close proximity to garlic, leading to the myth that vampires could be repelled by garlic. I confirmed with Kin, no scampi or garlic bread.

Oh, and the other senses, sight, hearing, taste, touch: Vampires can see perfectly in the dark. They can hear the faintest sounds and from great distances. Their sense of taste, well, since it's pretty much restricted to blood, there's not much to say. But apparently they can tell some things about a person by what they taste in their blood. I didn't ask him to elaborate because it's gross. As for the heightened sense of touch, I said he didn't need to explain that. I'd cross that bridge if and when I came to it.

7. Vampires have no reaction to Holy Water. This was another myth perpetuated by the vampire community. If a person was seen, not just to be out in the day time, but to touch the Holy water without it burning their skin, they could not possibly be a vampire.

This myth originated during the period in history when Catholicism was the chief religion in Europe and surrounding countries, and people were expected to attend services weekly, if not daily, as well as on the numerous feast days and Holy days.

8. Vampires can't eat or drink. Partially true. They can drink simple things, like water and certain wines. I know nothing about wine, so I have no idea why some wines are ok and some aren't. Also, some vampires are able to eat small quantities of fruits and vegetables, though Kin said it is extremely rare. Because vampires are technically dead, they can't digest things. They can try and eat and drink the things they were used to when they were alive, but it will often cause them to vomit and suffer enormous abdominal pain. In many cases, a vampire attempting to eat something will find themselves unable to swallow and will choke. Some vampires have learned to eat and drink enough to keep from arousing suspicion and then excuse themselves to go to the

nearest rest room and purge. Makes you wonder about the origins of bulimia.

9. Vampires are very strong. They are also very fast, as we already knew. They can run so quickly that even to an attentive observer, they are no more than a momentary blur. They can lift things hundreds of times their weight and are capable of enormous feats of strength, though they try not to let them be witnessed. Vampires never compete in sports or athletics because their abilities are too extreme to avoid notice. I had mixed feelings about this. It was a comfort to know Kin was so strong, but at the same time, it meant the bad guys, whoever they were, were just as strong.

10. Vampires can turn into bats. Untrue. This was a myth started by humans because of the vampire bat, which likes to feed on blood. Some vampires do have extraordinary abilities, such as being able to jump several stories, or being able to read the minds of humans. These are rare and are, for the most part, an extension of some talent or gift they had when human. Kin did, however, say that he once heard of a werewolf who was turned vampire. Talk about a nightmare!

11. Vampires don't hypnotize people. They can influence those humans that are easily susceptible to outside influence. Some call this 'glamour'. This ability varies from vampire to vampire. As in human life, our ability to influence people is a matter of our personality, experience and skill. I found that oddly comforting. Got to take it where I can get it I guess.

12. A vampire must obey his or her maker and elders. The vampire world has a very set hierarchy and they follow it religiously. Hmm, that seems like an oxymoron, doesn't it? Because it requires an exchange of blood (explained below), there is a mystical bond between a vampire and the vampire who created him. If your maker calls you or orders you to do something, you are compelled to obey and cannot refuse, even if

you want to. With elders, it is more a matter of what is expected. Honor is a huge thing among vampires and to disobey an elder dishonors you both. Depending on your vampire age, it may dishonor your maker too. Due to the importance of honor and the violent nature of vampires, if you do not obey your elder, you will probably find yourself staked.

13. I saved this one for last. Unlucky number thirteen. How someone becomes a vampire. According to Kin, and since he is one, I have no reason to disbelieve him, in order to be made vampire you must be bitten three times by the same vampire within the same cycle of the moon. After the third bite, in which the vampire drains you of your blood, you must then drink the blood of the vampire who bit you.

Now, I told Kin I'd rather die than drink someone's blood, but he said because you are so weak and lightheaded at that moment from the loss of blood, your own natural survival instincts kick in, and you can't help yourself. You just hear that you can live and, before you know it, you're drinking blood. Also, the moment a vampire in the making tastes the blood of his or her creator, they become insatiable for it. A vampire who chooses to make another vampire must be careful not to let his creation drink too much of his blood.

So there you have it. The Vampire World According to Hero. There are a few other tidbits I wasn't allowed to include because they are closely guarded secrets. But I did tell you everything I dared.

Kin was thoughtful enough to share a few little tips that might save my life, but I was sworn to secrecy, as there are some things that vampires are a bit touchy about humans knowing.

This educational talk about the myths and realities of the vampire world still seemed like a dream. I'm mean, I'm here writing it all down in black and white and even as I'm doing that,

I can't help but thinking 'this can't be real'. And after some reflection, I'm ok with that, because I'm afraid of what it will take to make me really believe it's all true.

I'm sure there are some of you out there that have other ideas about vampires and you may disagree with some of what I've said. Well, you go right ahead and disagree if you want to, but don't bother me about it. I've gotten it straight from the vampire's own blood stained lips, so I'm not too interested in any human's theories and notions. Sorry, but that's the way it is.

This encyclopedic divulgence of all things vampire took a couple of hours. Needless to say I had a lot of questions and interrupted him a lot. I have to give him credit, he was very patient with me and didn't laugh at any of my questions.

I knew we still had a long night ahead of us, so I asked if it was ok for me to take a shower. He said that was fine, of course, and got me some clean towels. Kin lived in a condo, and as luck would have it, it was a security complex. You had to have a sticker on your car to enter, or the security guard at the gate had to call to get permission to let you into the complex, so my lie to Debbie and Bob wasn't too far off.

The hot water felt good on my back and shoulders. I had been so tense for the past twenty four hours or so. I stood beneath the spray as long as I dared. I didn't want Kin to think I was never coming out, or one of those women who took forever in the bathroom. Typically, I'm pretty low maintenance. The crisp smell of his soap was pleasant and combined with the hot water, I felt relaxed and more alert, which I know sounds contradictory, but you'll just have to trust me on this one.

I got out and toweled off quickly. I pulled on the nightgown I had packed in my bag earlier that day and ran a brush through my hair. Since I was there, I brushed my teeth too. Might as well take care of everything at once.

Thankful that I'd chosen a modest nightgown, I was none the less a bit shy about walking back out into Kin's living room. Why hadn't I packed a robe? I held my overnight bag in front of me as I walked into the room. Smiling sheepishly, I shrugged my shoulders and said "Thanks."

"I'm sorry," Kin said when he noticed the bag. "I should have shown you to your room. It's right down here," he said as he reached and took the bag from me. I was glad that he was leading the way because I felt very exposed. "Just in here," he said as he opened the door and reached in and switched on the light.

It was a comfortable little room. There was a double bed with a down comforter, a nightstand with a lamp on either side, a comfortable chair by the window with a small table and a floor lamp, and a little closet. The walls, bedding and chair were all a soft sage green. The hardwood floor was almost entirely covered by a floral carpet.

"Thank you," I said as I entered the room. Kin placed my bag on the chair. Things became awkward. I didn't know what to say or do. I just stood there with a stupid smile on my face.

"So," said Kin, obviously feeling as awkward as I did. After a long, uncomfortable pause, he concluded, "You must be pretty tired. I'll let you have your privacy."

"No," I said as he headed for the door. "Actually I'm wide awake now."

"Oh, uh," I'm sure he was thinking 'Now what?'

"I don't suppose you have tea or anything?" Why would he? He was a vampire.

"Yeah, I do." When he saw my surprise he explained, "I do keep some things in case a visitor wants something. Also, because it would look strange if my cabinets and refrigerator were bare."

"You buy food and things that you'll never eat or drink just to keep up appearances?" Seemed like an awful waste to me.

"We have to do a lot of things in order to hide what we are." He smiled at me. The smile that I liked, the one that made my heart beat faster. "Come on, I'll make you a nice cup of tea and see if I have anything else you might like." That was a loaded question. Oh, all right, it wasn't a question. I guess it was a loaded statement, or offer or whatever, but it was loaded.

I followed him to his pristine kitchen and watched as he filled up the kettle and put it on the burner. Then he opened a cabinet that revealed an overly organized interior. All I could think of was Monk. He's a TV detective with OCD. He would love this kitchen. Everything in the cabinet what sorted by size, shape and perfectly aligned. I'd be afraid of touching anything.

Kin reached up to the second shelf and took down a large wooden box. He carried it to me, opening the lid as he came. "Which kind would you like?" The box was full of several kinds of tea. After a quick inventory of the offerings, I selected chamomile. I figured I needed any and all help to relax. He removed the little foil pack holding the tea bag and put the box back on its shelf. "I have some shortbread if you'd like."

Yum! I love shortbread. At first I was inclined to say no because I didn't want to eat if he wasn't, but then I realized I was never going to see him eat, so it was stupid not to eat when I wanted to. Ew! At least I hoped I'd never see him eat. Ok, bad mental image, think about something else.

"I suppose you want to talk about the snuff box?" he asked, his back to me.

The snuff box had not been on my mind for a little while, and I wasn't too happy to have it brought back to my attention. Though, I figured we should talk about it and get it out of the way. "I guess," I said. Way to be decisive Hero!

He took a plate down from another cabinet and arranged some shortbread biscuits on it. Then he tore open the little foil packet and placed the tea bag into a tall mug. "How do you take it?"

"Oh," I said, still thinking about what I might learn about the snuff box. I realized he was asking me about my tea. "Just sugar please," I told him. We stood there in silence while we waited for the kettle to boil. Apparently the saying about watched pots also applies to kettles.

As I stood there thinking 'Boil damn you, boil!', I suddenly heard a tinkling version of Patti Smith's 'Because the Night'. Before I could really wonder where the sound was coming from, Kin reached into his pocket, pulled out a cell phone and flipped it open. "McIntyre," he said gruffly.

"Yes," he said, turning is eyes to me. Uh oh. I didn't like that. "Yes, I understand." He had turned his whole body to me now. Definitely not good. "Yes," he said again. "We'll be right there." He closed the phone and put it back in his pocket.

"We'll be right where?" I asked, both nervous and upset. Who was he to say I'd be anywhere?

"I've been summoned," he said simply, as though it were the most natural thing in the world. Well, maybe it was in his world. "And I've been instructed to bring you."

The kettle boiled. Good timing. He reached and switched off the burner and slid the kettle onto a cool place.

"I'm sorry, but your tea will have to wait. You need to get dressed. We have to leave right away."

"Wait a minute! What is this all about? Where are we going and why do I have to go?" I asked as he steered me back towards the hallway.

"It's about the snuff box, and Leontine and Nigel and everything that's been going on the past twenty four hours. You need to be there because it concerns you, whether you like it or not. I'll tell you more about it in the car, but right now you need to hurry up and get dressed. He doesn't like to be kept waiting."

"He? He who?" I'm sure that was probably horribly incorrect grammatically, but really, who cares?

"'He, is Darius. And he is my elder and the Magistrate for the North East sector."

"Excuse me?" I asked, stopping in my tracks and turning to face Kin. "Magistrate for the,"

"North East sector," he finished. "I'll explain on the way. Just hurry up and get ready. He doesn't like to be kept waiting."

Unusually obedient, I closed the bedroom door, whipped off my nightgown and pulled on a change of clothes as quickly as I could. I had a very bad feeling about this. Being summoned could not be good. I rushed, hoping it was possible to be moving too quickly to think about what this could mean.

I pulled open the door and nearly ran in to Kin in the hall. "Oh! All set. Let's go." I skittered past him into the living room and grabbed my pocket book up off of the floor.

We went out the door and into the entry way of the building. I had to walk quickly to keep up with Kin's long strides as we hurried to his car. He let me in to the passenger side and then appeared as fast as the speed of light as his own door. As I fastened my seat belt I asked, "This isn't good, is it?"

Kin shook his head slowly. "I'm not sure. It's hard to tell." He waved to the guard as he approached the security station. As soon as we were on the main road, he floored it. I hoped we wouldn't get pulled over, but then I figured Kin probably had a way with dealing with the police.

"Hero, make sure you stay close to me. Don't speak unless spoken to." That wouldn't be easy. "And, I hate to ask you this, but, while we are there, you need to address me as 'Master.'"

"What? Are you kidding?" Like hell I was going to call anyone 'Master'!

"Hero, listen to me!" he said loudly. He was not kidding around. He meant business and he reached out and grabbed my arm to make sure I got the message. "Your safety, your life, may depend on it. You must do whatever I tell you. Do you understand?"

I gulped, swallowing hard, and nodded. "Yeah, ok," I said hoarsely. What new level of Hell was I about to enter now?

CHAPTER 11

Vampires are organized. Who knew? It's not like you'd associate civilized things such as a legal system and government with the supernatural. Then again, since few know the supernatural are actually real, they definitely wouldn't think about the structure of their community.

I suppose it should make it seem better to realize that they had these things, seem a little less wild and dangerous. Just a little. But all it did for me was make it seem more like a weird dream.

We were in the waiting room at the palatial home of the Magistrate of the North East sector. Any moment we would be shown in to see Darius, the Magistrate. I couldn't help thinking about the stories I'd read of the Three Musketeers. Throughout all of Dumas' stories of Athos, Porthos, Aramis and D'Artagnan, he depicts over and over the process of soldiers, courtiers and citizens waiting in a large room for the privilege of an audience with the king.

The waiting room Kin and I were seated in was nothing like the scope of the palace of the King of France, but it was a large, ornate room full of chairs, all lined up along three of the four walls. These chairs were covered pale rose fabric that looked like silk. The frames of the chairs were painted gold. The walls were covered in a cream damask paper. The ceiling had a large gilt medallion in the center with a crystal chandelier hanging from it. The floor was checked in black and white marble. Here and there were large potted plants, or small trees. There were several mirrors on the walls, all with matching golden frames. Over all, it looked like something from another time. I half expected to see a string quartet playing in the corner while women in crinolines and men in tail coats waltzed around. Though the vampire standing guard next to the door to Darius' chamber didn't look like he'd be willing to dance.

I wasn't sure if the position Darius held required such opulence and pomp or if he felt he deserved to be treated like a king of a tiny country. Then again, I had no idea how old Darius was or what he had been when he was human. Ok, I jumped aboard that train of thought too easily. It was disturbing that I seemed to be acclimating to the vampire world so quickly.

Kin hadn't told me too much about Darius himself on the ride over. I did get a crash course in the structure of the vampire government, but frankly, it was mostly a blur. The world was divided up into sectors. Each sector had a magistrate. Each magistrate had officers and the officers were divided into different ranks. Each country had a Supreme Judicator that the magistrates reported to. Also, vampires didn't recognize a lot of the newer countries. Or at least countries that were newer to them. Vampires don't like change. They kept their countries, sectors, etc. exactly as it had been since they first became organized. Apparently, Istanbul was still Constantinople.

As for the snuff box, Kin did his best to fill me in on its significance, but I wasn't sure I understood it all. There was just so much information all at once. I knew the box was part of some puzzle that was supposed to reveal the location of some important ancient text. I still didn't know what this text was or why it was so important, and I was still glad about it. But Kin had told me that the vampire who made the snuff box, Grigoryi Aleksey Sereysky, had created other items which contained clues to the location of the text. Grigoryi Sereysky had deliberately scattered these items, hoping to ensure the puzzle would remain unsolved until he chose to reveal it by reclaiming his works.

Unfortunately, when it was discovered that he knew the location of the text, a very powerful vampire named Marek Nikita Rostislavitch tortured him for the information. When Sereysky refused to give the location, he was torn to pieces and burned.

I don't know where this text came from or how Grigoryi Aleksey Sereysky came to be the only one who knew where to find it, but I did know that for centuries vampires and other supernatural beings had been searching for it. I also discovered that Darius held, or had held, nearly all the artifacts Sereysky left behind at one time or another. Well, at least all that had been found so far. There were still a lot of pieces missing.

We had been waiting a long time. I was getting kind of ticked at being summoned and told to get there right away and then kept waiting for ages. We had to have been waiting over half an hour. My leg started shaking from nerves. Kin laid his hand on my leg gently to stop it. Funny that I never noticed how cool his skin was. Just another dippy broad so happy to have someone to hold hands with you don't even notice that the guy's hand is several degrees cooler than norm.

I wanted to ask Kin why we were still waiting if we had been sent for so urgently, but the waiting room was as quiet as a tomb. Oh - bad simile. Instead I looked at him and raised my eyebrows in an expression, that I hoped conveyed what I was wondering. Kin responded with an apologetic grin and a squeeze of my hand. Not what I had hoped for, but then again, he was hardly any more likely to speak out loud than I was.

The urge to scream was becoming more and more difficult to suppress. And not a 'Help! I'm surrounded by vampires!' scream, but a 'Who the hell do you think you are making us come out here on the double and then keeping us waiting!' kind of scream. To my credit, I knew a scream of any type would be bad, so I held it in. That didn't mean I still didn't want to do it though.

Kin sat there as calm as you please. Still as a statue with just as blank an expression. That only made me more irritated. I suppose when you're a vampire you get used to just waiting around. After all, they've got all the time in the world, haven't they? That reminded me, I had no idea how old Kin was. He had told me on our first date that he was 34, but I figure that was just how old he was in human years when he became a vampire. I sighed. Another long and possibly horrifying talk to look forward too.

When I sighed Kin looked at me with an expression that showed he was sorry for the long wait. I knew it wasn't his fault. How could he know this would happen? Or could he? Was this the SOP? Did Darius always keep people, I mean vampires, waiting? I started to get worked up again at what I felt was our lousy treatment, when suddenly the door to Darius' inner sanctum opened.

The stoic vampire guarding the door moved his head a fraction of an inch to the left as he leaned toward an invisible someone who was giving him instructions. He gave a very faint nod of the head and then turned to look at Kin. They looked each other square in the eye. After a moment of staring, the guard shifted his eyes to the left, toward the open door. Apparently, that was the signal to go in. I had figured the guy probably wasn't much of a talker, but he wasn't much on moving either.

We both stood and Kin took my hand again. He gave me a reassuring smile, that didn't really reassure me at all, and then we headed for the door. As we approached the guard he turned his cold black eyes on me and I thought I saw hatred in them. Why? I'd never done him any harm? Perhaps he hated all humans. Maybe he just hated that a human was in his master's house. I didn't know, but I'd be lying if I said I didn't care.

The interior room was even more grand than the outside had been. There were frescos on the high ceiling and an enormous white desk with a marble top and gilt edging. Old fashioned divans covered in rich fabrics were located in several places throughout the room along with matching high back chairs. Closer to the desk were chairs very similar to those in the waiting area. The walls in the first half of the room were covered in paintings and the second half were lined with bookshelves crammed with old books.

Darius sat behind his desk. I half expected to see him in a velvet or brocade jacket and cravat or scarf, but he was wearing a charcoal gray button down shirt with the top couple of buttons open. I couldn't see what was on his bottom half because of the desk. He had dark blonde hair, cropped short in an almost Roman style. Perhaps he was. As we got closer and I could see his features better, I could imagine him as a Roman soldier with lorica segementata and a centurion helmet. He had a straight, aquiline nose, a strong jaw and dark brown eyes. He was thin lipped and very stern looking. Even had he not been a vampire, I wouldn't want to tussle with him.

"Magistrate," Kin said as he bowed his head. The corner of the Magistrate's mouth curved upward ever so slightly. Then he looked at me. I had no idea what was expected of me so I just stood there looking back at him. Kin hadn't told me to bow, so I didn't. After a tense moment where Darius stared me down, he finally returned his attention to Kin.

"You have it with you?" he said, not really asking.

Kin pulled the box out of his pocket. It was wrapped in a small blue velvet pouch. He stepped forward and placed it on the desk, then stepped back to stand beside me. Darius reached for the pouch and slowly untied the strings. He removed the snuff box and ran his cold fingers over it. "Lovely," he said to himself as he examined it. Gently, he opened the box and inspected the inside. Then he closed the lid and set the box on his desk, upside down. He took a small magnifying glass out of one of the desk drawers and bent his head to have a closer look.

"Yes, this is the one," he said. "Good work," he said to Kin as he straightened up. "You done good, kid, as Mr. Moran used to say," he added with a smile. It wasn't a real smile. It didn't go past his lips.

"Thank you, sir," Kin said formally. "It is my pleasure to be able to present it to you." That seemed a bit much.

"Ah, yes. About that." Darius' expression altered. He was looking at Kin as though Kin were an annoying little bug he'd like to squash. I was trying not to panic, but Kin seemed perfectly calm. "It was fortunate that my plans had been changed and that I could be here to accept this," he said, gesturing towards the box. "I was displeased when I learned that you were no longer in possession of the object." The word displeased was uttered in a very ominous manner.

"Forgive me, I did what I thought was best. I was unaware that Leontine had already dispatched Nigel to spy on me."

"Tch, tch. After all this time, Kinley, I thought you would know better than that. Surely you knew that Leontine could contact Nigel and have him follow you to your pet's home just as quickly as you could get there in an automobile." Pet! That was right up there with Lunch! I wanted to be angry and indignant, but I did my utmost to keep from reacting.

"Yes, Magistrate, you are right. I should have anticipated it, but I underestimated them, and I apologize for this." I didn't like this Kin, all subservient and slavish. It was not a good side to see in any man, human or vampire.

"And you gave it to this human? You allowed it to be at risk in the possession of a human?" Clearly Darius did not think well of the living.

"Yes, I did. I thought it would be unexpected. I believed Leontine and Nigel would come after me for the box, never thinking I would entrust it to a human," Kin explained unemotionally. I had to give him credit for that. I'd have been plenty ticked if I was him, but I guess vampires are good at this stoic stuff.

"Obviously, a poor choice," Darius commented with a sneer. Hey! I was not a poor choice. They hadn't gotten it, had they? Oh, wouldn't I just love to give him a piece of my mind. Unfortunately, he'd have taken a piece of me in return. Literally.

"The box is safe, sir. Miss Fletcher did manage to keep them from obtaining it while it was in her possession." Thank you!

"Yes, well, you lucked out there, didn't you?" Jerk. "What would have happened had I not been able to return so soon? Surely you don't think this human could have kept it safe for four more days?" Big jerk.

"I took possession of the box early this afternoon. I had not intended for her to keep it the rest of the week."

"Hmmm. That's quite interesting," Darius murmured. He leaned back in his chair and placed his hands in front of his face, tips touching. "My information tells me that you had intended for her to keep it and she insisted you take it back. Have I been misinformed?"

Kin stood silently. A cruel smile curled Darius' lips. I didn't like where this was going at all. "Yes," I interjected.

Darius's eyes became huge saucers. Apparently, a human was not supposed to address the Magistrate. "Indeed. Tell me, Miss Fletcher, in what way have I been misinformed?"

Well, that didn't take long for me to regret. Having those cold eyes piercing through me was damn nerve racking. I swallowed and said "As soon as Kin, I mean, my Master, realized he'd made a mistake, he took the box back." Darius raised a doubting eyebrow. "Yes, I did ask him to take it back, but it was unnecessary. He said he would never leave it with me once he knew I was in danger. I did make a show of giving it back to him though because I didn't know if anyone was watching us and I wanted to make sure they knew I didn't have it any more." I spewed it out so fast I hoped I made sense.

Kin kept his eyes on the Magistrate. Darius looked at me and then at Kin, trying to decide if I was telling the truth. And probably whether or not the truth mattered.

"Interesting," Darius said, noncommittally. "This is good news, Kinley. I didn't relish the idea of punishing you. Still," he let it drift off.

Still? Still what? How did you punish a vampire? I felt queasy. I swallowed, trying to keep the nausea away. I tried to peek at Kin out of the corner of my eye. I didn't dare turn and look at him. He hadn't moved, but I couldn't see his expression.

After a very, very tense moment, Kin spoke. "Magistrate, I have always served you faithfully. In hindsight, I did not make the best decision, but I did handle it and we do have the box. I have never given you any reason to consider punishment before this."

"You admit you have given me reason to punish you?"

"I admit that without full knowledge of what had taken place, it was more than understandable that you would wish to punish me."

Darius sat forward and rested his hands flat on the desk top. "Kinley, are you saying that I made a mistake?"

Uh oh. This was bad. Swallow after swallow. Keep it down, don't get sick.

"Forgive me, Magistrate. Perhaps my words were poorly chosen. What I meant was that your informants did not provide you with all of the pertinent details, and in light of that fact, your decision to punish me was very logical, and right of course."

"So, you claim that I was misinformed, and as a result of that misinformation, you do not deserve punishment. Is that right?" His voice was as cold as ice.

"I would not presume to say what you should or should not do, sir." Kin said in an almost monotone voice. In black and white it may sound sort of sniveling, but it didn't sound that way in person, yet it wasn't sarcastic either. Vampires had a strange way of dealing with one another.

Darius squinted slightly and considered Kin for what seemed like ages, but was probably no more than a minute. "You are correct that you have never before given me reason to punish you. Normally, you are a good and faithful servant. Therefore, I choose to ignore your lack of judgment this one time. I trust we will never have cause to revisit such issues, Kinley."

"Never, sir. You are very kind. I thank you."

I was beginning to think I might never breathe again. The tension eased slightly, but only slightly. Kin continued his statue like stance. Darius had sat back in his chair, but he still had the air of a king about to pronounce a death sentence. If I wasn't so scared I would have laughed at the irony of the undead pronouncing a death sentence on each other.

He reached out and picked up the snuff box again. "Obediah," Darius said softly. Suddenly another vampire stepped forward. I hadn't even noticed him. He had been standing off to the side beside one of the numerous book cases. He had been so still all this time that he seemed like part of the décor. I was mortified that I jumped a little in surprise, but I couldn't help it.

Obediah was a short man with olive skin and dark, greasy hair. He was dressed in a cream suit with a Nehru jacket. He stood erect at the side of the desk, eyes forward, waiting for his master to speak. "Show Miss Fletcher back to the waiting room, please Obediah. Then retrieve the ledger and bring it to me."

This time I did dare to turn and face Kin, though I didn't dare speak again. Once was enough. Kin turned his head only slightly, just enough to make eye contact. He looked into my eyes and gave the tiniest, almost imperceptible nod. Had I not been concentrating on his face so hard I wouldn't have noticed it. I guess that was all the reassurance I was going to get.

Before I knew what was happening, Obediah had my arm and was leading me from the room. I didn't want to leave Kin and I sure as hell didn't want to be out in that big empty room all alone. I was quickly ushered through the door, past the guard and escorted to the nearest chair. After he released my arm, he turned to me and gave a little bow. Then Obediah returned to the inner sanctum.

Great. I was back in the enormous waiting room with nothing to do. I'd already counted how many chairs there were. Forty two. I had already counted all the mirrors. Sixteen. There were a dozen potted plants and trees. I had no interest in counting the crystal drops on the chandelier.

Dare I take my cell phone out and play solitaire? What else could I do? Would the guard care? Did I care? I had just eased my pocket book onto my lap and was trying to undo the zipper without making any noise, when the door at the other end of the room opened. It was thrown open by a man, a vampire presumably, with no care for the noise he made. He tramped loudly upon the marble floor in his flat heeled boots. The newcomer was all in black, from head to toe, including a black duster that would have looked ridiculous on anyone else. His head, however, was adorned with a heavy mop of long almost white blonde hair that reached past his shoulders. The duster billowed out behind him as he strode confidently across the great room.

As he got closer, I could see he had very pale skin, paler than Kin's and his eyes were light, though I couldn't tell what color they were. His nostrils flared and his brows furrowed. He slowed his pace. The man in black seemed confused. He looked around the room and his gaze rested on me. I had nowhere to hide. I had to sit there on the stupid gilt chair and watch him look me over. The stranger turned and headed towards me. Oh, joy!

He stopped about two feet in front of me. "You are a human," he stated unnecessarily.

"Yes, I've been aware of that for some time," I answered.

His nostrils flared even more and his lip curled in distaste. "You are either very brave or very foolish to address me in such a manner." He spoke with a slight accent, perhaps German.

"You tell me that I'm a human and I'm foolish?" Ok, perhaps I was, but I'd had enough and I wasn't going to take any crap from this guy. I'd had more than enough for one person to endure for a lifetime, and I'd had it all in a little more than twenty four hours.

My remark didn't go over well. He pulled back, offended that a lower life form such as myself would speak to him in such a manner. "You are very lucky that we met here at the home of the Magistrate. I am forbidden to kill here," he said. He emphasized 'here' in such a way that it was very evident that were we to meet elsewhere he would have no qualms about killing me.

"I'm sorry that you are so easily offended. I didn't realize vampires were so thin skinned." If he couldn't kill me, why stop? I know, but I wasn't exactly in the most reasonable frame of mind. His eyes flashed and he bared his teeth, fangs and all. "Oh, just lighten up. You've got hundreds of years to go, potentially. You need to not take yourself so seriously."

Two deliberate strides brought him practically toe to toe with me. He bent down, close to my face. "You had best hope that the Magistrate has some use for you, or I will make you regret every word you have uttered." His rancid breath was enough to do that. I don't know who or what he'd been eating, but he was in dire need of a bottle of Scope. I had to fight the urge to cover my nose.

Just at that moment, the door to Darius' office opened and Obediah stepped out. He said something in a language I did not understand and the black clad vampire spun on his heels and marched himself in to see the Magistrate.

I bet he and Nigel were on the same bowling team. Ok, that time I had to chuckle. A vampire bowling team! Just imagine them all there in matching shirts! The stifled chuckle grew to a giggle and soon I couldn't hold it in. I blamed the stress. The stone faced vamp guarding the door looked at me like I might explode and that only made it funnier. The sound echoed in the big empty room and I bit my lip and even my fingers to try and stop. Eventually, I managed to calm myself down. As I wiped the tears of laughter away, I realized I'd been very stupid and made another enemy. I didn't need another enemy. Well, really, who does?

I decided I was very near the end of my rapidly fraying rope. The short nap at Debbie's was not enough to repair my wrecked nerves and there had been so much more to wreck them since I'd awoken. I feared I'd just about reached my breaking point and wondered what did happen to someone when they went past the breaking point? All at once I felt so very tired. Exhaustion overcame me. The tears of laughter were very quickly replaced by the tears of someone who doesn't know what to do or how to get out of trouble and is too tired to help themselves, but even tears required more effort than I could muster.

If only I could lie down. I didn't care that there were five vampires in close proximity, and one who was very eager to kill me, I wanted to sleep. And I wanted more than sleep. I wanted my mother. I wanted someone to take care of me. Someone to hold me and stroke my hair and tell me that everything was going to be ok. But I didn't have a somebody like that anymore. I was alone. Perhaps I could manage a few tears after all.

I tilted my head back against the wall and closed my eyes. Silent tears ran down the sides of my face. I tried hard to think of something relaxing, but it was no good. My head was full of vampires and a shape shifting bitch and insensitive police detectives and a ruined home and that damned stupid Russian snuff box.

Finally, Kin emerged from Darius's room. I don't know how long I had been sitting with my eyes closed. "Hero," he whispered, seeing my closed eyes. I lifted my head and opened my eyes. He reached out a hand and cupped the side of my face, wiping a tear away with his thumb. "Let's go home," he said quietly. I nodded and stood up. Kin put his arm around me as we walked out. He kept it there all the time, until we were out of the mansion and at his SUV.

We rode home in silence. Neither of us wanted to talk. Kin because he was a man of few words and me because I was too damned tired to hold a conversation.

When we arrived at Kin's, he swooped around to open my door so fast that I couldn't see him do it. I didn't care. I was beyond caring about how fast he could move. He helped me out of the car and held my hand as we entered his condo. Once inside he asked, "Would you like that cup of tea now?" I just shook my head 'no'.

"I think maybe you should go to bed," he suggested. Good call.

"Yes," I said softly. "I'm so tired." I went to the room Kin had designated for me and got undressed. As soon as I got my nightgown on I climbed right into bed. I didn't care about brushing my teeth or anything else. I wasn't even sure if I had picked my dirty clothes up off the floor. I just needed to get my head on the pillow. Sweet relief! Even that nearly made me cry. I was just about to nod off when there was a knock on the door.

"Hero, can I come in please?" What did I care? I grunted something that I hoped sounded like 'yes'. Kin opened the door carefully. Seeing that I was in the bed, he came fully into the room and walked over to me. He sat on the edge of the bed and looked at me. It was all I could do to keep my eyes open. "I'm so sorry that I've gotten you involved in this. I really did think Leontine and Nigel would come after me and not you. And now with Darius, and I gathered you did not make a friend of Jaeger." Jaeger? Who the hell was Jaeger? Oh, must have been the guy in black. I think. I didn't care.

My eyes fluttered. It was such an effort to keep them open. "I won't let anything happen to you. I promise, Hero. I will protect you." I grunted again. Then I felt him lie down behind me. He spooned with me, draping his arm over me. "Nothing will harm you, Hero. I swear it." Then he kissed the top of my head.

That I did care about. I sighed a tiny happy sigh. Someone was around to take care of me after all.

CHAPTER 12

The sun did its best to force my eyes open, but I wasn't giving in. I pulled the covers up over my head, determined to sleep as long as possible. It felt so good. Sleep. A comfy pillow, snuggly blanket and a body curled up beside to me. A body? Body, beside me? Everything came flooding back. No! No, no, no. I was feeling so good. I was content. Now, sun or no sun, I was awake and probably going to stay that way, damn it.

I lowered the blanket and gently rolled on to my back. Kin was sound asleep. Why is it that men always seem to be able to sleep? I looked at his tousled hair, his dark eyelashes, handsome face. I had to admit, it was nice not to wake up alone, especially after the events of the past two days. Funny, considering that Kin was a vampire, I would never have thought I would see him sleep. Nice to know he didn't climb into a coffin at dawn.

So, we'd spent the night together, in the literal sense. This was moving along faster than I normally like. Of course, nothing about this relationship was exactly normal. And what kind of relationship did we really have, anyway? I mean, we'd only had two dates and then all this chaos happened. It did make it difficult to sort things out clearly. There was an unspoken requirement to be together now for the sake of my safety. It forced us into a more intimate situation and I had to ask myself if what I felt for Kin was influenced by all of this. Would I feel as strongly for him if nothing unusual had happened? Would I have taken it in stride, well, sort of in stride, when he told me he was a vampire, or did I only accept it now because of the predicament I was in? And was it possible to separate my feelings with all these other emotions jumbled in?

Still, I had to own up that lying here next to him, watching him sleep, was one of the nice things to come out of all of this mess. Well, the only nice thing really. As I lay there, committing every inch of his face to memory, his beautiful green eyes fluttered open. "Good morning," he muttered in a sleepy voice. I smiled in reply. He reached up and brushed a strand of hair off of my face and then trailed his fingers across my cheek. "Did you sleep well?"

"Yes," I said, still smiling. "Did you?"

"Mm hm," he answered, returning my smile.

"I didn't think you could do this."

"Do what?"

"Sleep. In a bed. I mean, I always thought vampires slept in coffins or something."

Kin laughed. "Well, that's one of those sort of half-truths."

"Half? How do you half sleep in a coffin?" I was curious now.

"Well, many ages ago, new vampires were often buried, the townsfolk thinking they were dead. And when the new vampires awoke, they would have to claw their way out of their grave. Fortunately, they were strong enough that this wasn't as big an ordeal as you might imagine. Also, it was much more common to have family mausoleums and such, where the vampire would have to break through stone. The new vampires would consider themselves dead and would often return to their graves to rest."

"But didn't they realize they didn't have to?"

"Some did, some didn't. Our reaction to sunlight, the burning sensation. Many an old vampire thought they would burst into flame if they stayed out in the sun. They thought retiring to a coffin that would securely block out all of the sun's rays was the safest place for them. Not to mention that damn few people would ever dare disturb a coffin. Remember, vampires were once humans. When they are turned, they are still as ignorant and superstitious as they were before they were made vampire."

That made sense. Not that I'd ever really thought about it, but it wasn't like they would instantaneously know all there was to know about being a vampire. "What about their makers? Weren't they around to teach them these things?"

"Some vampires didn't have much conscience about creating new vamps. In fact, some did it out of some warped sense of justice. They were angry that they'd been made vampire, so they'd go around taking it out on others, creating more vampires and abandoning them."

"Oh, my God! That's horrible!" As if the knowledge that vampires were real wasn't enough!

"Yes. That was one of the main reasons that vampires became organized. Now, being a maker is serious business and there are severe penalties for those who do so irresponsibly."

I hated to ask, but I couldn't help myself. "Um, why create more vampires at all? I mean, if you're all organized and everything, isn't it irresponsible to create a new vampire no matter what?"

He smiled wryly. "Some vampires don't think it's such a bad thing to be vampire. Some even think it is an honor if they deem a human worthy of being made vampire. There are those that do it because they love the person and don't want to lose them, and there are even those that do it out of sympathy for a person who is terminally ill and doesn't want to die."

"Oh." I wasn't sure how I felt about that. I suppose I could understand if you didn't want to lose the person you loved, and they were willing. "Have you ever made a vampire?" This wasn't a question I was eager to hear the answer to, but I figured it was better to get it over with. I couldn't look in his eyes when I asked or while I waited for his reply.

"No, I have never turned anyone." Kin seemed to understand I was uncomfortable asking this, and his tone was kind and sympathetic. "Would you rather not talk about this?"

"It's ok. It's just that it's so much information to process. The past couple of days have been very," I searched for the right word, "well, weird. Sometimes I feel like I'm stuck in a bad dream."

"I understand. I'm so sorry you've gotten mixed up in all of this. I never meant for it to happen," he said sincerely.

"I know," I replied with a smile. Now that I was awake, I had to pee. Did vampires still have bodily functions? Ok, kind of gross, but it's not like you wouldn't have thought about it too. "Um, I need to, ah. I'm going to get up." I pulled back the covers and swung my feet onto the floor.

Kin was still dressed from last night. I hadn't noticed that all he'd done was take his shoes off. Isn't it strange the things you notice and the things you don't? He sat on the edge of the bed and watched me walk out of the room.

After I'd answered Nature's call, I washed my face. My toothbrush was in the other room, so to make do for the moment I squeezed a bit of Kin's toothpaste onto my index finger and rubbed it around on my teeth. At least I wouldn't have morning breath. Scrub. Rinse. Spit. Why can't they make a toothpaste that's safe to swallow? Seriously, how hard would that be?

I took a long look at myself in the mirror. Though I'd only just woken up, I had the look of a woman who hasn't been getting enough sleep. My complexion was dull and I had dark circles under my eyes. Lovely. And as was usual first thing in the morning, my hair looked as though a family of raccoons had been living in it. What a gorgeous site I was for Kin to wake up to! I ran my fingers through my hair, trying to make it look at least presentable. I didn't want to use Kin's hairbrush. That just seemed too personal. Too personal? You just spent the night in the same bed with the man. Not that anything happened. He hadn't even gotten undressed. He hadn't even tried to kiss me or anything.

Women are a strange breed. I can say that because I am one. It's allowed. Here I am trying to decide whether or not to be offended that he didn't try anything. And the really silly part is, had he tried anything, I'd probably be having this same inner monologue with myself. To be offended or not to be offended, that was the question.

Ugh. Poor choice of words my mind picked. It made me think of my father. I hadn't even given him a thought with all of this mess. What would he say when he found out about the house? Did he already know? I had some well-meaning but nosy neighbors who were still in touch with my dad. I'm sure one of them would let him know about the police and the devastation. There were enough of them standing around trying to get a glimpse when Debbie and I had left Georgia Road the day before. Another life observation; neighbors feel it's their God given right to have a good look at whatever's going on at your house. They'll stand right out there on the street, or at the end of their driveways or wherever they can get the best view, and watch without an ounce of shame whatever ordeal one of their neighbors is experiencing. They don't even bother pretending to have a reason to be out there, or act like they're not straining to catch every word that might be passing. It's like socially acceptable vulturism. Is that a word? Vulturism? I don't know, but if it's not, I want credit for it when Webster's add it to their dictionary. You heard it here first!

Ok, back to Dad. What was left at the house that he'd care about? The books. The things I could care the least about. I can easily replace books. It's not as though any of them were first editions or signed by the author or anything. What else? Not Mom's fancy ladies. He always thought they were a waste of her money, but as it was her money that bought them, he couldn't complain. The crystal maybe. It had been a wedding present and he had liked to use it. It wasn't saved for holidays and special occasions. He had his evening cocktail and his after dinner brandy in the crystal every day. No, I couldn't think of anything that would grieve him as I had been grieved. But then, he wasn't sentimental like I was. Neither was William. William wouldn't care a bit about any of it. He would just say 'Oh, Hero, they're only things. There are worse tragedies in this world.' Which of course would be of enormous help to me. Sarcasm again.

No, Dad would say he was glad I wasn't hurt, offer help he had no intention of actually giving, offer advice that wasn't wanted and that would be the end of it. I know this is going to sound like a really mean, horrible thing to say, but at times like this, I have to wonder why would God take my mother away and leave me with Dad and William? Why her first? Don't get me wrong, I don't wish my father dead or anything. It's just at times like this when I really need someone like my mother, I feel like God played a bit of a nasty trick on me. Sorry God, I can't help it. Maybe someday you'll explain to me why it had to be this way, but until then, I can't help what I feel.

Alright, enough hiding out in the bathroom. Kin's going to think I have some kind of problem. I ran my hands over my hair one last time and opened the door. The smell of toast met me in the hallway. Mmmm. Food. That smelled so good. And maybe I could finally have that cup of tea. Oh, yeah, forget sad, depressing thoughts, it was time to eat.

I walked into the kitchen just as Kin was setting a plate of hot buttered toast down. There was already a large cup of tea next to the plate. "I couldn't remember how you took your tea," he said when he saw me come in.

"Just sugar, thank you." I sat down and pulled my chair right up to the table. I reached for the sugar packets he had in a little bowl on the table and added two to my cup of tea and stirred. "This is very thoughtful of you. I really appreciate it." Perhaps I should have felt a little guilty because he couldn't eat, but it wasn't my fault that he couldn't, and I didn't ask him to make me toast and tea, and did I mention that I was hungry?

"Not a problem," he said as he took his seat opposite me, a bottle of Poland Springs in his hand. "It's nice to have someone to make breakfast for. I like being able to do normal things that I used to do when I was human. Is the toast enough? I don't have any eggs."

"Oh, no, toast is great. I love toast and tea. I'm not that fond of eggs anyway, so please don't worry." I munched a couple of bites of toast and took a small sip of the hot tea. It still needed to cool a bit. "Do you miss it? Being human I mean."

"Yes, I do. I miss lying in the sun. I miss eating my favorite foods. Though not nearly so much as I did at first. I miss the people I've lost or had to leave behind. I miss feeling," he paused and sighed, "normal."

Now I did feel guilty. I hadn't really taken the time to think about what or how much he might miss his former life. I'd been too busy thinking about how screwed up my own was. "I'm sorry, Kin. I shouldn't have asked."

"No, don't be silly. I'm glad you feel comfortable asking me questions. To be honest, you've taken the news that I'm a vampire better than anyone I've ever known."

There was a shock. It hadn't felt as though I'd taken it well at all. "Really? I certainly felt pretty freaked out."

(I'm sure there are some armchair psychiatrists and therapists out there who have a lot of very interesting theories as to why I reacted to the news that vampires were real the way I did. If you really want to delve into it, I strongly suggest you start a blog, maybe even a forum where others can come and discuss my reaction, as well as other aspects of this book. Or if you prefer a less technological method, join a book club and you can all read and discuss these points together. Just make sure you all get your own copy of the book, and tell everyone you know how much you like it. And remember, it makes a great gift!)

He chuckled a bit, but I knew it wasn't really at me. "I'm sure you did feel very freaked out. But you didn't scream or run away, and you're here now and sitting with me over breakfast and talking about my life as though I were a normal man. It's a far cry from what usually happens."

I could imagine what usually happened. "Well, I guess I kind of had to accept it, didn't I? I mean with all that's going on. Especially after Nigel frightened the shit out of me and finding out he was actually a vampire, it was good to know there was a vampire on my side. Besides, you're still you. I don't know, maybe if I actually saw you drinking someone's blood or something, then I'd have some real issues, but right now, it's just an, I don't know, abnormality."

Kin laughed out loud then. "An abnormality? I don't think anyone has ever called it that. Thank you, Hero. You can't begin to imagine what it means to me to hear you say those things. It's been very hard all these years."

"How long have you been a vampire?"

"I was made vampire in 1932." He took a sip of his water and toyed with the cap.

"Do you mind talking about it? We don't have to." I reached out and put my hand gently over the one playing with the cap.

Kin looked up at me. His beautiful green eyes stared in to mine. "I don't mind. I'd like to tell you, if you're sure you want to hear about it."

I nodded. "You can tell me anything you like. And of course I want to hear about it. It's part of who you are." I gave his hand a squeeze.

He squeezed back and smiled. "Ok, well, I was born in Chicago in 1898. I'm an only child. My father had a small haberdashery, a hat shop in The Loop. It did ok, but he had to work very hard to keep it going. There was a lot of competition and only so much need for men's hats. It got worse when men started going to Europe to fight in WWI. I started college at the University of Chicago in 1916. My major was Engineering. Unfortunately, at the beginning of my third year, my dad had a stroke and died. I'd never had any interest in his business, so I couldn't take it over. We sold it for what we could get, which wasn't much. I had to leave school and get a job to help support my mother."

Kin paused to take a sip of his water. My tea had gone cold, but I drank it anyway. "I got a job in a slaughterhouse." He caught my reaction. I couldn't help it. The idea of a slaughterhouse was repulsive. I'm a dyed in the wool carnivore, but that doesn't mean I want to be graphically reminded that I'm eating the flesh of a dead animal. Chagrin curled his lip. "You have no idea. The really ironic part is that it made me sick to my stomach to work there. But it was the best pay I could get and we needed every penny."

He shuddered a bit, recalling the grotesque animal corpses, split open and butchered, hanging and dripping blood. "Three or four times a day I'd have to run outside to heave my guts out. The old timers thought it was a riot. Well, they all did really, but it was entertainment to the old guys. And oddly enough, that was what led me to a career that would put me in the path of a vampire."

Ok, my curiosity was definitely peaked. "How?"

After another sip of water, he continued. "One day I ran outside to be sick and the foreman was out there talking to some big tough guy. A stereotypical looking thug. They were standing beside a fancy yellow car. The foreman, Mr. Czarnecki, laughed at me, pointing me out to his friend. 'Poor college boy', he said. All the guys at the slaughterhouse all called me 'college boy'. 'After all these months, he still gets sick like a little girl!' They both had a good laugh at my expense. The tough guy called me over. 'What's a college boy doin' workin' here?' I told him about my parents and how this was the best paying job I could get. He asked me a few more questions about myself and then, to my great surprise, he said to Czarnecki, 'He don't work here no more.' Then he turned to me and said, 'Be at the Green Mill Gardens at six thirty, kid.' After which, he climbed into his car and drove away. My foreman told me to leave and go home and get myself cleaned up. He said he'd send my pay to the Green Mill Gardens. I started to protest, but he told me that 'no one says no to Mr. McGurn'"

Kin paused, waiting for my reaction, but I had none. The name meant nothing to me, but it was clear that Kin thought it was a very important name. I shook my head and raised my eyebrows to convey my lack of recognition. "Jack McGurn? 'Machinegun' McGurn? He was one of Al Capone's henchmen. He was part owner of the Green Mill Gardens." Ah, Al Capone, now that name I knew. Once I was sufficiently impressed, he continued. "So, I did as I was told and went home and showered, shaved, clipped my nails, you name it. At six twenty-five, I walked into the Green Mill Gardens and told the guy at the door that Mr. McGurn had told me to come."

A smile brightened his face. He actually looked happy. "I wish you could have seen it, Hero. It was such a beautiful place. They don't make places like that anymore. Oh, and the music! All the big acts played there. Sophie Tucker, Al Jolson, Eddie Cantor, Joe E. Lewis. Ugh, that wasn't a good story. Poor Joe."

"Why? What happened to Joe?" I asked.

"You never heard that story?" he asked, genuinely surprised.

"I wasn't around back then," I explained.

He frowned. "It's a famous story. Frank Sinatra even played him in a movie. It was called 'The Joker is Wild'." Seeing that that still didn't shed any light on poor Joe, he continued, "The manager of the club, a guy named Danny Cohen, complained that Joe was going to leave the Green Mill Gardens to go to another club, so McGurn, uh, 'convinced' him it would be bad to leave."

A suspenseful pause. Very dramatic. "And?"

"And Jack slit his throat and cut off his tongue."

"Ah! Dear God!" I exclaimed, grabbing my own throat for some stupid reason. "Sort of a, if you're not going to sing for us, you're not going to sing for anyone, huh?"

"Actually, Joe did recover. His voice was never as good, but he did sing again."

"And he sang at the Green Mill Gardens," I concluded.

Kin nodded. "Oh, yeah. Violence really didn't happen that often at the club though. Usually it was a great place to be. A lot of fun, even when you were working. I started out as a busboy in the restaurant. It was fantastic. A big dance floor, inside and outside, lit with lanterns. The club was packed every night. And of course, because of Prohibition, there was a speakeasy in the basement, and a trap door that lead to a series of tunnels in case of a raid. Not that we got raided very often. Policemen were easy to buy off in those days. Their pay was disgracefully low, and many of them had families to support."

His cell phone rang just then. "I'm sorry," he said, as he flipped the phone open. "Yes?" I signaled to him that I was going to take a quick shower and I retreated to the guest room. I had no wish to eavesdrop on his conversation and I wanted to get clean. I grabbed what I needed and dashed to the bathroom. A fast in and out and I wrapped a towel around my head. I met him in the hallway as he came out of the kitchen. "I thought we might finish this in the living room. It'll be more comfortable." I agreed and we sat down together on the couch.

"Is everything ok?" I asked, referring to the phone call.

"Fine," he said, averting his eyes. I didn't believe him, but I was willing to be fooled for a little while.

"So, you were a busboy at the Green Mill Gardens. Then what?"

"Well, eventually, I worked my way up to being a bouncer at the club downstairs. Mr. McGurn liked me and sort of took me under his wing a little. He'd stop and talk to me most nights when he came in. Nothing important, just small talk. Sometimes he'd ask me what I thought about a horse race and I'd calculate the odds. He liked that. I was good at doing the numbers in my head quickly. So, I was able to work up through the ranks and get out of the kitchen and into the club."

"That must have been exciting, working in a speakeasy." It certainly sounded exciting and glamorous to me. "Did you ever meet Al Capone?"

He smiled broadly. "Yes, a few times. I was terrified of him!" he said with a laugh. "Yeah, it was a great time. Sure there'd be a scuffle now and then, or someone would get too drunk and we'd have to throw him out, but when the place was part owned by one of Capone's guys, people tended to behave themselves."

"When I think back now on the people I knew and the acts I got to see," he paused to sigh. "It was amazing."

I could tell he had enjoyed his life. It made me so sad to think that some damned vampire had taken it all away from him. You know, if you think about it, you really have to feel sorry for vampires. I mean, it's not like the vast majority of them chose that life. It happened to them against their will. Thinking about that put things into a new perspective. My life might suck at the moment, but hopefully, things would work out and I'd be able to put everything back together. But to wake up and discover that you've been turned into a vampire! What must that be like? I gave an involuntary shiver.

"Are you ok?" Kin asked when he saw me shiver.

"Oh, yeah, just one of those weird things." I didn't want to tell him I'd been pitying him.

"I'm sorry, I've been rambling on. I'm sure I must be boring you." I assured him that I was most certainly not bored and begged him to continue. "Ok. Well, one night, after we had closed up, I heard Angelo, he was sort of like a bookkeeper. He was in charge of all the cash. Money would be taken from all the tills at various times throughout the night so that if we were raided, there wouldn't be much money for the cops to take. Angelo would take the cash and record all the withdrawals and stuff. So, I heard Angelo giving the numbers to Mr. Cohen. We charged a two dollar cover charge for coming in the door to the club in the basement. Sort of insurance against a raid. You know, get some money out of them up front in case they don't have a chance to pay their tab. Since I worked the door that night, I had a good idea of how many people I'd admitted. The number Angelo gave was way below what it should have been. But, I didn't have any proof, so I kept my mouth shut. The next time I was on the door, I put a little notebook in my pocket and I kept track of each and every cover charge I collected. At the end of the night, I lingered as close to Angelo and Mr. Cohen as I could, hoping to overhear the take Angelo reported for the door. As I expected, it was off a good amount. Almost fifty dollars."

"Well, that wasn't very bright," I noted. "You had to be an idiot to steal from a violent criminal like McGurn."

"No kidding," Kin said in return. "When I came in to work the next day, I kept an eye out for Mr. McGurn. I knew if I told him, he would believe me. Not that I thought Cohen wouldn't, but I knew Jack would be right on my side with no questions asked. And I was right. When I asked him if I could have a minute alone, his response was, 'What's going down, Mac'. He used to call me Mac. I showed him my notebook and told him what I had heard. He didn't even question why I had a notebook. He understood. McGurn went straight to Cohen and the pair went up to Angelo and told him they knew what he had been up to. They didn't mention my name, which I was extremely grateful for. I didn't want to be known as a snitch. But McGurn had been really good to me. The job he gave me paid a lot more than the slaughterhouse, and I was able to provide well for my mother. I felt I owed it to him to let him know if someone was ripping him off."

"Naturally," I interjected. "It was only right you should feel that way."

He smiled and nodded. "Well, even though I felt strongly that I had done the right thing, I felt enormously guilty when they found Angelo dead the next morning."

"Oh, God! But it wasn't your fault. He would have been found out one way or another, and it's not like you were responsible for his stupid stealing."

"It's ok, Hero. I've had a long time to get over that guilt. I know what you said is right and Angelo would have ended up that way with or without me. But that's not what makes me wish I'd never done it." The smile was gone. He was somber and there was no spark in his eyes. I knew what was coming.

"Go on," I said gently. I reached out and took his hand.

"Cohen gave me Angelo's job. They felt since I was the one that ratted him out, I could be trusted. And I was trustworthy. I kept excellent records and was on top of everything. The one time we got raided, the cash was in the tunnel long before they broke the door down. But this was Chicago at the height of Prohibition. I was often the last to leave for the night. I would double check the books and make sure everything was in the safe, ready for the next morning's deposit and for the next night's opening tills. One night, when I was leaving, I had just stepped outside and locked the door. I'd barely taken a step when someone clocked me on the back of the head. I woke up hours later in a strange bedroom. A woman I'd never seen before was sitting on the edge of the bed, wiping my forehead with a cold cloth."

This was the painful part of the story. I squeezed his hand. I was touched that he was sharing this with me. It couldn't be easy to relive this.

"I asked where I was and what had happened. All she would tell me was that I should take it easy and be patient. Easier said than done. I made a ruckus and two thugs came into the room. Seeing as I was conscious, they decided I didn't need to be in bed any more. They dragged me into the next room and sat me down in a chair. They wanted to know all about the club, Jack, Mr. Cohen, when Capone came in, the combination to the safe, every bit of info I could possibly know. I refused to tell them. I told them to kill me, that'd I'd never betray Mr. McGurn. As you might expect, they roughed me up pretty good. I was beaten up one side and down the other, but I wouldn't talk. I figured they were going to kill me and I started to pray under my breath. The head guy laughed at me. He told me God wouldn't touch me once they were done with me. One of the others laughed and called the head guy Bugs. I knew then that he wasn't nearly finished with me."

"Why? Who was Bugs?" Stupid me and my TV age upbringing. All I could picture at that moment was the Bugs Bunny cartoon with the two dumb gangsters, where they're hiding out after a robbery and Bugs keeps getting them to hide in stupid places. I'm not proud of that, but I figured just in case it happened to any of you I'd mention it so you wouldn't feel alone.

"Bugs Moran was one of Capone's fiercest enemies. The St.Valentine's Day Massacre, that was between Moran and Capone. He got the nickname 'Bugs' because he was a nut case. I was determined not to talk, but I tell you, I was scared." I didn't blame him. "After they worked on me for a few more hours, I finally passed out. When I came to, I was back in the bed again, only this time the dame wasn't mopping my brow, she was cleaning blood off of me."

The dame? Apparently this trip down memory lane was also bringing back his old 1920's lingo.

"I assumed it was all just blood from the beating I'd taken. I was in such rough shape, I didn't notice the wounds on my neck. In fact, it was probably the only wound I had that didn't hurt. And it wasn't like I could see it. There was no mirror and I didn't feel like looking at myself. The cycle of beating me unconscious and then putting me to bed to recover went on for two more days. The last day, when I came to, there was a man in the bedroom that I'd never seen before. He asked me how I felt. I told him I felt like crap. He said he was going to make it all better. I didn't like the sound of it; I thought he was gay or something. He came over to the bed and sat on the edge. I was really anxious, but I couldn't move. They had tied down my arms and legs while I was passed out. I hadn't noticed right away because my attention had been on this weird guy. He put his wrist up to his mouth and bit it. It was disgusting. The noise, the sight of the blood, the smell, not to mention seeing the blood trickle down his chin and his ghastly smile, with blood stained fangs. I wanted to scream but I couldn't. He put his wrist to my mouth and told me to drink. I turned my head. He grabbed my head with his other hand. He was too strong, I couldn't turn away. And as I told you yesterday, once you get that first drop of blood, you become insatiable for it. As repulsed as I was, I couldn't stop sucking on his wrist once I'd started. Oh, sorry," he said when he noticed my nauseated expression.

"Did you give them the information?"

Kin nodded. "I had no choice. I was compelled to obey my maker. It was like taking a truth serum."

"What happened? Did you have to stay with Moran's gang?"

"No, much to my pleasant surprise. After a few days, Clive, my maker,"

"Clive! You were turned by a vampire named Clive?" I couldn't help laughing.

"That was his name." Kin didn't appreciate the humor of a vampire being named Clive, so I held in my laughter. I suppose since we were talking about the guy that ended his life and cursed him for all eternity he wouldn't have much of a sense of humor about it. "Anyway, my maker didn't want to give me any more of his blood and certainly none of the gangsters who came to the apartment would tolerate being bit, or allow the woman to be bit. So I was turned loose on the streets of Chicago."

"Why? That doesn't make sense. Not to mention irresponsible making. Wouldn't Clive have gotten in trouble for that?"

"I don't know what they thought. I think they figured what they had turned me into was worse than death. As for Clive, he met his responsibility. He told me what it meant to be vampire, about our government and the rules of my new race. And, of course, he taught me how to feed."

Eww! Gross! "But you could have told your boss what they were up to, or waited for them and bitten them, or told where their hideout was."

"No, actually, I couldn't. Clive gave me a long and detailed list of orders to obey. I could never enter the Green Mill Gardens again. I could not speak to Jack McGurn or Danny Cohen. I could never reveal the location I was taken to to anyone. The list went on and on. They covered all of their bases. All except one. They knew nothing about the few months I'd worked at the slaughterhouse years before. I went to see Mr. Czarnecki at the slaughterhouse. I asked him if he would do me a favor. He said he would. I wrote a note, explaining as much as I could and asked him to deliver it to the club. Naturally, he agreed. He told me that everyone had been looking for me and the word on the street was that I'd been whacked. Czarnecki told me that McGurn had sworn to kill whoever had done the hit if it was true. I told him it was more true than he knew. Then I asked him to deliver a second note, to my mother. He agreed to that as well. Then I went to my bank, withdrew all I had, and got on a bus for New York."

"Why? Why didn't you go home?"

"Couldn't. It was on the list," he said simply.

I felt awful. I wanted to cry. It was terrible and sad. "Oh, Kin. I'm so, so sorry," I said, holding back tears. I leaned over and hugged him. It just seemed like the thing to do.

He put his arms around me. "It's ok, Hero. That all happened a very long time ago. Besides, if it hadn't, I'd have never met you."

I chuckled and pulled my head back to look at him. "Has anyone ever told you that you're very cute when you're sappy?"

He laughed too. "No. Was it terribly sappy?"

"Not terribly, no."

"Oh," he said, leaning his face in close to mine. "Good. I'd hate to be accused of being too sappy." Then he bent his head and kissed me. And then I kissed back. And then... his phone rang.

CHAPTER 13

You know, there are times when I think the invention of the cell phone will bring about the downfall of civilized society. But, I could write a whole other book all about my love-hate relationship with cell phones. Let's just deal with one book at a time.

Kin gave me a look that clearly indicated this was an important call, so I left him alone and went to the spare bedroom to get my own cell phone. After all, I'd promised Debbie that I would call her. She picked up before it finished the first ring.

"What, were you sitting on top of the phone?" I asked after she said 'hello'.

"I thought you were going to call me this morning?" she said irritably.

"It is morning Deb. It's barely ten o'clock. I'm fine. I told you I would be."

"Well, I thought you would call me first thing, as soon as you woke up," she explained.

"Sorry. I'm at someone else's home. Kin cooked breakfast for me and I had a shower and we talked about some things." I wasn't going to feel guilty about this.

"Doesn't he work?" A reasonable question.

"He deals in antiques. It's not like he has a nine-to-five job."
This reminded me that although I'd learned an awful lot about
Kin in the past forty five minutes or so, I still didn't know exactly
what he did to earn a living. What fun! Another series of
questions and answers to look forward to. Just add it to the list.

"Oh," she said simply. There was a pause as she considered
this. "Well, at least he hasn't left you alone."

"No, I'm not alone."

"By the way, did Detective Joyce get a hold of you?"

"No. Why was he looking for me?" Oh, what now?

"You have to go to the station to fill out some paperwork."

I groaned. Just what I felt like doing. Going to sit with my
pal Detective Joyce and fill out paperwork about my destroyed
home. I'd rather have a root canal.

"I could go with you," Debbie offered.

"Thanks, but you've already missed work on account of me.
Actually, shouldn't you be at work now?" I really hoped she
hadn't taken another day off.

"No, I'm working a later shift today. I switched with someone
who had something to do this afternoon."

"Oh, ok." That was a relief. "It's no big deal about going to
the police station. Just a pain, you know?"

"Yeah, I know. Are you sure you'll be ok?" I felt bad that she was worried. I hated it really. I didn't like people being worried about me.

"Debbie, I'm fine. Please don't worry about me."

"I'll try, but I'm not promising. I told Sue I'd have you call her."

I'd forgotten about Sue. Poor Sue! Only my best friend. I'm sure she felt left out and even a bit hurt that I'd pawned her off on Debbie to find out what had been going on. "I'll call her tonight when she gets off work. Thanks for talking to her. I just couldn't go through it all over again last night."

"It's ok. We both understand." I hoped that was true. It probably was, but I worried none the less.

"Well, I'd better check my messages. I just called you straight away as soon as I turned my phone on." I hoped that little tidbit would make up for not calling as soon as she had expected.

"Yeah, ok. You've probably got a message on there from Detective Joyce. And you've got one from me too."

I could just imagine the message from my friend. Chuckling, I said "Thanks for the warning."

She laughed too. "Call me later on, ok? I should be home from work about ten thirty."

I promised like a good girl and hung up the phone. Then I punched in my pin number and checked my messages. Yup. Two messages from Detective Joyce and a call from Debbie. Debbie's message was exactly what I expected, please call me.

The messages from Detective Joyce were brief and business like. He wanted me to come to the station ASAP to fill out paperwork. The first call was just after eight and the second one just after nine. If this was the beginning of a pattern, call number three should be arriving any moment. Deciding to beat him to the punch, I sighed and dialed the number he had left for me. I had a good memory for phone numbers. Can't explain it. Just one of those otherwise useless talents. The call was answered by another officer and I waited while they tracked Joyce down and let him know I was on the phone.

"Joyce," he barked. Such a pleasant fellow. I wondered if he had a wife. If he did, I seriously considered sending her some flowers, the poor woman.

"It's Hero Fletcher, returning your calls. I'll be down to fill out the paperwork within the hour." I wasn't going to give him a chance to dictate when I should come in.

"Fine. As soon as you can get here." Oh, good. He wasn't going to argue with me.

"Do I need to bring anything with me?" I asked.

"Bring your ID and your homeowner's insurance information if you have it." I did. I'd taken it from my office the day before.

"Ok. I'll see you soon," I said as I hung up. What were the odds he'd be this agreeable while I was there filling out paperwork? I don't know, but I wouldn't take the bet. Still, there was hope.

After I put my phone back into my purse, I gathered up all of my belongings, such as they were, and neatly placed them into my overnight bag. Then I put on my shoes and swung my pocketbook onto my shoulder.

I went back out to the living room to see if Kin was off the phone. He was standing, looking out of his front window. "Is everything alright?" I asked.

"Just fine," he said, turning to face me. "How about you?"

"Yeah, fine. I've got to go to the police station and fill out some paperwork."

He just nodded. Looking thoughtfully at the floor. "I have something I need to do for Darius," he started.

"That's ok, I can take my own car. Oh. No, I can't. We left it at Debbie and Bob's. Well, you can just drop me off there and I'll pick it up." That didn't sound too bad. Seeing how Darius liked to keep people waiting, I doubted he'd notice if Kin took the time to drive me to get my car.

"No. I'll take you to the police station and come back for you." It was said simply, but I felt there was something more there.

"You don't have to do that," I began, but he stopped me.

"Hero, I will drop you off and pick you up."

"Ok, what aren't you telling me?" Something stunk and it wasn't me. I'd showered.

"I would just feel better if we did it this way, that's all."

"Oh, no, that's not all. There's got to be a reason why you'd feel better about it. What's going on Kin? Whatever it is, I have a right to know." I realized our relationship had been short, but surely he must know by now that I'm the kind of woman who demands answers and explanations.

"It would be safer."

That was it. Just that. The missing 'because…' hung in the air and I didn't like it one bit. "Safer?"

"Yes," he said.

"Elaborate, Kin. Don't make me drag it out of you. It's easier if you just come clean."

"If you're alone, you are vulnerable to Leontine and Nigel and anyone else who wants the snuff box. Or any of the artifacts that Darius has for that matter."

"Well, that's just great. You mean they will be after me forever because we had two dates?" It seemed to me that an enormous injustice was being done and I had no idea what to do about it. I had no intention of becoming Buffy the Vampire slayer, but I didn't want to live looking over my shoulder all the time either. What the hell was I supposed to do?

"No, not forever. We'll take care of it, but I need a little time."

"We? Who's we? You got a mouse in your pocket?" Sarcasm rears its ugly head again.

Kin furrowed his eyebrows in confusion. Clearly, he had never heard that expression in the hundred years or so he'd been on the Earth. "Darius and Jaeger and I."

"Jaeger? Who's Jaeger?"

"You met him last night, don't you remember?"

I met someone named Jaeger? Oh! Ok, I knew who he meant. "You mean that vampire with the long black coat?"

"Yes," he said, raising one eyebrow. "I'm surprised you didn't recall him right away. You certainly made an impression on him."

My ill-advised conversation came back to me. "Well, he walked up to me and told me I was a human. How stupid was that? And then he got all bent out of shape and said I was lucky we'd met there because he couldn't kill me in the Magistrate's home and I told him to lighten up."

In that very short span of time that it took to tell Kin this, his face went from surprise to shock to utter disbelief; closing his eyes and pinching the bridge of his nose. "Oh, Hero. Why did you do that? You should have just kept quiet."

"Well how was I to know he was so high strung? And I'm sorry, but vampire or no vampire it was a stupid thing to walk up to me and say 'You are a human'. What, like I didn't know?"

Kin just looked at me. It was the kind of look you give a puppy who's just piddled in the kitchen, but he's so cute, you can't be mad at him. I wasn't sure I appreciated it. "Fortunately, Darius told him you are off limits, but you may not be so lucky the next time you insult a hunter."

"I didn't insult him! And what's a hunter? I mean, in vampire terms?"

"Jaeger is employed by Darius to hunt down vampires who break the law. He is ruthless and enjoys his job. He is not someone you want to make an enemy of."

Ugh. My toast sat like lead in my stomach. "I still say he was very thin skinned for a vampire," I protested petulantly.

"Yes, well, as he is protecting you now, you should try to stay on his good side."

"Are you sure he has one?" Kin shot me a dirty look. I decided I'd behave myself. Well, I'd try and behave myself. I made no promises. "Ok, so let's get this show on the road then."

We went out and got into Kin's SUV. After we passed by the guard house, I turned to Kin and said, "You never did tell me what happened with Darius after I went back out to the waiting room? Did you get in trouble?"

"No, I'm not in trouble. After we discussed the matter a little more, he decided I had been trying to act in his best interest. We also discussed how to deal with Leontine and Nigel, especially in regards to you. That was why Jaeger was brought in."

"Oh." I wasn't sure what to say to that. "So what did you all decide?"

"Darius will issue and edict that you are under his protection and not to be touched. That will keep you safe from most vampires."

"Most? Only most? Why most?" I would have thought an edict from Darius would have been followed by all.

"There are some vampires who do what they please and until they are charged with a crime and caught, they will continue to live that way. Also, if a vampire is sent from another area to here, he or she will follow the orders of their own Magistrate. They can still be charged with breaking our laws, but normally, by the time we know about such things they have already returned to their own sector. However, that only applies to vampires"

I sat quietly as I sorted through all this news. Something was missing. "Leontine isn't a vampire."

"No, she isn't. That is where I am going with Darius after I drop you at the police station. He has set a meeting with the head of her Menagerie."

"Menagerie?"

"Yes, shape shifters belong to a Menagerie. It is part of their form of government."

"But why should the leader of her Menagerie help you?" If Leontine was after the snuff box that must mean her leader wanted it too. I saw no reason for him to call off his dogs. Um, I mean cat.

"I'm not sure if he will. Shape shifters and vampires have been trying to live together in harmony for generations. Unfortunately, it hasn't always worked. But Ilderim is a good man who has always worked with Darius to promote good will between our peoples. Darius thinks he can get Iderim to make Leontine leave you alone."

"Ilderim? That's an odd name."

"I believe it's an old Arabic name."

"But doesn't Ilderim want the snuff box too?" I thought that was a pretty obvious point of contention.

"Yes, but he may be willing to negotiate. It's complicated."

Seeing as that was probably all I was going to get out of him on that subject, at least for the moment, I changed the topic. Sort of. "And that call you got earlier this morning, was that about this meeting?"

"Yes. That was Obediah letting me know that Ilderim had agreed to meet and I would be called again when a time was set."

"How long will this meeting take?"

"I really don't know. Hopefully not too long." He didn't seem very concerned about the meeting. I wasn't even going and I was nervous as hell. It almost made having to go to the police station and deal with paperwork and my favorite Detective appealing. Almost.

"So, you have no idea when you might be back to pick me up?" That could be awkward.

Obviously, Kin hadn't really thought about that part. "No, I'm sorry, Hero, I don't. I will get back to you as quickly as I can. You'll just have to wait for me."

"Why? Couldn't I take a cab back to your place or something?" I really didn't want to have sit around the police station twiddling my thumbs.

"No. You're safer with the police. Leontine and Nigel wouldn't try and take you in there."

There was a comforting thought. And when the police asked me why I was hanging around, I could tell them I was waiting for my boyfriend to pick me up because there was a vampire and a shape shifter out there waiting for me. Seeing as I really had no other choice, I agreed to wait for Kin to return.

We pulled right up to the front door of the police station and Kin told me to wait. In a flash, he was beside me, opening the door. I worried that his super-fast movement might be noticed, but no one in the parking lot or in the lobby seemed to notice. He walked me inside and stood with me as I waited my turn to ask to see Detective Joyce. Once the officer at the desk had called down to let Joyce know I was there, Kin kissed me on the cheek and said softly, "Remember, don't go outside. Stay around people until I come for you."

"I will," I said, smiling at him. What a sap I was. All it took was a peck on the cheek to change my disposition. He smiled back and then turned and went to meet Darius.

Kin had barely gone out the door when I heard the Detective behind me. "Miss Fletcher?"

I spun around and faced him. "Good morning, Detective. Let's get started." I held out my hand for him to lead the way. He grunted something in response and led me back to his desk. He motioned to an old wooden chair that was probably as old as the building, and I sat down while he went around to the other side of the desk and plopped into a green leatherette swivel chair. Not as old as the wooden chair, but probably thirty years old at least.

He pulled out a folder from amid a huge stack on the corner of his desk. Somehow, without looking, he managed to reach in and grab mine. Years of practice or sleight of hand? Who can say? The Detective flipped open the folder and started shuffling things around. "Ok, ok," he kept muttering to himself. I was kind of ticked that he hadn't been ready for me, but then I remembered that I might have an awful lot of time to kill, so it didn't really matter.

Joyce bent down and reached into a drawer that squeaked in protest when he opened it. He straightened up and slapped down a pile of blank forms. "Here we go. You just need to fill these out. You can use the pics the forensic team took to help you out." The stack of forms was slid across the desk, accompanied by a large pile of photographs.

"Uh... ok. Where am I supposed to fill all this out?" There wasn't any free space on his desk and I didn't really relish the idea of sitting with him while I filled the forms out.

The Detective didn't seem to know where I should go either. Glad to know he was on top of things. I know that it's wrong for movies and TV to portray law enforcement personnel as clueless dim wits, but the fact of the matter is, you find clueless dim wits in every walk of life, and baby, I'd found me the king! He told me he'd be right back and he went off in search of some place where I could work on all this crap. Fortunately, he wasn't gone long and he led me to an interview room that wasn't in use.

I put the pile of papers and photos on the table. "No one's going to be watching me, are they?" I asked, indicating the one way glass mirror on the far wall.

"Nah, don't worry. We can't use this room right now because the video shorted out. Someone's coming to fix it tomorrow, so you're good. If you need anything, let me know. If you can't find me, talk to whoever's at the front desk." He left, closing the door behind him before I could reply.

Plopping down on the blue vinyl chair, which emitted a soft whoosh as I sat down, I resigned myself to the unpleasant task ahead. First, I opened the file of pictures from my home. It seemed unreal, looking at these photos of destroyed rooms, destroyed possessions. The items were familiar, but it didn't feel like I was looking at my own home. Deciding that this was probably a good thing, versus the alternative and getting all emotional, I started sorting them out by room. I have to say, I would have thought they would have been already, but, then again, what do I know about police work?

Once that was sorted, I pulled a pen out of my pocket book and drew the pile of forms towards me. I just knew I was going to have writer's cramp before this was over.

Hours later, I emerged from my solitude with cramped fingers and a headache. I went straight to Detective Joyce's desk. As luck would have it, he was there. I guess that was luck. Anyway, I handed him all the pics and papers. "All done."

He looked up in surprise. "Wow. You got that done quick," he remarked as he looked over my forms.

"Quick? I've been in there for nearly three hours. I couldn't believe I had to list all my belongings. My right hand may never be the same." Just to prove my point, I held up my poor, over-worked hand and gingerly flexed the digits as best as I could. He was unimpressed.

"Whatever. Thanks for coming in. I'll let you know when we have any info for ya." That was it, I was dismissed. I was going to miss him. Not!

"Yeah, yeah," I muttered as I turned and made my way back to the lobby.

My hand did ache. I wasn't being a baby about it. Really, I wasn't. You'd think with all the computer work I do, I'd have been ok, but you don't hold your hand all tight like you do when you write. I kept flexing my poor little hand as I pushed through the double doors that led to the lobby.

The same officer was behind the desk that was there when I came in. She was helping a man and woman who looked to be in their fifties. I didn't want to eavesdrop, so I hurried past them and slipped into the ladies room. Now that I was vertical, I realized I hadn't gone since I'd woken up this morning, and my tiny little bladder was protesting. I'll spare you the grisly details. You're welcome.

After washing my hands (just so you knew I did), I opened the door and stepped back into the lobby. And right there, two feet in front of me, was Leontine. She had her back to me. I considered retreating into the restroom, but I feared getting trapped in there with her. At least out here there were witnesses. I slid quietly to the right, sat down in the first chair and tried to hide behind a magazine. Out of the corner of my eye, I saw her turn and look at me. Damn. Oh, well, it's not like I really expected the magazine to protect me. I looked out the glass doors that led to the street and hoped to see Kin out there, but no such luck. Leontine walked toward me. I got up quickly and walked over to a vending machine that was closer to the reception desk and further away from the doors. I reached into my bag and took out my wallet. As I dropped some change into the machine, the Amazon came close up beside me. "Come with me," she hissed.

"No fucking way," I replied without taking my eyes off the snack pack of Oreos that were slowly inching their way to the drop off. I bent and retrieved the cookies and turned to face the big, blonde baddie.

Her eyes were flashing and her jaw was clenched. "You will come with me."

"No, I will not. Have you been dipping into the catnip? Like I'm really going to leave here with you." I opened the cookies and popped one into my mouth. Don't judge, those vending machine Oreos are smaller than the regular ones. Besides, I was in a tight bind and needed chocolate.

She reached out to grab my arm, but I pulled back. "You even try to touch me again and I will scream like a banshee. Besides, don't you know that Kin and Darius are meeting with Ilderim right now to get him to call you off?" Hmm. It had been three hours since Kin left. I didn't know how far they had to travel to see this guy. Had things gone wrong? Had the leader of the pack not agreed?

"How dare you speak his name?" she hissed.

"Oh, please! You super natural people take yourselves way too seriously. Get out of here before you get yourself in trouble with your boss. He might decide to have you spayed."

Her face went scarlet. She opened her mouth, no doubt to cut me with some scathing remark, but all that came out were funny little choking noises.

"Hair ball? Aww, that sucks." I popped in another cookie.

"Miss Fletcher," a voice called happily. "How are you doing?" The nice young officer who had responded to my call the night Nigel scared the crap out of me walked up to us.

"Officer Salucci, isn't it?" I greeted him with a smile.

"Yes, it is. I'm sorry to hear about your place getting trashed." He did seem sorry. A nice guy, Officer Salucci. He looked at Leontine, waiting to be introduced. He didn't seem to notice that she was uptight.

"Thank you, I appreciate that. It's funny you should bring that up. Because this woman here," I said, waving my hand in Leontine's direction. I paused to give her a very smug look before I continued. "I'm pretty sure she's the one who did it."

Both the officer and the cat woman gaped in surprise. "Uh, um," stammered the nice young policeman.

"Preposterous!" cried Leontine. She turned and stalked towards the doors. I wondered if he'd let her go or not. He seemed to be torn between taking me seriously and thinking I was playing a mean joke.

"Miss Fletcher, are you joking?" he asked.

I smiled and said, "No, actually, I'm not. I have no proof, you understand, but I think there is a good chance that that woman is responsible for ruining my house."

Officer Salucci was facing me and had his back to the front door of the police station. He didn't see Leontine hurry out the doors and change into an orange cat. No one seemed to see it but me. I could still see her green cat's eyes reflecting from under the bush next to the door. He turned to look for her and was amazed that she had seemed to disappear.

"Who is she? Do you know her name and address?"

"I just know her first name. Leontine."

"Leontine?" he repeated. I could tell he still didn't believe me. "And what makes you think she is the one responsible?"

Oh, damn. He had me there. I couldn't exactly tell him the truth. "She's ah." Quick, Hero, think of something. "Well, she's jealous. I went out on a date with her ex-boyfriend. He said she just can't accept that they've broken up." That sounded plausible.

"Oh." He was looking out the door again, as though trying to figure out where she'd gone so quickly. "Have you told Detective Joyce?"

Crap! "Uh, no. I didn't realize it until just a minute ago, when she came up to me here. She told me to leave her boyfriend alone. She's nuts."

"Well, we'd better let him know. Come on, I'll take you to him."

Great! Now look what I'd gotten myself into. As I followed him across the lobby, I stole one last look out the front doors. Leontine was still there, peering at me from under the bush. I hoped she'd get fleas.

Explaining my theory to Detective Joyce was every bit as painful as I'd feared. He wanted to know why I didn't mention her before. I lied and said I didn't think she was nuts enough to do such a thing until she approached me in the police station. I was constantly amazed at my ability to lie. What did that say about me?

I stuck to my story and he gave in and let me go, though I could tell he thought I was holding something back. Once I was back in the lobby, my first thought was whether Leontine was still waiting for me in the bushes. I didn't see any eyes reflecting back at me. Then I noticed that Kin was standing in the far corner of the lobby, reading notices on a bulletin board. At last! The Calvary was here!

"Hey," I said as I walked up behind him. He turned and smiled at me.

"Sorry I took so long. Have you been waiting?" Kin asked as he reached out and took my hand.

"Oh, I've been busy." My tone clearly indicated that something out of the ordinary had taken place. He started to ask, but I shook my head. "Later," I said.

"Okay. Let's go home."

That sounded good to me.

CHAPTER 14

"Oh, God, you didn't," Kin said, laughing. "Hero, you do love to antagonize people, don't you?"

"I thought Leontine didn't consider herself a person? Anyway, what else do I have? I'm not a vampire or a shape shifter or werewolf or witch or whatever. I'm just a human. All I have is my wit and sarcasm. The most damage I can do to her is annoy her." That wasn't a comforting thought, but I felt it was better to be realistic about my limitations.

"Well, not really. Shape shifters are as easily injured as humans, they just heal faster. Werewolves too. Except you can't kill a werewolf like you can a human, but you can injure them. Shape shifters are just a susceptible to death as a human."

"Good to know. How do you kill a werewolf? I mean, since we're talking about such things."

"Silver. You have to either get them through the heart with silver, thus the silver bullet method, or you have to cut off their heads with a silver sword," he said, very casually, as though it were the most normal conversation in the world.

"Okay. So what happened with Iderim or whatever his name is? Is he going to call her off?" I really hoped he would. I enjoyed all the shots I got in on Leontine and especially putting the cops on to her, but I knew a direct order from her boss was the best bet to keep her away from me.

"Yes, he agreed. I'm certain that by now Leontine has been told to leave you alone."

"What about Darius? Did he have to give up the box?"

Kin nodded. "Once we've had a chance to thoroughly examine and document it, we will turn it over to Ilderim."

"So, Leontine gets what she wants in the end. What did this cost Darius?" I wasn't naïve enough to think there wasn't a bargain of some kind struck beyond the sharing of the snuff box.

He sighed, just a little, but I caught it.

"Or did it cost you?" I hadn't considered that. Had I caused trouble for him? Not that he hadn't caused enough trouble for me, but still, it's not like I want to be responsible for anyone being in trouble.

He nodded again. "Darius will have something for me to do soon. I'm not sure when, but it won't be easy and will probably require me to travel." Kin's face was placid but I could tell he was uneasy.

"I'm sorry," I said.

"Why?" he asked, genuinely surprised. He turned for a moment to look at me. "It's not your fault, Hero. It's my own doing."

Kin was right of course, but I still felt badly. "Will it be something to do with this manuscript thingy?"

"The text? Yes, I believe it will be. I expect it will be to recover another artifact."

"Well, you never know, it might be an exciting trip. And you might even find some nice antiques while you're there." At least I could try and be positive. Kin smiled, but it wasn't a real smile. Clearly there was something he wasn't telling me. I decided not to pry. I was probably better off not knowing. We were nearly back at his condo, so we just rode the rest of the way in silence.

Once inside, Kin stopped short and slapped his forehead. "Oh, damn, I should have thought to stop and get you something to eat. I'm not sure what I have."

"That's ok. I'm sure we can scrape together something." I followed him into the kitchen. A quick perusal of the cabinets showed he really didn't have much, but considering he didn't eat, it was good there was anything at all. I settled on a can of minestrone soup and some saltines.

"I'm going to have to go shopping and pick up some more food if you're going to be staying here."

That reminded me. Detective Joyce had said I could go back to my house this afternoon. The thought of having to go and sort through all of that mess took the wind out of my sails. I suddenly felt drained and had to fight the urge to cry. Kin noticed my sudden change in mood. "Are you ok?"

"Yeah, I'm just not looking forward to having to go and make sense of all the destruction. It's going to be hard." I'd had so much going on that I'd been able to keep my mind from dwelling on all the wreckage waiting for me on Georgia Road. Now that Leontine had been called off and I'd taken care of all the paperwork, I had to face the task of trying to put everything back together. Not to mention that I had to get back to work.

Fortunately, the forensic team had not felt the need to confiscate my computers.

"You know I'll help you," he said, reaching across the table to cover my hand with his.

"Thanks. There's just so much. It'll take days. I should probably hire some people to help me." I thought about all the food in the kitchen that had been spread all over the floor and things. Oh, God, what would that be like to go home to? And there would probably be bugs. I hate bugs! Really, really hate bugs.

"Let me take care of it. I'll make a few calls and get everything set for you."

"No, Kin. You don't have to do that," I didn't relish the idea of strangers going through my belongings. Getting someone in to do the gross stuff in the kitchen was one thing, but having people I don't know go through my bedroom or office, no way.

"Yes, actually, I do. You wouldn't have a mess to clean up if it hadn't been for me getting you involved in all of this," he replied emphatically.

"Well, I suppose I could use some help, but there are parts of the house I'd rather do myself."

Kin said he understood. Then he suggested I take a nap, and I had to agree that that sounded like a good idea. I asked him to only let me sleep for an hour though, because I wanted to go to Debbie's and get my car and go to my house and try and work out what to do first. Kin walked me to the bedroom door and kissed me. "Sweet dreams," he said as he pushed the door open. Then he turned and went back down the hall. I had to admit, he was pretty cute.

Sleep might have sounded like a good idea at the time, but it didn't turn out that way. I dreamt I was in my poor wrecked house, and it was almost dark out and I couldn't get the lights to turn on. As I stepped over the shattered and torn piles of what was once my home, searching for a flashlight or candle or something to light my way, Leontine leapt out of the shadows. Her eyes were glowing neon green and her fingernails were several inches long and sharpened to points. She hissed at me, baring her tiny pointed teeth, like a cat's, not a vampire's. I jumped back and ran into another room. Leontine beat me there, hissing again. Everywhere I ran, she was there first. I couldn't get away from her. I tried to leave the house, but she blocked the door. I was running and tripping and sliding on all the mess on the floors, frantically trying to escape. Then, mercifully, Kin woke me up.

Apparently, I had not shown any signs of having a bad dream, which I was very thankful for. "Did you have a nice nap?" he asked thoughtfully.

"Mm hm," I lied. "Thanks." I sat up and swung my legs over the side of the bed. "Well, let's get this over with." I added a bit reluctantly.

"Good. Some of my friends are meeting us at your place in about an hour."

"What?" More vampires? In my house? What if they were like Jaeger and hated humans? No wait, Kin would know that, and wouldn't ask someone who would hate me. Not to mention if they hated humans they'd hardly agree to help one.

"While you were resting I called a few friends and asked them to come help. I told you I would take care of things." He strode out of the bedroom very confidently. Clearly the man felt as though he'd done his duty and fixed things for the poor damsel in distress.

I didn't like it. I hated being a damsel in distress. I preferred being the damsel who kicks butt. It may seem ungrateful, but I wasn't thrilled that he'd taken it upon himself to invite a group of strange vampires to my home to help go through all my things.

"You shouldn't have done that, Kin. I was just going to sort of go through and make a list, you know? Figure out where to start and what's the best way to go about things. At this time of day it hardly seems worth it to start on such a huge project."

"Ah, you forget. My friends and I work best at night. Besides, you'll soon learn that there are benefits to having vampires do your dirty work for you." He smiled and wriggled his eyebrows.

Was he joking? What was with the eyebrow thing? What sort of benefits? Ugh! It was only Tuesday but it had already been a very long week. I slipped my feet into my shoes and followed Kin out to the living room. Soon we were back in his SUV and on our way to Debbie's to get my car.

Debbie had taken a later shift and Bob wasn't due home from work for a couple of hours still, so I just got in my car and started it up. Kin followed me across town to my house.

When I pulled in to my driveway, I noticed there was a strange car parked across the street. I wondered if it belonged to one of Kin's friends. Before I barely had time to undo my seatbelt, Kin was beside the car, opening my door for me. "Aren't you afraid one of my neighbors will see you do that?"

"Nah. I move too quickly for them to actually see me moving and if they did notice it, they'd think their eyes were playing tricks on them."

"Glad you're so sure. Is that one of your friends over there?" I asked, nodding towards the car across the street.

"I think so. I believe that's Angel's car."

I stopped short. I turned to Kin, laughing. "Oh, no! Are you telling me you have a vampire friend named Angel?" It was really too funny.

Kin frowned and tried to shush me. "Hero, trust me, you don't want to make fun of him. He's very sensitive about the TV show. He had to deal with a lot of crap from other vampires over it and he won't take it well if you tease him too."

Nodding my head, I managed to say "I promise," while holding in my laughter. What a disappointment. I really needed a good laugh, especially after that awful dream. I just hoped I could hold it together.

I heard a car door close and I turned to look as two men, I mean vampires, crossed the street. One was about Kin's height and the other was shorter. Probably a little under six feet. As they came closer, I could see the shorter one was of Hispanic descent, though his skin was paler than it should have been. The taller one was fairly nondescript. He had unremarkable brown hair, pale brown eyes, unremarkable features and, of course, pale skin.

"Hero, I'd like you to meet my friends, Angel," he said, indicating the Hispanic vampire, "and Mike," indicating the other.

"Hello. Thank you both very much for agreeing to help me. I really appreciate it." I smiled broadly at them both, hoping that no sign of my mirth still showed.

"No problem," Angel said.

"Yeah, sure. Kin told us what happened. I hate that bitch. Oh, sorry! Excuse my language."

I smiled at Mike. How cute was that, apologizing for swearing? "That's ok."

I went to the door, unlocked it and walked in. Kin followed me and quietly cleared his throat. As I turned to question him I noticed the other two hadn't followed and were standing, awkwardly, on my front step. "Oh! Sorry. I wasn't thinking. Angel, Mike, would you please come in?"

"Thank you," they said in unison as they came inside my home. Not that I had doubted Kin when he told me that part of the vampire myth was true, but it was a comfort to see it in action.

If possible, it was even messier than when I first saw it. The forensic team hadn't made the situation any better. There was an unpleasant aroma from the direction of the kitchen. "Whoa," said Mike in a loud sort of whisper. "This sucks, man. You must want to kill her, huh?"

That was a bit extreme. I think. "Well, she's certainly not my favorite person. Or cat, or whatever she is."

"Oh, God, Hero." Kin took my hand and looked at me tenderly. It was worse than he had imagined. I was glad of his sympathy. It was genuine and he felt for me. I was feeling pretty bad for myself at the moment and the sympathy fit in nicely.

Angel stood there shaking his head slowly. He muttered something in Spanish under his breath. "Should we wait for Hazel or just get started?" he asked a moment later.

"Hazel?" Who was that? I wanted to laugh again, picturing Shirley Booth in a maid's uniform cleaning my trashed living room.

"Another of my friends. She had a little farther to come, but she should be here soon."

"Well," I started, seeing as it was my house and my show, "why don't we have a look at what needs to be done first. Then we can decide who's going to do what and by then Hazel should be here. Ok?"

Everyone agreed and we began the grand tour. I told them that my office and bedroom were off limits to anyone but me. They had no problem with that, thankfully. I was unsure of my mom's bedroom. After careful consideration, I asked Kin to handle that room and whispered that I would explain more about it later.

Angel, God love him, actually volunteered to clean the kitchen. He said messes like that didn't bother him a bit and as it was the most undesirable job, he figured he might as well take it on. It also helped that vampires don't have to breathe, so he wouldn't be inhaling the rancid stench or the spoiled food all over the floor. I promised myself I wouldn't laugh about his name anymore, even if it was just in my head.

Mike took the living room and we assigned the dining room to Hazel, whenever she got there. Since I needed to get back to work, I settled on cleaning my office first. Kin would clean the spare room first.

"I've got tons of trash bags," I told them. I'm a sucker for those community service groups that sell the trash bags to benefit someone or other, so I had about half a dozen boxes.

"Please save any photographs, regardless of the condition. Anything that can be repaired put to one side for now. If you're unsure of something, put it in a pile and I'll look at it later. Does that sound ok?" They all agreed and my vampire cleaning crew got to work.

I went in to my office and tried to block out what was going on in the rest of the house. I started scooping up papers and stacking them in neat piles. I'd go through them after and sort them out. The torn painting was propped up against the far wall, out of my way. I gathered up the disks and piled them off to one side. Getting them in order wasn't that big a priority as they were mostly back up. The drives got replaced on the shelves along with my manuals and books. The drawers were a pain to put back in because they never want to line up, but I managed to get them in. Then I grabbed the hanging files at random and just shoved them in. The papers that belonged in them had been scattered everywhere, so it didn't really matter about the order they went in at this point.

Now that the floor was mostly cleared of large items, I focused on picking up pens and pencils and the larger office supplies. Little things like paper clips and thumb tacks I left. I couldn't be bothered to fuss with them. They were cheap enough to replace. I got the dust buster I kept plugged in next to my desk and vacuumed up at the smaller bits and debris. After emptying and repeating a few times, the office actually started to look something like an office again. It was messy and disorganized, but it was clearly my office.

Sitting down at the desk, I cleared myself a space and reached for the nearest pile of papers and began sorting them. What a pain in the butt! But it was a damn site better than cleaning the kitchen! Eww!

I wondered how the others were getting on and whether or not Hazel had shown up. Considering the amount of work to be done, things were kind of quiet. Resisting the urge to go have a peek at everyone else's progress, I made a deal with myself that I would check only after I had sorted through the first three piles of papers.

The third pile done, I stood and stretched. I didn't know how long I'd been in there working. Quietly, I went to the door and opened it slowly. I don't know why I bothered being quiet. It was my house, after all. I guess I didn't want anyone to think I was slacking off.

I expected to hear the sounds of things being put in trash bags and the clanging of pots and pans being put away, but all I heard was voices. I stepped out into the hallway. Looking to my left, I was shocked to see a gleaming kitchen. Every surface was sparkling clean and it appeared that everything was in its place. I couldn't believe it. I went down into the living room and there were Kin and his friends all standing around chatting. The living room was clean. It was also devoid of furniture, which was hard to take.

"Oh, did you finish your office?" Kin asked as he crossed the room to come to me.

"Uh, almost. How did you guys get this all cleaned so fast?"

"We can move very quickly, remember?" he replied with a twinkle in his eye.

"Yeah, but, still." I was just so flabbergasted.

"I didn't know what you wanted to do about your furniture," Mike said. "I put it out at the end of your driveway. You could probably have the sofa and the chair reupholstered, but, you know, I didn't know?"

"No, that's fine, thank you. I'll probably get new stuff."

"I'm so sorry about your home," said a tiny woman with shockingly red hair.

"Thank you. You must be Hazel?" I said, shaking her hand.

"Yeah. It's nice to meet you. I saved some of the broken pieces of china in a paper bag for you. I thought you could use them for like a mosaic top on a table or something and then you'd still sort of have them with you."

"Oh, what a nice idea. Thank you. I wouldn't have thought of that." I started to well up thinking about my grandmother's china. Kin must have told her about it.

Turning to Angel I said, "The kitchen looks amazing. I can't thank you enough for doing that for me."

He shrugged. "No problem." I found that hard to believe. It had been such a grotesque mess, but I let it go. Angel didn't seem the type who liked to have a fuss made.

"Well, um, thank you all so very much. I don't know what to say." It was kind of awkward. If it had been a group of humans, I would have offered to send for some pizza or take them out for a beer or something, but what did you do to reward vampires? Eww! I got a visual there. Didn't like it.

Instead I turned to Kin with, what I hoped was, a subtle expression that indicated I wasn't sure what to do. Thankfully, he picked up on it. "Yeah, thanks guys. I really appreciate your coming over on such short notice and all."

Hands were shaken, shoulders slapped, niceties traded and I even got a hug from Hazel. Then Kin's friends left and we were alone.

"So, you want to finish up in your office, or would you like to go get something to eat?"

My stomach growled, casting its vote for option B. "I'll come back tomorrow and finish up. Let's go get some food, I'm starving!"

Quickly I ran around and shut off most of the lights. I left the light on in the front hall and front steps and hurried Kin out the door. We decided to take his car and as I climbed in he asked, "Where would you like to go?"

I thought about it for a minute. Steak. I wanted steak. After naming my favorite steak place, Kin hopped into the driver's seat and we were off.

When we got to the restaurant, we stood in the lobby, waiting to be seated. It was crowded, especially considering it was a Tuesday. The aromas made me salivate. The soup at Kin's had taken away my hunger, but it wasn't very satisfying. The hostess told us it would be a fifteen minute wait for a table. Kin was about to tell her that was fine, when I told her we'd order to go instead.

Kin looked at me quizzically. I ignored him and placed an order for two meals and a dessert. "Just one dessert?" she asked?

"Yeah, we'll share." I told her.

Kin pulled me back a step and whispered "Why did you do that?"

"One, we'll get the food faster, and two, it occurred to me that I'd be sitting here devouring a huge steak while you sipped water. Not the image I want to present to the world. It'll be better if I just eat at your place."

"But you ordered two meals?" he added, confused.

"Well, it would have looked pretty strange if I ordered only one. Besides, I'll take the other one home to eat tomorrow." It seemed a perfectly sensible decision to me.

We sat on a bench in the lobby and made small talk about the restaurant, the patrons, the décor and all the other crap you drivel on about while killing time. The food came in good time and we were soon back in the SUV and on our way to Kin's. The second meal I ordered had fries with it and I stuck my hand through the opening in the bag and pried open the corner of the Styrofoam container and liberated a few. Kin smiled at me while I munched on the fries to take the edge off my hunger. I probably would have been embarrassed, doing this in front of another guy, but seeing as Kin hadn't actually eaten since before World War II, I wasn't going to bother hiding my appetite.

Back at Kin's, I practically inhaled my dinner. When you're really hungry, there's nothing like a nice big steak and a baked potato loaded with butter. Yeah, yeah. Tell me how bad that is for me, I don't care. I'll die someday and I doubt it'll be because I love steak. Besides, it was delicious.

As expected, Kin sipped from his usual bottle of Poland Springs. I did feel a little bad that he couldn't eat, after all, it was hardly his fault that he couldn't. I wondered what his favorite foods had been, but had the decency not to ask.

My dinner eaten, I dug into my dessert of chocolate cake with dark chocolate icing and chocolate chips and almonds. It could do with a scoop of ice cream, but that didn't stop me from eating it anyway. Fortunately, I have a fairly fast metabolism, and I do try and exercise, though I should probably do so more often.

"Did you enjoy your meal?" Kin asked when I finally pushed the dessert box away.

"Oh, yeah." I answered as I wiped the chocolate from my mouth.

Kin reached out and stopped my hand. Suddenly, he was at the side of me, facing me. He bent his head and licked the dab of icing from the corner of my mouth. "I can't remember the last time I tasted chocolate," he said in a husky voice.

"Oh," I whispered, rather stupidly. Great reply, huh? I turned my head towards him and we kissed. I half expected to hear a phone ring. This was usually when it happened.

Nope, no phone. Just more kissing. He put his hand behind my head, drawing me closer and deepening our kiss. I uttered a little moan. He kissed really well. Then again, he'd had a great many years to practice.

"Hero," he whispered, as he turned his attention to my neck and ear. "I want to make love with you. Will you let me? Will you let me make love with you?"

Silly question. I wrapped my arms around his neck by way of response and arched my back towards him. In a flash he had scooped me up in his arms and carried me down the hallway to his bedroom.

Gently, he laid me down on his bed. It was huge, must have been king size, and it was covered in a red and gold patterned comforter. There was light coming from a small lamp on the bedside table, but the rest of the room was pitch black. I heard the 'thunk, thunk' of his shoes landing on the floor just before he slid next to me on top of the bed. My shoes had been left behind in the kitchen.

Kin thrust his hand into the mass of my hair and pulled my head close to his. His kisses were passionate and expert. I twined my own fingers into his hair and pressed my body against his.

He trailed kisses across my face and down my neck. When he nipped a little, it dawned on me that I was about to have sex with a vampire. I gently pushed him back and looked into his face.

"What's wrong?" he asked.

"You're a vampire," I said, stating the obvious. He looked crushed and started to disentangle himself from me. I grabbed his shoulder. "No." I said, pulling him back. "I just didn't know… I mean, my neck and everything. Could you get carried away and, you know, bite me?"

"You don't have to worry about that, Hero. You should know that my fangs will come out, I can't help that, but I won't bite you or hurt you in any way." He still seemed unsure of me.

"Oh, ok. I just didn't know, that's all." I brushed my fingertips along his cheek and smiled at him. "Thanks for telling me," I said as I leaned in to kiss him again. And he eagerly kissed me back.

This time there was no pausing for questions or hesitations of any kind. Clothes went flying and bedclothes were tousled and no small amount of noise was made by both parties. Kin was a wonderful lover and, even if I do say so myself, he seemed more than satisfied with my abilities.

I was exhausted when we finished. I snuggled up to Kin's hard, cool body and rested my head on his chest. I've got to tell you that when you're all overheated from a round of really great sex, having a cool body next to you is vastly preferable to another hot, sweaty body. I highly recommend it.

He held me close and kissed the top of my head. "Will you stay the night with me?" he asked.

"Is that allowed?" Well, I didn't know, did I?

He chuckled softly. "Yes, sweetheart, it is. And I'd like it very much if you would."

"Ok then," I replied with a contented sigh. It hadn't occurred to me that I would be able to spend the night with him, literally I mean. It was a nice surprise, and I was overdue for a nice surprise.

(And if you were hoping for scintillating specifics or ridiculous euphemisms for the male anatomy, you're out of luck. I may kiss and tell, but I don't 'you know what' and tell. Well, you know, not in detail. Oh, heck! Go get your own vampire!)

CHAPTER 15

Kin drove me back to my house in the morning. He walked me inside, but said good bye to me in the hallway. "I have some things I need to do. I should be back around lunch time. Would you like me to bring you something?"

How thoughtful. Especially considering that he didn't eat. I had left my second meal from the night before in his refrigerator. "Yes, please, if you don't mind. Could you get me a salad and an iced tea?"

He leaned forward and kissed my forehead. "Not a problem. Be back as soon as I can." Kin smiled at me and stroked my cheek gently before turning around and leaving. Before he closed the door behind him, he looked over his shoulder and gave me a little wave. I couldn't help thinking how lucky I was to have him, despite everything. Now if only he weren't a vampire. Well, we can't have everything.

I went straight to my office and booted up the computer. I still had a few stacks of papers that hadn't been sorted and filed. Sighing, I decided that I just didn't want to do any more of that right now. Instead, I chose to catch up on my emails and get in touch with my clients. Surely they were wondering what was happening.

The morning passed quickly and I was able to get caught up more easily than I had expected. I'd even finished the leftover filing. One of my clients had requested a new logo for a new product line she was going to be offering. She made homemade candles and used different faeries for all her logos. Her company was called Faerie Lights. Cindy was actually my very first client. I loved working on her account. Faeries were a favorite of mine and I liked the challenge of creating new ones with the effect of candle light for her. As I tweaked the lighting, trying to get the right angle and balance of light, my doorbell rang.

I hurried to the door. Kin was standing there with a white paper bag and a large Styrofoam cup. "Someone ordered a salad and an iced tea," he said with a grin. I laughed and stepped aside for him to come in. As I was closing the door, I suddenly realized something.

"Kin? Yesterday, how did Hazel manage to come in here? I didn't invite her in?" I couldn't believe I hadn't noticed that before.

"Hazel's not a vampire. She's a Sidhe," he explained.

"She's a she?"

"Yes," Kin replied simply.

"Hazel is a she?" I asked again.

"Yes."

Ok this was getting nowhere. "A she, as opposed to a he?"

"What?" Now he was confused. "Hazel is a Sidhe."

I felt like Abbot and Costello. "Third base!" I exclaimed.

"Huh?" Now he was really confused.

"When you say Hazel is a she, do you mean she is a female, or am I missing something?"

"Oh!" he exclaimed, finally seeing the problem. "No, not a she, s-h-e. A Sidhe. Sort of Celtic faerie. It's spelled S-i-d-h-e."

"You pronounce that 'she'?" My turn to be confused again.

He laughed. "In Celtic, Si is pronounced like Sh. You know, like Sinead O' Connor?"

Whatever. I was beyond caring. The conversation had gone on too long and I was hungry. I sat down at the kitchen table, now spotlessly clean thanks to Angel, and pulled the salad out of the bag. "Why didn't you just say she was a faerie?"

"Because she's not. Not exactly. There are different kinds and there are some who are known as just faeries, but Hazel is a,"

"A Sidhe. Yeah, I know." I chomped a large bite of salad while unwrapping the straw and stabbing it into the lid of the iced tea. "So what have you been up to this morning?"

Kin looked down at his hands, fiddling with the scrunched up wrapper from my straw and shrugged his shoulders.

Not good. "What? Can't you tell me?"

"Of course I can," he replied with a fake smile. "I was meeting with Darius and Jaeger."

"Uh huh. And...? Sorry, I'm being too nosey. It's none of my business." I realized that I didn't really have any right to pry into his affairs. Unfortunately, I have a knack for not realizing things like that before I speak. I focused on my salad and hoped I hadn't overstepped my bounds.

The silence didn't help. Neither did the look on his face. It read 'Do I tell her the truth or not?' I found myself wishing I could think of a good reason to get up and go back to my office, but seeing as I still had a tray half full of salad, (notice the positive attitude - I was trying anyway) I didn't know how to excuse myself without being obvious.

Ok. Change of topic. "I got pretty much all caught up on my work," I said, and then shoved a forkful of lettuce into my mouth to keep from having to talk any more.

"Oh, good. I'm glad." So much for that topic.

I decided to abandon my salad in favor of retreating to my office. "I'm working on a new logo for my candle lady. It just needs a bit more tweaking." Pushing the chair back, I carried the salad to my bare refrigerator and placed it in the center of the top rack. Poor lonely little salad. The last of the iced tea was slurped up in a most undignified manner and the cup deposited in the trash.

"Thanks so much for bringing me lunch."

"You're welcome. I'll let you get back to your work."

Before I could respond, he was gone. For a moment, I didn't know where he'd gone. I stared at the front door trying to decide if it had moved or not, when I starting hearing faint sounds from upstairs. That had better be him. I wasn't in the mood for a new crisis.

Quietly, I went up the stairs and found Kin whizzing around my mother's bedroom. I had told him about it while we were lying in bed together the night before, but I hadn't actually expected him to do anything with it just now. I hadn't gone in there myself since the break in. It was too much to deal with. Now my vampire boyfriend was whipping around like the proverbial white tornado, clearing away the mess and putting things back together faster than I could take it in.

This wasn't what I had wanted. It was like watching some movie on fast forward - super fast forward. Things seemed to be moving on their own. Objects disappeared and reappeared in another part of the room in the blink of an eye. It seemed inconceivable that he could be being careful with anything or salvaging any of my mother's fancy ladies.

"No!" I cried. Literally. I hadn't noticed the tears rolling down my cheeks. Before I could even draw another breath Kin was in front of me, putting his arms around me.

"Hero, what is it? What's wrong?" Kin pulled me to him, enveloping me in his cold embrace.

"You're going too fast. You have to be gentle. They're my mom's things," I sniffled into his chest.

"Oh, honey, I am being very careful. I'm so sorry that you didn't realize. Or that I didn't realize, for that matter. I should have told you. Just because I can move so quickly doesn't mean I'm being careless or rough. I've had a great many years to get accustomed to my abilities and I assure you that I can be just as careful using my vampire speed as I can if I went at a human pace. Honest."

I sniffled again, in a most undignified manner, and peeked out at my mother's room. He was right. He had been very careful. Surfaces were cleaned of the dust made by smashing figurines and other delicate items. The figures that weren't broken or could be fixed were lined up on the top of her dresser. Kin had folded the bedclothes and stacked them neatly in a corner and the mattress and box spring that Leontine had shredded were propped against the far wall. In fact, the room was very nearly clean. Or at least as clean as it was going to get under the circumstances.

"Thank you, Kin," I squeaked as I tried to wipe my nose without him seeing. "I'm sorry, I should have known better."

"How? How should you have known? It's ok, Hero, really. You've been through so much the past few days and I can't believe how well you've been coping with it."

Had I been coping with it well? It didn't feel like it, but it's not as though I had some frame of reference for how well someone should deal with finding a fanged freak on your front lawn, having your home ransacked and your belongings destroyed, finding out your boyfriend is a vampire and being threatened by a shape shifting cat woman. They don't make a Chicken Soup book for that.

I shrugged and reached up to give him a peck on the cheek. "Thank you," I whispered.

Chocolate. I needed chocolate. I'm sure the women reading this know what I mean. There are times in life where the consumption of chocolate is an absolute imperative for both mental and physical well-being, and this was one of those times.

"I think I'm going to go to the supermarket and pick up a few things. I mean, there's nothing here. I can't even offer you a spring water." Smilingly weakly, I cupped my hand against his cheek and told him I'd be back soon. He kissed my forehead and said not to worry about anything, that he'd take care of the house. My heart knew it was true and it was a nice feeling.

The drone of the supermarket was somehow comforting. A familiar hum punctuated with the squeak of wobbly cart wheels and the "click clack" of shoes against the linoleum. And lest we forget, chocolate. I was a good girl and stopped by the produce aisle first and got a few Granny Smith apples and a container of cantaloupe, already cut into nice big chunks. The next aisle was full of juice, juice boxes and the week's specials, and there in the very first section, as if ordained, were two shelves full of Hershey bars, buy one, get one free. The Shopping Gods were on my side. I picked up a pack of eight regular chocolate bars and an eight pack of Special Dark bars. As I pushed my cart up the aisle, I punctured the cellophane and helped myself to a bar. What? I'm going to pay for it.

The chocolate melted slowly on my tongue as I continued up one aisle and down the next, filling my cart with essentials and not so essentials. Milk and bread, obviously, but also barbecue chips and a big jar of creamy peanut butter, which I suppose could be considered an essential, depending on your outlook.

I made sure to get a 24-pak of Poland Springs water for Kin. Luckily, it was on sale. A sign! First the chocolate and then the water. Were things beginning to turn around? Ok, maybe that sounds a bit desperate, but if you'd been through what I'd been through, little things like that would seem big to you too.

Ah! The last aisle. Frozen foods. Frozen pizza, check! Frozen French fries, check! Frozen Boston Market dinners, check! Frozen Ben and Jerry's New York Super Fudge Chunk, check, check, check and check! Don't judge me. I'd been through hell.

As I swung my cart around to head to the checkout line, the hairs on the back of my neck suddenly stood up and a shiver ran through me and made me shudder. My hand flew to the back of my neck and I spun around to look behind me. There was a little old woman at the end of the aisle and another woman about my age four feet or so away with a little boy in the seat of her cart. None of them were paying the slightest bit of attention to me. I told myself it was just because of the cold from freezer cases and continued on to the registers.

I got the same feeling again as I was loading the groceries into my car. No freezer cases in sight. This time I had the presence of mind not to react. Instead, I pretended to be arranging things in the back seat while a checked the reflection in the car window opposite me. No one and nothing stood out. At least not at first. Just as I was making up my mind that I was paranoid, I reached to pull the rear driver's side door closed and caught a reflection in the glass.

I opened the driver's door slowly, looking to see if I could catch the reflection again. I knew once I was inside and had the aid of mirrors, the watcher would be gone. There it was. He was definitely there, in the row behind me, standing half behind a paneled work van. Jaeger was watching me intently.

In the time it took to get in and close the door, he was gone. I did my best to appear nonchalant as I adjusted the rear view mirror and pulled on my seatbelt. He was nowhere in sight, but I know I hadn't imagined it. He had been there, but why?

Carefully, I backed out of the space, and then put the car in drive before continuing slowly through the parking lot. I held up my receipt in front of me, so if anyone was watching, they'd think I was checking it, but what I was really doing was using it as a ploy to go at a snail's pace while I cautiously darted my eyes to the right and left to see if I could catch another glimpse of my vampire stalker. Correction. My second vampire stalker. Naturally, there was none.

Why was he watching me? Was he keeping an eye on me for Kin? If Leontine and Nigel had been told I was off limits, why would that be necessary? Was he still angry at me because he felt

I had insulted him the other night at Darius' home? Neither was a comforting thought.

On to the next non-comforting thought. Should I tell Kin? There was obviously something he hadn't wanted to discuss with me earlier. Did this have anything to do with it? If so, did I want to force his hand or do I trust him and let him decide if and when to tell me about it? Ordinarily, I'd have my nose out of joint and insist on being told everything, but considering all the unsettling things I'd seen and heard in the past few days, I was beginning to believe that sometimes ignorance might truly be bliss.

My heart continued to thump against my rib cage as I drove the two miles or so back to my house, constantly checking all my mirrors for any sign of being followed.

Was this nightmare ever going to end? Would this be my life as long as I was with Kin? That was an unpleasant thought. I really cared for Kin. I know we hadn't known each other long, but recent events had caused us to bond quickly.

I decided the coy approach was not the way to go and I looked all around conspicuously as I gathered the bags out of the back seat of my car. If I was being followed, there would be no doubt now that I was aware of it.

"Kin?" I called as I pushed through the front door with plastic bags dangling from my wrists and paper bags pressed against my chest. There was no answer. I considered calling again, but I remembered Kin's super vampire hearing and knew that he had heard me.

Depositing the bags onto the kitchen floor near the fridge, I began unpacking items which required refrigerating or freezing, expecting any moment to find Kin behind me or beside me. That moment didn't come. I began feeling uneasy, but reminded myself that if Jaeger had followed me home, he could not come into my house without and express invitation. It offered a little comfort. Not enough though. Where was Kin?

I closed the freezer door and walked to the front hallway, calling his name as I went. I knew it was silly, that he wasn't there, but I didn't know what else to do and the feeble hope that he'd answer helped keep me from being afraid. In the front hall I found a note on the table. I hadn't seen it when I came in with the groceries.

"Hero,

I'm so sorry. I must go to Darius. Unavoidable. I will be back as soon as I can.

Love, Kin"

Well, at least I knew where he was, and I was glad to see he was thoughtful enough to have left me a note. The 'love' at the end brought an involuntary smile to my face and flutter to my still nervously beating heart.

I folded the note and slipped it into my pocket and turned to head back to the kitchen and finish putting the food away. As a last minute thought, I changed directions and threw the deadbolt on the front door. Maybe it was unnecessary, but I wasn't taking any chances.

CHAPTER 16

The sun was setting and still there was no sign of Kin. In my mind, I had been sure I would either see him or hear from him before dark. I don't know why, but somehow I had unconsciously decided that that was how it would be.

I'd never been afraid of the dark, even as a child, but now that I was aware that the stuff of childhood fantasies and nightmares actually existed, and more specifically, that they knew I existed, I discovered I didn't like being alone once it was dark out.

The afternoon had been productive. I'd made calls about getting rid of the decimated mattresses and box springs, since I couldn't put them out with my regular trash pick-up. The clerk at Town Hall informed me that there would be a special collection the second weekend of the following month, so I decided that until then I would have to find a way to stuff them into my shed in the back yard.

I'd gotten an empty cardboard box and filled it with all of the photographs that were in need of new frames and albums. I'd also made a list of things that needed to be replaced, such as light fixtures, furniture and my blender. The list was longer than I'd imagined it would be, but at least it was down on a list in black and white now. Somehow that made it more manageable than just thinking about it all in my head.

For the past hour or so I had been looking on the internet for deals on mattresses and couches and such. Until I heard from my insurance company, I'd have to wait to replace a lot of things, but there was no getting around the fact that I needed a bed and at least one place to sit in the living room.

I bookmarked several pages of things to go back and look at when it came time to make my purchases. The clock on the bottom corner of my screen read six thirty. My tummy rumbled, reminding me of how long it had been since the chocolate bar in the super market.

Sighing, because I had hoped I wouldn't be eating alone, even if I was the only one eating, (yes, I was aware of the irony) I pushed my chair back and headed for the kitchen. I selected a TV dinner and ripping open the box as I walked over to the microwave, I resolved not to allow myself to feel down. After all, I'd been eating my dinner alone here ever since Mom passed on. This wasn't anything out of the ordinary.

Returning to the fridge, I pulled out the remainder of my salad and a can of Diet Sprite. Yeah, I know, I couldn't wait to check out to eat a candy bar but I'm drinking Diet Sprite. Leave me alone.

At the sound of the beep I took my beef tips with egg noodles out of the microwave and brought it to the table. Mmm. It smelled good! I sat down at the table and dug in. Thank God for TV dinners. It's not that I can't cook, I can. In fact, I'm a really good cook, but who wants to cook this kind of stuff for one person?

By the time I finished it was pitch black outside my kitchen window. I washed my lone little fork and wiped down the table. As I turned to leave the kitchen, I tossed the rinsed soda can into the recycling bin. Aimlessly I wandered down the hall, unsure of what to do with myself. There were plenty of projects to be done and there was no end of laundry that needed doing since I didn't want to wear anything Leontine had touched without a hot wash and a tumble in the dryer first.

Sighing in self-pity, I leaned my forehead against the cool glass of the window beside the front door. No sign of Kin. I amused myself by breathing on the glass and making little steam clouds and watching them slowly disappear. Pathetic. I heaved another sigh, and determined not to wallow in my mood and instead find some useful employment to occupy myself, when a car came down the street. Pausing to see if it might be Kin, I was surprised to see the headlights pass over a tall figure at the edge of my drive way by the hedgerow.

My breath caught as I recognized Jaeger watching my house. Quickly, I backed away from the window. I knew he couldn't come in, but that wasn't much comfort.

"First thing in the morning, I'm cutting that hedge down," I muttered to myself as I stomped off to my office.

Enough was enough. I pulled out my cell phone and dialed Kin's number, without a care as to where he was and what he might be doing. There was another vampire stalking me, damn it, and I wanted answers!

The phone rang several times. I didn't care. I was going to let it ring and ring and ring. If it went to voice mail, I'd simply hang up and call again. Finally, Kin answered.

"Hero, what is it?" he asked, obviously my own cell number came up on his display. His voice was quiet, but he sounded quite concerned. I probably should have felt bad, but I didn't.

"I want to know why I've got another vampire stalking me," I demanded peevishly.

"What? Stalking you? What are you talking about?"

"Jaeger. First he was following me around the grocery store and now he's hanging out at the end of my driveway. Why, Kin? What's he doing?"

There was silence on the other end.

"Kin?" I asked after a moment.

"I don't know, Hero, but don't worry. Jaeger won't harm you." He didn't sound as though he thoroughly believed it himself.

"Well, not as long as I stay inside anyway," I answered sarcastically. "But he made it pretty clear to me the other night at Darius's house that he wouldn't think twice about making a meal of me."

"He won't, Hero. Even if you walked out to him now, I promise he will not hurt you." He sounded more sure that time, but I still wasn't buying it.

"Why is he here, Kin?"

"I already told you, I don't know. Look, I can't talk right now. I will find out what I can and be back at your place as soon as possible, ok?"

"Like I have a choice?" I spat.

"Yeah, you do have a choice. If you don't want me there, I'll just go home. I won't force my presence on you."

Now I did feel bad. "No, that's not what I meant. I meant about the waiting."

"I'll be there as soon as I can. That's all I can do, Hero."

"Ok," I said, softly, feeling like the bad guy.

Don't you just hate that? When you've got a perfectly good reason to be upset and somehow by the end of the conversation, you're the bad guy, the one in the wrong. It sucks!

I flipped my phone shut and slammed it down on the desk, taking my frustrations out on the little piece of technology. Well, calling Kin had turned out to make matters worse instead of better. I was still here alone for God knows how long with a homicidal vampire lurking in the bushes, only now I also had guilt. Great! I decided to channel my energies into killing something on the computer and jiggled the mouse violently to get the screen to pop on.

An hour or so later, with many various electronic opponents vanquished, I rose from my chair and stretched. The harmless mayhem had done its job and I felt much better than I had after my phone call to Kin. I went to the kitchen and got a bottle of water from the fridge. Instead of going back to my office, I walked down the hall to the front door. Without thinking too much about it, I pulled it open and called out.

"Jaeger, I know you're out there. What the hell do you want?" I had the presence of mind to stay within my house as I did this, consciously calculating the space between me and the top step, hoping his arms weren't abnormally long.

Everything was still and quiet. The nearest streetlight was three houses away. More light shone from the hall light behind me than from the street. I stood my ground, hoping he was in fact still out there so I didn't look like a fool. Oh, the irony!

"Come on," I yelled, "I saw you at the store and I saw you at the end of the driveway. It's silly to just skulk out here. What's going on?"

Another moment of quiet. The night was completely still. There was no breeze, no sound of insects, no neighborhood dogs barking, nothing. A shape emerged from the shadows. Jaeger's black silhouette, with billowing duster, crept forward and halted a few feet behind my car. In the blink of an eye he was suddenly right in front of me.

"You called?" he said with a sneer, more of a statement than a question. I could see his topaz colored eyes flashing and the mouth that seemed to be in perpetual snarl.

"Yeah, I did. What the hell are you doing?" I demanded.

"That is none of your concern," he said simply.

"Uh, excuse me? How is you stalking me none of my concern?" I asked, incredulous.

"If it were your concern, you wouldn't need to ask me, you'd already know." Jaeger smiled a cold cruel smile. I liked the snarl better. "Do not call to me again, human," he said, emphasizing the 'not' by drawing it out. Then he began to turn to the right and was gone in a flash. I was left standing with an open door and a stunned expression. Another plan gone awry.

I adopted what I hoped was a 'fine, what the hell do I care' face and calmly closed the door. There was no way I would give him the satisfaction of seeing me upset, even going so far as to consciously walk slowly to my office, in case he could hear my footsteps.

When I got there I sat gently in my chair and hit the space key on my keyboard. I took a deep breath and reached for a stack of CD-ROMs on my shelf. After flicking through them, I found the one I wanted. A couple of minutes later, I was playing Doom and viscously blowing away things that might possibly pass for vampires or their fellow supernatural beings. It was very therapeutic. I found my skill at the violent game improved greatly when I envisioned the various demons as Jaeger or Leontine. This realization caused my lips to spread into a sinister smile. After the past few days I had to take my satisfaction where I could find it.

Eventually I had to concede to the miserable headache that was throbbing at my temples and call it quits. I pulled open the top right drawer and grabbed a bottle of Excederin. I popped two in my mouth and washed them down with the remains of my bottled water.

I instructed the computer to shut down and switched off the monitor. The empty bottle got tossed into the recycle bin as I passed the kitchen on my way to the front hall. My pride prevented me from checking the window for either Kin or Jaeger. Instead I marched straight upstairs to my room.

And then, the wind went out of my sails. I'd forgotten. My room was in no condition for me to sleep in, unless I wanted to sleep on the floor. I sighed, yet another self-pitying sigh. I was getting rather good at it. Then I turned and went to sit on the top of the steps.

What now? I was sick of the computer. I couldn't watch TV because Leontine had broken it and even if she hadn't I'd have had to sit on the floor to watch it. I couldn't go to bed, despite being tired because I had no bed. No beds anywhere in the whole damn house! If I could have found a book that hadn't been ripped to shreds that I was interested in I might have read it, but it would have been too much effort to try and find one. I contemplated drowning my sorrows in a container of Ben and Jerry's, but honestly, at this point, that felt like too much of an effort too.

This sucked ass big time! I couldn't even wallow in my self-pity because there was nowhere to throw myself down. No beds, no couch, no comfy chairs. I hated that cat woman bitch more than ever at that moment. Not only had she destroyed my home and possessions, but she'd robbed me of the ability to indulge gloriously in feeling sorry for myself. After all, what's the point if you can't throw yourself histrionically on the bed or collapse dramatically on the sofa while sobbing your eyes out and wailing woefully?

Because I wasn't already pathetic enough, I inched my way down the stairs on my behind, like a little kid, bumping down one step at a time. Silent tears ran down my cheeks. I was in my own home and I couldn't relax, couldn't go to sleep, couldn't do much of anything at all. I didn't know what to do with myself.

I schlepped my way to the kitchen and reached into the cupboard for a Hershey bar. Unable to decide between milk and dark, I took one of each, telling myself it was better than scoffing a whole container of New York Super Fudge Chunk.

I unwrapped both bars as I scuffled miserably towards the living room. In front of the bay window that overlooked the front lawn were the remains of some of the sofa pillows. Mike had re-stuffed them, the sweetie, even though they were beyond sewing back up. I arranged them as best as I could, taking care to find ones that weren't ripped too much on one side and have those sides facing up. Then I lay down on them and munched my chocolate. Nothing like chocolate to help you immerse yourself in a fit of self-pity.

Before I knew what was what, I was being gently shaken. "Hero? Wake up honey." Kin was kneeling beside me, his hand on my shoulder as he tried to rouse me.

"What time is it?" I mumbled still half asleep.

"It's late," he offered apologetically. "I'm sorry. I got away as soon as I could."

I wanted to roll over and go back to sleep. However, when I tried I was painfully reminded that I was lying on the hard floor and not in a comfy bed. Whimpering pathetically, I brushed the empty candy wrappers aside and sat up. "I hate this!" I announced petulantly. "I want my house back. I want to sleep in my own room."

Kin brushed my hair aside and tucked it behind my ear. "I know honey, it's lousy. We'll go shopping tomorrow and get you a new bed and whatever else you need."

"I haven't even heard from my homeowner's insurance yet. I don't have the money to buy stuff."

"Don't worry about it. It's my fault this all happened," he said with a sympathetic smile.

"Oh, no! No way! I am not letting you pay for stuff." My female pride was hurt, and no matter what they might tell you, it is nothing compared to an injury to the male pride. "I can handle this myself. Thanks for the offer, but I don't need someone to fix things for me."

Kin sat back on his heels and looked surprised. "Well, I certainly didn't mean to offend you. I just thought since this was all my fault to begin with, I should help you out instead of you being at the mercy of your insurance company. You can pay me back once they manage to close out the claim and send you a check."

Oh. He meant it as sort of a loan. Well. Damn! There I go again, feeling I had a right to be pissed and he turned the tables on me. I shrugged my shoulders and began picking bits of fluff out of a cushion that Mike had so thoughtfully re-stuffed. "I suppose as long as it's just a loan," I conceded quietly.

"Good!" he said happily as he got to his feet and offered me his hand.

Grabbing his hand and pulling myself up, I added, "And only what I really have to have to get by. Nothing extra."

"Whatever you say," Kin replied, dropping a little kiss on the tip of my nose. "Now why don't we go back to my place so you can sleep in a bed instead of on the floor?"

That sounded too good to argue with. "Ok, hold on," I said. I ran out to the kitchen and opened the door to the laundry room. Well, it wasn't a laundry room really as much as a big closet with a counter where we always folded the laundry after bringing it up from the cellar. Mom hated the cellar too. I grabbed a clean nightgown and a clean change of clothes from the couple of loads I'd managed to do throughout the day. Seeing as my overnight bag was already at Kin's, I grabbed a plastic shopping bag and shoved the clothes inside. Charming.

Ducking into my office, I grabbed my purse, my keys and my poor abused cell phone. Then I met back up with Kin in the front hall. "All set," I declared, lifting my arm to display my not-so-designer luggage. "I'll follow you," I said as I reached into my bag for my keys. He agreed and we were soon out in my dark driveway.

Involuntarily, I found myself searching the blackness for Jaeger. Kin noticed and asked if everything was ok. "I was wondering if Jaeger was still here. Or did he leave when you came?"

"I don't know," he said, avoiding my gaze by appearing to fumble for the key to open his door. He had a remote. He didn't need a key.

"What aren't you telling me?" I asked, making no effort to hide my suspicions.

"Hero, I truly do not know if Jaeger is here or not. Or whether he was here when I arrived, for that matter."

"But you do know why he was here, don't you?"

"I told you when you called me earlier that I had no idea why he was following you."

He was avoiding my gaze. Kin wouldn't look at me. I was convinced he was hiding something. "Fine, Kin. You want to play it that way, fine. But when we get back to your place you're going to tell me what's going on."

I stomped to my car, pulled open the door, climbed in and slammed the door as hard as I could, just in case he didn't know I was pissed. Half of the clothes I'd packed tumbled out onto the floor of the passenger side. Cursing a blue streak, I leaned over and gathered them up and shoved them back inside the plastic bag.

The engine made a horrible grinding sound as I turned the key in the ignition unnecessarily, forgetting that I had already started it. Kin had already backed out of my driveway so I hoped he hadn't heard it. I put my car in reverse and backed up, wishing

Jaeger would step out from the bushes and I could run him down. And then put the car in drive and run over him again. Then back up again. What? He's a vampire, it wouldn't kill him.

It wasn't a long ride to Kin's place but it certainly felt that way. I hit every light, and Kin made most of them. Soon there were several cars between us and at one large intersection I lost sight of him completely. Once again, I suppose I should be flattered that the entire universe was out to get me. I kept waiting for my engine to seize or to get broadsided by some coked-up lunatic trying to outrun the police or a record setting sink hole to open up and swallow me. What can I say? When I wallow in self-pity I don't do it half way.

Eventually, I managed to make it to the condo. The security guard recognized me and waved me right in. Kin must have told him I was coming. I pulled into a spot opposite Kin's SUV. He was standing next to it waiting for me.

As I approached him, I noticed he had a shopping bag in his hand. "What's that?" I asked, with no shame at being nosey.

"I picked a few things up at the market. I didn't have much to offer you food and beverage wise," he explained.

"Oh. Thanks." I will not feel guilty, I will not feel guilty. I repeated the mantra to myself as we walked to his door.

Kin held open the door to the shared entryway where the mailboxes for his unit were kept. While walking past him into the vestibule I noticed a sharp change in his expression. He'd sensed something. A sound, a movement. I spun around quickly and peered back into the parking lot.

"What's wrong, Hero?" he asked.

"You tell me," I said as I turned back to face him. "I saw the look, Kin. You heard something or saw something."

"You're imagining things, Hero. Come on, let's go inside," he replied. Kin gently put his hand on my back and guided me further inside the building. He thought he had fooled me, but I paid close attention to his reflection in the glass and saw him dart another concerned glance at the parking lot. Before the night was through, he was going to wish vampires really didn't have reflections.

"Just stop it!" I yelled, throwing a sofa cushion on the floor. "Stop lying to me, Kin. I know you're not telling me something. I saw you! I saw you look back out at the parking lot, so just stop the lying!" I demanded as I stomped around his living room.

We had been going round in circles for about fifteen minutes. I told him I'd caught all the looks, all the deceptive behavior, and he steadfastly maintained that he had no idea what I was talking about.

"You're imagining..." he started, but he never got the chance to finish.

"Ok, fine. Have it your way. Obviously, I can't trust you." In a huff, I marched down the hall to his spare bedroom and grabbed my overnight bag. I pushed past him in the hall as I tramped back to the living room. I swung my purse onto my shoulder, and with the other hand I picked up my disposable plastic luggage and headed toward the door.

"Hero, wait! What are you doing? Where are you going to go?" Kin asked as he followed helplessly behind.

"I'm going to go stay with someone I can trust!" I spat out viscously.

Without warning, Kin was suddenly in front of me and blocking the door. "You can trust me, Hero. Please."

"No, I can't. I know you're keeping something from me, and no matter how much I plead with you, not only won't you tell me, but you lie to me and tell me there's nothing. How am I supposed to trust you?" I tried to push him out of the way, but I might as well have tried to put my Camry into my purse. Neither was going to move where I wanted them to.

"Please move," I requested simply. Kin just stood there. He was immobile and I was implacable. Not a good combination. "Ok, either move and let me out, or tell me the truth about what's going on." Whether or not I was in a position to give ultimatums to a vampire didn't enter my mind. I was fed up.

Minutes passed as he remained stone faced in front of the door and I stood giving him my best death stare, oblivious to the irony of using it on a vampire. "I won't change my mind, Kin. If we have to stand here all night, that's ok with me, but I will never trust you again if you don't tell me the truth right now. This is it. Now or never." And to punctuate my demand, I haughtily crossed my arms across my chest and turned my back to him.

Total silence. My own breathing was all I heard for several minutes. My arms and legs longed to move, but I stubbornly kept still. Finally, I remembered there was a back door in the kitchen. Quickly, I bent and grabbed my things and bolted for the kitchen. Kin beat me too it. I turned to run for the front door and he blocked me from leaving the kitchen.

I screamed in frustration. Throwing my things on the floor, I stormed the cabinets, pulling open the doors looking for something to hurl at him. I found a heavy sauce pot and turned and hurled it at his head. Then I reached into the cabinet and emptied it of its contents, throwing everything in it at Kin as hard as I could. When it was empty, I opened the next one and started bombarding him with plates and salad bowls, not caring that they shattered on the floor.

Kin pinned my arms to my sides. "Hero, stop it! Stop it!" He shook me to try and calm me down. It didn't work.

"Let me go! Let me out of here! I hate you, I hate you!" I screamed at the top of my lungs.

Kin let go of me suddenly and backed away. "You don't mean that." His face showed clearly how much I had hurt him.

"I do mean it. All this crap that's happened to me, it's all your fault! Even if I could get out of here, I still can't sleep in my own house! It's because of you this all happened, and last night I let you make love to me because I thought you cared about me, but you don't! You lie to my face and keep secrets from me and have psycho vampires stalk me and you won't admit it." I charged at him and started pounding my fists against his cold, rock hard chest. "I know something is going on, but you won't tell me, after everything. No, no, you lie to me instead! I hate you, I do, I do!"

That was it. The dam burst. Everything I'd been holding in for the past couple of days came spewing forth with a vengeance. I slid ungraciously to the floor and began sobbing my heart out, wailing like a wounded animal. There was no stopping it now that it had been unleashed. Rocking back and forth uncontrollably, I wrapped my arms around myself and gave in to it, holding nothing back. My reaction to every shock, every upset, every disappointment, every fear, every uncertainty, every anger and rage, every everything I had gone through was finally getting its chance to be fully expressed.

Part of my brain wondered if Kin's neighbors would call the police after all the shouting and pot throwing, and now my very noisy breakdown. Kin was kneeling in front of me, but I wouldn't look at him.

He reached out to put a hand on my shoulder, but withdrew at the last moment. A wise choice. Physical contact was not what I needed or wanted right now. After a moment, he stood up and left the kitchen. I cried harder, though I would have thought it impossible. Then Kin was back. Carefully, he sat Indian style in front of me and placed a Dixie cup of water on the floor before me, followed by a square box of tissues. Then he held out his hand, revealing two aspirin in his palm.

Roughly, I grabbed a couple of tissues from the box and snuffled into them. I was still crying too hard to attempt to take the aspirin. Choking and hiccupping, I fought to calm myself down, but I'd been too far gone to rein it in so quickly.

Kin waited patiently, keeping his open hand extended, while I worked through my anger and grief. I was still completely pissed at him, but I couldn't deny that it was sweet of him to go and get Kleenex and aspirin for me. If only he wouldn't lie and keep secrets from me.

Eventually I felt safe to attempt to swallow the pills. I crunched the tiny paper cup in my hand and added it to the litter of used tissues scattered on the floor around me. Kin remained in front of me, his hand now resting on his knee, but didn't make a sound. The occasional sniffle and shuddered breath were the only noise aside from the faint ticking of the kitchen clock.

"Please, let me go," I whispered in a husky nasally voice. He made no reply. Unconsciously, I began rocking myself gently to the rhythm of the ticking clock. "Why?" I squeaked.

"I can't," Kin stated simply.

"That's not good enough, Kin. Whatever's happening, I deserve to know the truth. Why are you lying to me and keeping secrets from me?"

Silence.

I continued rocking.

Minutes passed, and I counted the seconds mindlessly as I moved back and forth. It had a numbing effect. My mind shut out the rest of the world. There was nothing but the soft 'tick tock' and the comforting swaying of my body.

I was so tired, I felt as though I could fall asleep right there, sitting on the floor. Suddenly, I wanted nothing more but sleep. More than wanted it. Needed it. My head flooded with the idea of sweet, deep blackness. No more thinking. Just sleep. Without much more thought, I raised myself up off of the floor and shuffled down the hallway to the guest room.

"Hero?" Kin questioned gently as I left the kitchen. I didn't answer. I let him follow me and left him staring at the door as I shut it behind me and locked it. I didn't doubt that he could easily break it down if he wanted to, but I knew the sharp click of the lock engaging would send a clear message. 'Stay away from me.'

I didn't undress or even kick off my shoes. I crawled onto the bed and as soon as my head hit the pillow I felt the delicious relief offered by a dreamless sleep envelop me. The last thought I had before I met the unconscious world was this: Tomorrow, I would not take no for an answer. No matter what.

CHAPTER 17

Isn't it just my luck? Only I would end up dating an honest to God vampire, and he doesn't have to sleep during the day and avoid the sun. If this were a movie, all I'd have had to do was wait for dawn to break, and I could have just walked out of the condo, no problem. But, no. Not me. Of course, with me involved, it turns out that the sun isn't that big a deal after all and with his super natural hearing, I'd never get anywhere near the door without him beating me to it.

Think I'm exaggerating? I tried creeping out of the guest room and attempting to make it seem like I was just going to use the bathroom. When I first cracked open my door, Kin's bedroom door was shut. As I was tiptoeing down the hall, I felt a whoosh of air. Then, lo and behold! There was Kin, poking his head out of the kitchen. "Oh, you're up early," he said, in a disgustingly cheerful voice.

"Bathroom," I muttered, waving my hand towards said bathroom. Out of the corner of my eye, I peeked back at his bedroom door, now standing wide open. Trapped. Great. Just great.

To compound my misery, upon arrival in the bathroom, I caught a glimpse of my reflection in the mirror. It wasn't pretty. My hair was a mess, my eyes were all bloodshot and showed that my sleep had not been restful. The smear of mascara beneath each of them only added to my dreadful appearance. The irony of looking like death warmed over while looking in the mirror belonging to the undead was not lost on me. I smiled and chuckled softly in spite of myself before splashing cold water on my face.

After a few moments strenuous effort, I at least looked somewhat normal and ventured out into the hallway. I considered going back to the bedroom and changing, but then I remembered my clean clothes had been left in the kitchen the night before. Oh, well. No big deal really. Not at the moment anyway.

Taking a deep breath, I steeled myself for battled and strode into the kitchen. The delicious smell of bacon filled my nostrils and I almost forgot that I was supposed to be angry. I love bacon.

"Good morning. I wasn't sure how you liked your eggs, so I was waiting for you."

Kin stood at the stove carefully turning strips of delectable smoked pork. A tea pot sat steaming in the middle of the table. He had set a place for me with a large tea cup and a sandwich plate stacked with hot buttered toast. Damn him! How did he learn so quickly that I can be ruled by my stomach? "Over medium," I said as I slid into the chair and reached for the teapot, mentally calling a temporary truce. Note the word temporary. He wasn't off the hook yet. Just a reprieve while I ate.

A second later there was a pair of 'cracks' followed by loud sizzling. By the time he slid the eggs onto my plate and added three pieces of crisp bacon, I had eaten nearly half of the toast and finished my first cup of tea.

Kin placed the frying pan back on the stove top and then sat down across from me. "Thank you very much for the nice breakfast," I said, but added, "though, as much as I appreciate it, and I do, it doesn't excuse what you did to me last night, Kin. As soon as I'm done eating, I want answers."

He sighed. It dawned on me that he sighs pretty often. Was this just a habit of his, or was it something I brought out in him? "Hero, I'm so sorry for last night and," he fumbled, looking for the right words. Shaking his head, he continued, "I never, ever meant to upset you so. It broke my heart to see you like that."

"But not broken enough for you to tell me the truth about what's going on? Even though it involves me and I have a right to know?" I'd eaten most of the bacon and was ready to put up a fight.

His guilty look spoke volumes. He truly did know he'd been in the wrong and I believed he regretted it. That was something at least. Another sigh. "I was told not to say anything to you, Hero."

"Well, why didn't you just say that? That would've been a whole lot better than just lying to me over and over and denying that anything was wrong."

"I suppose it might have. I thought that if I kept pretending everything was fine that you would eventually believe me and stop worrying. If I told you the truth, you'd know there was a problem and what you might imagine could've been worse than the reality. I really thought it was the best way to handle it, and I was wrong. I'm so very sorry."

There went the wind out of my sails. How could I be furious with him now? "But when you saw how adamant I was, that I refused to believe you, why didn't you tell me? Why did you just let me get angrier and angrier? I mean, by the time I got around to throwing pots and pans at you, you had to know your plan wasn't working?"

He laughed a quiet self-deprecating laugh. "By then I didn't know what to say to you, or if I should say anything at all for that matter. I had to resist my own impulses."

"What impulses?"

He raised one eyebrow. "I'm a vampire, Hero."

I gulped.

"No, I don't mean I wanted to bite you, but obviously, I could have more than overpowered you. I could have restrained you and stopped you from throwing a single thing, but I didn't. As much as I hated seeing you like that, I felt you needed to get your anger and frustrations out, so I let you trash my kitchen, even though I really wanted to stop you. Also, I was afraid I might accidentally hurt you, or that you might be afraid that I'd hurt you."

I hadn't thought about that part. Of course I knew he could have stopped me from throwing everything I could get my hands on, but I hadn't given any thought to why he didn't. "And now?" I asked quietly. "Can you tell me anything at all? Like why Jaeger was stalking me?"

He kept his gaze on his folded hands as he slowly shook his head from side to side. "Can you at least tell me if it was Darius who ordered you not to tell me?" Kin looked up at me knowingly. That told me what I wanted to know. He was under orders.

Suddenly, Kin leapt up and stood in the kitchen door, fully alert and ready to pounce. "What is it?" I asked. He answered by placing his forefinger to his lips.

I could tell by his eyes that he was listening to something, but that he wasn't certain what it was. "Don't move, Hero," he hissed through clenched teeth. "I mean it, stay exactly where you are."

Before I could react, he was gone. The soft click of the front door latching was the only clue to his whereabouts. I wanted desperately to run to the front window and look out. I even stood up, twice. It was against my nature to just sit still, especially when told not to move. I hated just doing nothing. Nervously, I ran my palms up and down the thighs of my jeans. My heart pounded in my chest. What had he heard?

Without getting up, I scooted my chair closer to the doorway so I could lean forward and peek out into the living room, not that it did me any good. "Damn, damn, damn!" I muttered under my breath. How long was I supposed to wait here? It seemed like ages, but in reality, it was probably only a matter of seconds. I stood and began to pace. Yeah, Kin said not to move, but I figured as long as I stayed in the kitchen I was technically ok.

At last the front door opened and Kin came back inside. He had his cell phone to his ear and I heard him say, "Yes, I understand. Of course. I would never have asked if I didn't think it was necessary. I am. I believe it is, yes, sir." Kin caught me watching him from the kitchen and gave me a weak smile. "Naturally. Yes, sir. That won't be a problem. Yes. Yes. Thank you, sir." Then he flipped his phone shut and sighed heavily. So, it wasn't just me that caused that.

"Hero," he said, turning to me. "I... I, uh." Kin pinched the bridge of his nose. "I'm not certain where to start." he admitted as he lowered himself to the couch. He patted the seat beside him, beckoning me to sit down. Quietly, I padded over and sat gingerly on the edge.

"I'm sure you can guess to whom I was just speaking." I nodded. He nodded back. "I have received permission to tell you some things." Now that I was allowed to know, I wasn't so sure that I wanted to, not after the look on his face.

"When you called me yesterday, I truly did not know Jaeger was watching you. I know now that Darius had sent him to keep watch." Kin paused to let that sink in.

"Why would Darius think I needed to be watched?"

Kin sat silently. I could almost hear his mind trying to form the words to tell me. At last he said, "Leontine. Ilderim told her that you were under Darius' protection and not to be touched. However, she insisted that since you had insulted her so, that she be allowed to..."

"To? To?!? To what, Kin!? Don't stop there. To what?" I demanded in a panic.

Yet another sigh. "She has received permission from her Menagerie to punish you for your insults. Because of Darius' edict, she will not kill you, but she can, and will, do you as much harm as she can."

The bacon threatened to come back up. "Oh, God. I was alone most of the day yesterday. Why didn't she..." I couldn't finish the question.

"Jaeger was protecting you. Even though Leontine is a shape shifter, she is no match for a vampire. Particularly one as old and ruthless as Jaeger. Even in her feline form, we can hear her footsteps. If anything bigger than a fruit fly came near your house, Jaeger would know it and have been there to protect you."

I sat rigid and tried to process this. Something was wrong though. I didn't know what, but there was a flaw. "Kin?"

"Yes?"

"How would Jaeger have protected me if she had gotten into my house? What if she had gotten in while I was at the market? I'd have had no chance to invite Jaeger in to defend me." The thought terrified me. I had been alone for hours and hours. She might very well have gotten in before he could get to her. Some of her shape shifting friends could have distracted Jaeger while she slipped in through a window or something. She could have torn me to pieces while Jaeger waited helplessly outside.

Kin's eyes grew as large as saucers. He hadn't thought of that. That was less than comforting. A lot less.

"What now?" I asked, deciding not to dwell on that, as I'd likely drive myself crazy over it.

"Well, that's kind of the problem."

"Kind of?"

"Yeah. You see, I have to leave the country tomorrow."

"What?" I cried, my voice rising at least an octave, my eyes filling with frightened tears.

"That other object. I have to retrieve it and I must leave tomorrow."

"Let them send someone else!"

"I can't do that, Hero. I promised to go."

"But, Leontine! And I don't want to have to deal with Jaeger. He gives me the creeps." The thought of having Jaeger stay in my house was terribly unappealing.

Kin cleared his throat. "Well, uh, that's what I needed to tell you." He took a deep steadying breath. I knew instinctively that I was going to absolutely hate whatever he said next. "Darius has decided that you will stay at his home."

"No!" I yelled, standing up. "I will not stay there! It would be like being a prisoner. And God only knows what other vampires I'll run into and have to deal with. No, Kin, I won't go there, I won't!"

"But, Darius,"

"I don't care," I cried, cutting him off. "Darius may be in charge of you, but he's not in charge of me! I'm not going I tell you."

"Hero, it's the only way we can be certain that you'll be safe."

"Great! What am I supposed to do? Spend the rest of my life in that miniature palace? What about my work, my friends, my family?"

"You can do your work from there. You can still talk to and see whomever you want."

"Gee, thanks! And how do you suggest I explain my new living arrangements to them?"

He didn't have an answer to that.

"No, Kin," I continued. "I refuse to go there. There's got to be a better idea."

After a moment, Kin said "I suppose we could have Jaeger move into your house."

"Over my dead body!" Poor choice of words. "No way!"

"Hero, we need to protect you," Kin pleaded.

"Don't you know any female vampires?"

Kin threw up his hands. "Of course I do, but I don't want to get them involved."

"What about your friend Mike?" At least he seemed almost normal.

"Mike is a nice guy, but as vampires go, he's very young. You need someone with more experience protecting you."

I paced the floor, trying to think of some way out of this disaster. "Why don't I just come with you?"

"I'm sorry, Hero. You can't. I'm going to a place where the vampires are very ruthless. They are not as civilized as we tend to be here in America. It's far too dangerous for you. Besides, you don't have a passport."

He had too good a memory. Even I had forgotten about that. I started pacing again.

"Wait a minute. What happened outside?" I turned to him suspiciously.

A very large sigh, combined with rubbing both hands over his face. "Well, while Leontine typically turns into an orange house cat, she can become any type of cat. She must have turned into some type of jungle cat and, uh, she um, scratched the hell out of your car."

"She scratched it?" Something wasn't right.

"Yeah. Scratched. And um, well, some of the scratches, they actually, um, ripped through the body of the car." He was looking at his hands again.

"Ripped?" I repeated. "Ripped? The body? Ripped through the body? Are you telling me I have big gaping claw marks on my car? How the hell am I going to explain that to the insurance company?"

I was pacing again. "Holy crap!" I cried over and over. "What the hell is next, huh? Oh, man!" I ran my hands through my hair, resisting the urge to yank it out. I felt trapped in this stupid new reality with vampires and shape shifters and faeries and God knows what else. "I wish I could just twitch my nose and put everything back the way it used to be."

Kin's face fell. I didn't mean to hurt his feelings, but how much could I be expected to take? It was as though this nightmare would never end. It just kept spinning out of control.

Then Kin unrepentantly perked up. "That's it!" he declared.

"What's it?" I asked.

"What if Hazel stayed with you?"

"Hazel?" It wasn't a great idea, but it was better than the alternatives I'd been offered. At least she was female and she didn't drink blood. At least I don't think she did. "I guess that would be ok. If she doesn't mind."

"She'll probably love it. Hazel likes people."

That was comforting.

"I'll call and ask her," he said as he flipped open his phone and punched in the numbers.

While he waited for her to pick up, I wandered over to the window. Lifting back the edge of the curtain, I could see my poor little Camry sitting in the lot. It looked like something out of a Stephen King novel. The paint was nearly scratched off all over, and the doors had big, gaping holes, torn in strips along the sides. How was I going to explain that?

"Hero," Kin called, breaking in to my latest round of depressing thoughts. "Hazel says she can protect you better at her house. She'll meet us at your place around ten o'clock tonight. Ok?"

Did I have a choice? "Sure, fine." It was my turn to sigh.

I was off to room and board at a faerie's house. I was going to need so much therapy.

CHAPTER 18

I was amazed at how quickly I settled in to life with a faerie for a roommate. Sure she's hyper, and always flitting around (yes, flitting. It's the only term that accurately describes her light, graceful darting from place to place). And yes, there are moments when her cute perkiness is anything but cute, but all in all, she was pleasant and cheerful, without being annoying, and just plain fun to be around.

Hazel insisted on cocktail hour every night before dinner. I thought it was kind of silly at first, but now I've come to look forward to it, and Hazel knows some pretty weird cocktails! What makes it even better is that, apparently, faeries have very little tolerance for alcohol, but they enjoy the buzz. No pun intended.

I introduced Hazel to Mojitos. She thought it was terrific to go and get fresh mint leaves from her garden to crush up for the drinks. She'd prepare me one in a regular tall drinking glass, but she'd have hers in a modest martini glass, half filled with ice. More than that would have knocked her off of her magical little legs.

Hazel would make that drink last through cocktail hour, nibbling on cheese and crackers or mixed nuts to help space it out. Often, she still had some left when we'd go in to have dinner.

Don't ask me how she did it, but whether it was faerie magic, or too many episodes of Martha Stewart, at the end of cocktail hour, there was always a delicious meal waiting to be served. I offered countless times to make dinner, and she always refused. She said it made her happy to have someone to cook for. I wasn't going to deprive her of such happiness.

After dinner we'd watch TV, especially old movies. We both were classic film buffs, which gave us something in common. Sometimes we'd play cards or other games, and once in a while, we'd just sit and talk. Hazel was very easy to talk to.

During the day, Hazel gave me my space. She graciously rearranged an extra room for me to use as an office while I was staying with her. I brought one of my computers with me, along with all the supplies and files I would need. I directed my clients to use my cell phone instead of my office phone for the foreseeable future and soon settled back into the rhythm of business.

While my business was getting itself sorted out, my personal life was still a mess. I talked to Sue and Debbie and Amy and Jennifer and just about all of my friends. Naturally, I couldn't tell them that Kin was a vampire and that I was living with a faerie because a woman who shape shifts into a cat was out to torture me for insulting her. Even just typing that sentence I can't help but wonder how long it's going to be before someone locks me in a padded cell.

Things were tense. They all knew I wasn't telling them something. They all were concerned that I was staying with some stranger instead of one of them while my house was put back together (that was the reason I gave them for not being at home.). They all called me daily to question me about what I was doing and when I'd be back home. They all wanted me to come to their homes instead. And worst of all, they were all talking to each other and plotting how to get me to break. Aren't friends terrific?

Don't get me wrong, I completely understand why they're upset and all that. It's just that there's so much going on already, that adding this pressure on top of what I already had to deal with was exasperating.

"Hey, Hazel?" I asked one evening during cocktails. "You know how my friends are all worried about me, right?"

"Yes," she answered. "It's nice that you have so many thoughtful friends," she added with a big smile.

"Yeah, I know. Well, I was wondering, do you think there's anything you could do to help them not be so upset over this?" I stabbed my straw around in my drink, avoiding her eyes.

"I'm not sure I understand what you mean?" Hazel leaned forward from her perch on her salmon colored chaise.

"Well, it's just that they're all so worried about me, and hurt that I'm not staying with one of them. I thought maybe there was something you could do that would help them. You know, like make them feel that this is best and that everything's ok?"

"I take it you're not referring to a reassuring phone call?" she asked, squinting at me with her bright turquoise eyes.

"No," I replied sheepishly. "I'm sorry. I shouldn't have asked. I just feel so guilty."

"No, that's ok. I don't mind, really. I just needed to be sure we were both on the same wavelength, ya know?"

"Yeah?"

"Yeah, sure." Hazel leaned back and took a tiny sip from her glass. "I'll have to think about it for a while though."

"That's ok. Thank you." I smiled at her. She was such a sweet person, um, faerie. I was really glad Kin had suggested I stay with her. The idea of having to stay with Darius gave me an involuntary shudder. Hazel's was best. She had all sorts of charms and magic on her house to help protect me. When I did have to go out, Jaeger was still keeping watch over me. Naturally, I went out as little as possible.

I missed Kin though. More than once I marveled at how close we had become so quickly. Every night I lay awake wondering if it was a question of circumstances that had forced a quick bond or if it was that Kin was just right for me. In the end, I always decided it didn't really matter. Though that didn't keep me from pondering the question again the following night.

Before he left for his treasure hunt, he had kept his promise to take me shopping for things I needed for the house. As agreed, he only paid for things I would need to get by until I got the money from my insurance company. Which was ironic really, since I wasn't even going to be staying there.

Angel and Mike were recruited once again. This time, they were there to receive the furniture for me. They also took turns keeping watch to make sure Leontine didn't return to mess up my new possessions. Mike called me every night to tell me things were ok. He was a nice young man. Made me feel so sorry for him that someone turned him into a vampire.

As for my poor assaulted car, there was no way that I could file a claim on it the way it was. It would raise so much suspicion. I was also nervous that between the house being wrecked and the car, that the insurance company would think I was trying to scam them. To my relief, and utter surprise, Darius bought me a new car. He explained that since it was due to a mission he had sent Kin on, that I had gotten involved in the whole mess, not to mention that if he had gotten to Ilderim faster, Leontine and I may never had our exchange of words that pissed her off so badly, that Darius felt it was the least he could do. He was right. In my opinion, it was the least he could do.

So, my faithful little Camry disappeared and was replaced with a Chrysler Sebring Convertible. I had mixed feelings. I had always driven a sedan. I liked a back seat. However, I had to admit, it was a very cool car. It was fire engine red with black leather interior. Hazel and I had been out in it a couple of times, and despite the cool weather, we put the top down. I'd be lying if I didn't admit there's a certain thrill from racing around in a little convertible.

But it wasn't all fun and games during those days at Hazel's. Even though we were protected, to a point, by the magic that Hazel and her friends had placed on the house, and even though we didn't know if Leontine knew where I had gone, there was the constant threat of danger hanging over me.

The first couple of days, I was afraid to be close to any of the windows for fear of being seen by Leontine or one of her cronies. I jumped a mile if anyone knocked on the door or if the phone rang. I even asked Hazel not to call me by my name in case anyone could hear her. Yes, I was paranoid. Wouldn't you have been?

After a while, I calmed down and tried not to think about it too much. Of course, as soon as I started to get comfortable, a knock came on the door. Hazel motioned for me to be quiet and stay put. Totally unnecessary. I was hardly going to volunteer to answer the door.

"Yes? Who is it?" she called.

"Jaeger," came the gruff, matter-of-fact response.

Hazel opened the door just enough for them to converse. I could make out nothing of their whispered conversation. After a minute, Hazel came back into the den.

"What's going on?"

"He thought he heard something. He asked us to stay in one spot and not move for the next few minutes while he searches the perimeter," she replied, so faintly that I could only just hear her.

For several minutes we sat like mannequins in a store window, only the shifting of our eyes betraying our living state. I strained my ears to try and hear if there was anything going on outside, but all I could hear was the sound of my own heart pounding in my ears.

I felt like one of those silly females in a cheap horror movie. One of the ones that just sits around and waits for the killer to find them. I wanted to bolt and run for my car and speed away. On further thought, hopping into an open convertible when someone who can turn into a panther is out there waiting for you didn't sound like a good idea.

Finally, Jaeger knocked again, announcing himself immediately. Hazel rushed to the door and they spoke once more in hushed tones.

"He didn't find anything. There were some tracks that might have been Leontine's, but he can't be sure since there are several cats living in the neighborhood."

I nodded, saying nothing. Had she been out there? Did she know where I was? Those questions dominated my thoughts for the rest of the evening. Even an old Stewart Granger movie couldn't keep my mind from pondering these questions.

That night, I didn't sleep a wink. I was afraid to close my eyes. Every time I began to drift off, I'd wake with a start, certain that someone or something was in the room with me. Eventually, I gave up, turned on a light and pulled out a book.

This scenario would repeat itself from time to time, bringing my happy mood crashing back to the reality that someone out there wanted to hurt me. Badly.

Twice, Kin called from wherever it was he'd been sent to. Cell phone reception was nearly impossible there. According to Kin, that place had barely made it into the twentieth century, never mind the twenty-first. I was flattered that he'd made the effort to find land lines that he could use for long distance calls. Our calls were brief and uninformative. Hello. How are you? I miss you. Good-bye. There wasn't much else. I felt like Ingrid Bergman in some suspenseful film noir where she and some handsome leading man were worried about being over heard by the enemy. Act normal, say nothing. It seemed unnecessary, especially since he wasn't using his cell phone, but he knew the people we were dealing with better than I.

He had no idea how long he'd be away. I had no idea how long I'd have to stay with Hazel. What a pair we made. The only thing we knew for certain was that we didn't know anything. Great!

One night, Hazel knocked on the door to my make-shift office. "Come on in," I called.

"Hey," she said as she came in and sat on the corner of the desk. "I've been thinking about what you asked me. You know, about your friends."

"Oh!" I replied, having forgotten, at least for the moment, about my request. "Yeah?"

"I think I can help relieve their worries, but I'll need you to help."

"Of course! What do you need me to do?"

"Nothing difficult. I just need you to call each of them, one at a time," she answered. "Maybe a reassuring phone call is the best way after all." Hazel smiled and wiggled her perfectly arched eyebrows.

"Ok. I can do that," I said, curious to know what she was going to do.

"Good. You'll need to get each one of them to talk to me. Once they are speaking to me, I can cast an enchantment on them."

"Over the phone? Really? Wow!" I was impressed.

"Yeah, well, it's not ideal, but it's not really feasible for us to go door to door either. It won't make them forget or anything, but I should be able to get them to agree that this is the best way for you to handle your situation. That way, at least they won't be so worried." She seemed apologetic as she explained.

"That's great, Hazel, really. Thank you so much," I gushed as I went out to the living room where I'd left my cell phone.

Hazel shrugged. "Thank me later, if it all works." I had no doubt it would. Hazel was modest by nature.

"Hi, Sue," I said as my best friend answered the phone. "How are you?"

"Ok. How are you doing?" she asked pointedly. "Any news from the insurance company yet?"

"No, not yet. They said it could take a few weeks to process my claim."

"So you don't know how long you're going to be out of your house?"

"No," I replied. "Remember? I told you this the other day. That's why I'm staying with Hazel. She's got lots of room and she's hardly ever here."

"Yeah. And who is this Hazel again?"

"She's one of my clients," I lied, crossing my fingers like I did when I was a child. "As a matter of fact, she happens to be home tonight. Would you like to talk to her?"

"Uh…" came the reply on the other end of the phone. Before she could come up with a response, Hazel grabbed the phone from my hand.

"Hi! Is this Sue? Oh, Hero's told me so much about you! I hope we can all get together some time."

"Yeah, sure. Funny, Hero never mentioned you before she moved in with you."

"Really? Well, probably since it's all through her work and everything it never came up. Sue?"

"Yeah?"

"I want to tell you something."

"Go 'head."

"Hero is safe with me. You have nothing to worry about. Hero is safe with me." Hazel's voice took on an eerie quality, as though amplified by an old fashioned microphone that made the voice echo. It made me shiver.

"Do you understand?" Hazel continued. "Very good. I'll give you back to Hero now. Bye!"

I took the phone from her and placed it to my ear. "Sue?" I said, unsure.

"Yeah?"

"So, um, I'll call you in a few days, ok?"

"Sure thing. Talk to you later. Love ya!"

"Bye," I said, somewhat bewildered.

"Wow! That was easy." I told her.

"Well, it will vary from person to person. It depends how much they want to believe that everything's alright versus how suspicious a nature they have," Hazel explained.

I nodded as though I understood perfectly. Mm hm. We're off to a good start at least. I flipped my phone back open and dialed the next number.

We made it through my list of concerned friends in a little more than half an hour. Hazel worked fast. Even the suspicious ones fell under her spell quickly. It was such a relief. I hated that they were all so worried for me, and that I had to keep lying to them. At least one of my concerns was eliminated.

Just as we were congratulating ourselves, my phone rang. I groaned. I'd called almost everyone I knew, so I automatically assumed it was my dad, whom I hadn't heard from since my birthday.

"Hello," I answered, hoping I sounded happy.

Apparently it worked because the caller said, "Well, aren't you a happy little camper!"

My blood turned cold. This couldn't be happening. "What is it?" whispered Hazel as she sprung off the sofa and took my free hand.

"Well, well. Cat got your tongue?" Leontine cackled.

"How did you get this number?" I chocked hoarsely.

"Tch, tch. You don't really expect me to answer that, do you? I see you've got a new car. Shame what happened to your old one. You really should be more careful."

"Darius bought me that car," I told her, hoping the information would keep her from damaging it.

"My, aren't we the spoiled little pet?" she purred.

"Pet? Ironic coming from you, Garfield." What the hell, I was already in it up to my neck.

"Watch it, human."

"Why? How could this be any worse than it is, you psycho freak?"

"Freak!" she screamed.

"Yeah, freak! What would you call a person that can turn into an animal? Not normal. Freak!"

"No, no!" whispered Hazel, trying to pull the phone out of my hand.

"How dare you!"

"How dare I? How dare you?" I yelled, getting into my groove now. "I was minding my own business, going on a date with a guy I had just met. You are the one who forced me into this mess. Did it ever occur to you to have Ilderim talk to Darius to begin with instead of ruining my home? Or at least waiting to see what would happen instead of destroying my home and priceless items that can't be replaced? Huh? I hadn't done anything to deserve that."

"You are a lowly human! I don't care for your feelings!"

"And I don't care for your feelings either, Felix! Why the hell should I care if I hurt your delicate little feelings? You act so tough, but the tiniest thing damages your fragile ego. You're pathetic!"

"Oh! This isn't good!" Hazel finally managed to wrench the phone from my hands. She switched it off and put it in her pocket. "Are you crazy? She already wants to kill you!"

"So what? She's got permission from her Menagerie to hurt me just short of death, so what does it matter what I say now? It's all just a matter of time, isn't it? I mean, it's not like she's ever going to give up. I'm sitting here like the proverbial mouse trapped by the cat!"

"Calm down, Hero."

"Are you kidding me?" I cried in disbelief. Did she seriously expect me to be calm?

"No, I'm not kidding you! Calm down!" Hazel yelled back at me. She grabbed a hold of my shoulders and shook me surprisingly hard, considering her small stature. "You can't think straight like that and we need to think."

"What's there to think about?" I started, but was interrupted by the sounds of screams coming from somewhere outside.

"Well, there's that," Hazel said with wide eyes.

CHAPTER 19

I'm not a big fan of horror movies, though I've seen my share. But let me tell you, no matter how scared you are in that big dark theater with its Dolby Surround Sound, nothing, and I mean nothing, scares the bejesus out of you like hearing blood curdling screams happening on the other side of a door. I'm talking too scared to even pee your pants, because that would involve some infinitesimal movement by your bladder or something, and there ain't nothing moving but your fiercely pounding heart that is going to explode any second. You don't move, you don't blink, you don't even breathe. Total paralysis.

After we heard the initial screams, Hazel and I ran to the front door. In those few seconds the screams grew louder and more feral. There were other sounds. Sounds I was afraid to put a name to. Now that it's over, I can tell you. It sounded like the tearing of flesh and limbs, and it's nothing like the movies.

A loud bang against the door made us both jump, shocking us back to animation. I turned, wide eyed, to Hazel, silently imploring her to tell me what we should do. More bangs. We could see the door shaking with the impact. I began backing away. "Hazel," I choked in a strangled whisper, barely audible.

"Get in your office," she said suddenly, turning to me and pushing me down the hall. "Hurry!"

I ran the last few steps to the little room. "Hazel, what…"

"There's no time," Hazel said. "Don't open this door to anyone but me or Jaeger. Do you understand me? No one!"

Before I could answer, she thrust my phone into my hands and slammed the door. I heard her mumble something followed by the sound of her retreating footsteps hurrying down the hall. She must have opened the front door, because suddenly, the screams and other noises were nearly twice as loud. I clapped my hands over my ears, leaning my forehead against the door.

What was happening? Was that Leontine outside? It sounded like more than just two people. It was excruciating to be locked in here, listening to a battle, and not knowing who the combatants were or who was winning.

Hazel had said not to let anyone in but her or Jaeger. What if neither one of them came back? How would I know what to do? Silent tears ran down my cheeks. I didn't think I'd ever been so frightened in my life. There I was, in a strange house, trapped like a rat, alone, defenseless, while some supernatural war raged outside.

I began pacing. I hated feeling so helpless. Looking around the room, I searched for something to use as a weapon, if it came to that. There was a floor lamp that might come in handy. After unplugging the lamp to make it usable (though it would have been so like me to try and use the lamp to defend myself and be jerked short by the cord being plugged in), I searched for other weapons. In the desk, I found a letter opener and put it in my front pocket for easy access.

Who was I kidding? If anyone but Hazel or Jaeger made it in here, what chance would I have of defending myself? My hand went to my throat as I wondered if Nigel was out there. Did Leontine have any other vampire friends out there? What about other shape shifters? Perhaps there was a shifter who could change into a wolf or a black bear or something huge and terrifying.

With a groan I plopped myself down in the desk chair. The noises outside were still raging. For the first time in my life, I seriously considered the possibility that I might die. The tears returned, but I was too afraid to make a sound. Just sitting there, waiting to see if my new friends would win or if I'd become cat chow, was unbearably nerve racking. I wanted to scream and scream and scream. I wanted to be home. I wanted my mom. Thirty years old and I wanted my mom. I didn't feel thirty. I felt like a child again, afraid of what I didn't know and couldn't control and wishing for my mother to come and take care of me and make it better. But I wasn't a child, and my mother wasn't going to save me.

Save me. Kin! I had no idea where he was, but surely he could call on someone to help me. I flipped open the cell phone that Hazel had, thankfully, given back to me. It took several tries to dial his number my hands were shaking so hard. I prayed that this once we'd get reception. Three tries, at last the call went through and I counted the rings while waiting anxiously for him to answer. Five rings, then, his voice.

"Hello?"

"Kin! It's Hero. There's a fight, a battle, going on here. Hazel locked me in a room. I don't know what's happening. It's awful! Oh, Kin! I'm so scared. Help me!"

"Hero, what...? Oh, God! I can't... Shit!"

"Call Darius! Call someone! I know you're far away, but you can still help me, Kin. Call in the cavalry, please! Hurry!"

I hung up without giving him a chance respond and clutched the phone to my breast as I said a silent prayer that whomever he called would get here in time. Yes, it was rude of me to just hang up, but I didn't know how much longer I could keep a hold of myself without freaking out on the phone. Plus, every second counted. He needed to get on the phone to someone without delay. I'd apologize later, if I lived.

"Oh, God, please help Hazel, don't let anything happen to her. Kin, please hurry. Get help here fast. And whoever is coming to help, hurry up! Please, please, please, let this all work out ok." My mind was full of so many pleas, all rushing through that they overlapped and intertwined until it was all just noise. I placed my hands on either side of my head, trying to quiet the noises within and without.

A deafening crash scared the hell out of me. I fell out of the chair and onto the floor. A large rock was on the floor, surrounded by shards of grass. The window on the far side of the room had been smashed. My heart hammered so violently I was sure I was about to have a major coronary. I actually wished I would. It would be a preferable death to what was coming.

An orange cat leapt through the hole and landed gracefully on the window sill. It paused only a moment before leaping to the ground where it almost instantly became a tall woman with honey blonde hair. "Well, well. We meet again." Leontine purred as she smoothed her hands over her blouse and slacks.

Like a backward crab, I scuttled toward the floor lamp. Leontine laughed. "Where do you think you're going?"

I reached the corner where the lamp was and carefully got into a crouching position. As I straightened up, I slowly reached out a hand for the long slender neck of the lamp. Cat woman came towards me, calmly, deliberately, enjoying my fear.

"No smart remarks, human? Hmm?" Her mouth was curled into an evil grin. "No? All out of insults and silly little quips? You're quite different when there's no one around to help you, aren't you?" Her eyes flashed with pleasure as she came ever closer.

As quickly as I could, I grabbed hold of the lamp and swung it at her head. It barely made contact before she got both of her hands around it and wrenched it from my grasp. "I don't think so," she spat angrily. "You're just a weak little human. You can't harm me."

"Seems I harmed your ego pretty bad, or you wouldn't be here. Darius and Ilderim had an agreement, but your poor little feelings got hurt," I said with all the disgust I could manage under the circumstances.

Her eyes were wide with fury. "I do not tolerate insults from humans!"

"If you hate humans so much, why do you even care what we say? Aren't my comments beneath you?" I taunted.

"Of course you are beneath me, but you cannot get away with insulting me!" Her voice was growing louder and louder.

"Yeah, because your poor little kitty feelings are so sensitive that you have to avenge yourself if someone says something you don't like." My sarcasm was like a tonic. I was feeling better and stronger with each passing comment. I might die tonight, but I wouldn't go quietly. "Poor wittle puss is so sensitive. She might get her wittle feelings hurt," I goaded.

That was it. I'd pushed the very last button. Leontine lunged at me and we both fell hard to the floor. Unfortunately, I was on the bottom and the angry Amazon's full weight knocked the breath out of me. Bright white, green and pink spots burst behind my eyelids after she punched me terribly hard on my right cheek. I felt nauseous, and couldn't help laughing in my head at the image of what Leontine might do if I were to vomit on her. I was losing my mind.

Another blow, this time to my left jaw, sent the spots into hyper drive and they exploded like a fireworks finale. My mouth tasted blood, followed by bile as I resisted the urge to throw up. Between the nausea and the pressure of her on my abdomen and chest, it was all I could do to draw breath, let alone cry for help. In a futile attempt to defend myself, I thrust my hands toward her face, intent on literally scratching her eyes out. She grasped both of my hands and pinned them above my head with one hand as she hit my face again and again.

I clung to consciousness like a drowning man to a life preserver. The pain and the fear were horrendous, but at least it meant I was still alive. With all my might, I struggled against Leontine, hoping to achieve something, even if my mind was too addled to think of what. I just tried as hard as I could to wriggle free.

A sharp pain in my hip reminded me of the letter opener I had tucked into my pocket earlier. Rocking feverishly from side to side, I managed to free my right hand. Once I managed to retrieve the opener, I forced myself to be still for a moment, as I focused on drawing as deep a breath as I could. Then, as loud as I could, I screamed "NO!" startling Leontine for just a second, but a second was long enough to raise my right arm and thrust the letter opener into her neck.

Blood sprayed across my face and ran down my hand and wrist as I pushed the silver opener as far as I could into her throat. She jerked backwards, clawing at my hands as she fought to remove the make-shift dagger. Eventually, I was able to knock her off of me and I scrambled to get up off the floor. I slipped in the blood that was quickly pooling on Hazel's nice hard wood, smearing the walls with crimson streaks as I reached out to steady myself.

There was a loud crash somewhere in the house and my nausea returned. What now? Before I had a chance to think beyond that, the door to my temporary office was splintered into hundreds of pieces. An arm, a leg and then a head and torso. It was Angel. He had come to rescue me.

"Hero, are you ok?" he asked with great concern.

"I think so," I replied as I stumbled over to him. "Leontine," I said needlessly. "I stabbed her in the throat," I explained as she lay on the floor, a sickly gurgling noise coming from her wound.

Angel stood over her and looked down without emotion at the tall warrior woman who was uselessly clutching at the opening in her neck. Blood continued to pour through her fingers. She narrowed her eyes as she recognized the vampire standing above her and she hissed her very last hiss.

In a flash, Angel was upon her, deepening the wound as he sank his teeth into her injured flesh and began to drink. That just about did it for my nauseous stomach. I clamped my hand over my mouth, remembering too late that it was covered in Leontine's blood. I barely made it to the kitchen sink as the vomit came rocketing up from my stomach.

I rinsed my mouth and scrubbed my hands, and forearms. Then I gingerly splashed water on my badly beaten face. Once I turned off the faucet, I realized how quiet things had become. Cautiously, I tip-toed toward the front of the house. The front door had been ripped off its hinges, obviously the loud crash I'd heard before Angel broke through the office door.

It was pitch black outside. I could barely see beyond the threshold. "Hazel?" I whispered. "Hazel, are you ok?" There was no sound. Not even crickets. Total silence.

I gulped down a new surge of bile and stepped out into the blackness. "Jaeger?" Still nothing.

Perhaps foolishly, I ventured out into the front yard, searching for some sign of my two body guards. Something glimmered in the moonlight under the willow tree to the right of the house. Heart thundering, I walked towards it. I couldn't identify the large black shape until I was nearly on top of it. Up close, I could finally see that the shine I had seen in the moonlight was the blood covering the neck and torso of what had once been Nigel. Even dead, I did not like to be this close to him. A branch from the willow tree had been used to stake him. It seemed ridiculous to see this gruesome body, covered in blood with what appeared to be a little tree growing out of his chest. Well, at least that was one for our side.

"Hazel?" I called again, a little more loudly this time. "Hazel? Jaeger?" The faintest sound of grass crunching beneath someone's feet made me jump. I spun around and came face to face, well, almost face to face, with a tiny woman with silver-white hair cropped very close to her head. Her amber eyes were almost yellow. She was only about four and a half feet tall and wore a violet tunic over a pair of black pants that looked as though they'd been made of strips of torn leather. Oddly, she was barefoot.

"Who are you?" I whispered, hoping I was right that her appearance indicated that she was some faerie friend of Hazel's.

"I am Lily. I have been sent to fetch you," she explained in a surprisingly deep voice.

"Sent by who?" I asked.

"The Vampire Magistrate, Darius. He is awaiting your arrival." Lily stood calmly as though there were no rush and she had all the time in the world to stand out here, barefoot, in the moonlight, talking casually after a battle between faeries, vampires and shape shifters. I admired her serenity.

"Ok." She smiled and turned and walked toward the street. "Can I ask, why did he send you?" I queried as I followed her. "Sorry, I don't mean any disrespect, but Angel is here,..."

"He has returned." Lily said simply.

"What? Who has returned? Kin?"

"Angel. He returned and told us the shape shifter was dead. Then Darius sent for you."

"Oh." I knew vampires were fast, but that seemed ridiculously fast to me. "Is Hazel ok?"

"She will be. Darius has summoned a healer. Hazel and the others shall be fine by morning."

"The others?"

"Yes. Jaeger, Mike, Anatol, Freesia, Brook, Glenn, Camille, Victor. I think that's all of them." Lily rattled the names off as though they were items on a grocery list. I hoped the lack of emotion meant none of them were seriously harmed and not just a matter of her personality.

We reached the street and Lily pulled something out from under her tunic. She took a moment to look up and down the street carefully, and then stepped back into the shadow of the short pine hedges that ran along the edge of the sidewalk.

"Come," she called. I walked up to her and she held out her hand. Lily dropped a shimmery pink stone into my palm. "Hold this tightly, please," she instructed as she closed my fingers around the stone. She took my other hand and stood directly in front of me, a few scant inches apart. "Do you trust me?"

"What?" I wasn't expecting that.

"Do you trust me, Hero?" she asked again, her glowing amber eyes staring into mine.

I was filled with tranquility, all the stress and fear of the past hour or more slipped away. "Yes, I trust you."

"Good," she said with a smile. "Close your eyes and let me lead you."

I closed my eyes, and waited to see where the tiny faerie would lead me. There was a sudden feeling of the ground disappearing beneath me. My stomach lurched as though going down that first big hill on a roller coaster. I must have cried out because Lily shushed me. "Shhh. You're fine, Hero. Try and relax and let me lead you."

I did my best to do as she asked. The night had been still, but now wind whipped my hair around and made my blouse ripple against my skin. Focusing on keeping my hands entwined with Lily's, I kept my eyes closed tight and tried not to think about what was happening.

The gusts of wind blew harder and took my breath away. It blew up the scent of blood from my injuries and I began to feel ill again. I slipped, feeling as though I was going to plummet from a great height as I felt myself sink down, reaching to keep a hold of Lily's hands.

"Nearly there, Hero. Hang in there." Poor choice of words.

"Come back to me, Hero. Listen to my voice. You are safe with me."

Her melodious voice had a calming effect. I forgot the plummeting feeling and somehow felt as though I were going towards that voice, though I made no motion on my own. "That's right. Just another minute and it will all be over."

"One, hippopotamus, two, hippopotamus," I chanted in my head like a child, counting off the seconds until it was over.

Before I reached sixty hippopotami, I felt my feet on solid ground and the air around us became still. "It's ok, Hero. You can open your eyes now," the little faerie told me as she gently released my hands.

Slowly, I opened my eyes and looked around. We were in Darius' mammoth antechamber. Unlike last time, it was full of vampires and possibly some more faeries too. I recognized the stoic doorman and Obediah, as he scurried from vampire to vampire, delivering messages. The hum of hushed conversations filled the room like the drone of bees in a hive. No one seemed to have noticed our arrival.

"Wait here," Lily said, with a light touch on my shoulder. She went towards Obediah, barely seeming to touch the ground as she glided across the marbled floor. They shared a few quiet words before Lily turned and came back to me. She smiled at me and gestured towards the chairs a few feet away. I smiled back, I think, and went and sat beside her in one of the many chairs that lined the walls in the great room.

"Obediah will let The Magistrate know you are here," she said simply.

"Thank you, Lily."

"Oh, it's nothing. Glad to help," she said with a big grin.

"Do you know why Darius wanted me brought here?" I asked.

Lily remained silent. I asked again, non-verbally by way of raising my eyebrows. "It is not our place to question such things," she replied.

"It may not be your place, but I'm not used to being ordered around." Frankly, if I hadn't been alone with at least two dead bodies lying around, I don't know that I would have come so willingly.

She shrugged her shoulders and smiled again. Realizing I'd get no further information, I rested my head against the wall and closed my eyes. I felt as though I hadn't slept in days.

"Oh, dear," Lily said quietly a few seconds later. "Come with me, Hero," she instructed and she took my arm and tried to lift me out of my seat.

"What? Why?" I asked groggily.

"Just come out into the hall with me for a minute, please. It's important." She looked so earnest as she tugged on my arm. I gave in and shuffled after her out into the hall.

There were a couple of vampires out there too, but they were further down and took no notice of us. Lily pulled me behind a large potted palm.

"What's up?" I asked.

"Your clothes. I should have had you change them before we came." She sighed and scratched her head.

"But why...." I began, but she held up her hand to silence me.

"I'm trying to think of something to.... Yes, that might do it," she said cryptically as she reached for a bag of stones that hung from her waist. The faerie rummaged in the bag for a moment, and after selecting the one she wanted, she clenched it in her fist and held it over my head. Just barely. Her other hand reached up to my shoulder to hold me still. Lily raised and lowered the hand with the stone several times, criss-crossing in front of me. My skin began to prickle slightly, almost in a ticklish way. I wanted to scratch but Lily tightened her grip on my shoulder. Somehow I knew that meant for me not to move.

The prickling feeling intensified and I wanted to scratch my face, shoulders and stomach and my right upper arm desperately. At last she stopped and opened her eyes. In the bright light of the hall, they seemed almost orange.

"That's better," she announced as she returned the stone to its bag, clearly proud of herself.

Free to scratch, I began chasing itches down all over my face, torso and arms. "What was that all about?"

"You were covered in blood," she said simply.

"Oh," I replied, looking at my shirt and seeing the blood was gone. I hadn't even noticed which made me feel pretty dumb.

Lily stepped out into the hall from behind the palm and headed back to the anteroom. "Come on, we'd better get you back before The Magistrate calls you."

"Oh, I get it. You didn't think it was right for me to meet The Magistrate with my clothes all bloody."

"Actually," she whispered to me, "I didn't like the way the vampires were looking at you. A human, covered in blood, sleeping with your neck exposed."

Hmm. That could have been very bad. "Ohhh," I said, finally realizing why she felt the need to get me out of there so urgently. "Thanks."

"No problem," she replied with a perky smile.

We had barely gotten our butts back in our chairs when the silent guard nodded frugally at Lily. "Come," she said, reaching out her tiny hand to me.

Gladly, I took her hand and allowed her to lead me through the group of anxious vampires and Lord knows what else. For once I had the presence of mind to keep my gaze lowered and not make eye contact with any of them.

Obediah greeted us as we walked through the enormous doorway. "Thank you for bringing the human to us, Lily," he said graciously as he bowed slightly toward the little faerie. Then, as a show of good manners, I suppose, he nodded briefly to me.

He led us to a pair of seats opposite the Magistrate's elaborate desk. Bowing his greasy head once more, Obediah motioned for us to sit down. This was an improvement over my last visit. Kin and I hadn't been invited to sit. I took it as a good sign.

Darius emerged out of the shadows in the far recesses of his office. I couldn't tell if he had been there when we came in or if perhaps there were some hidden door back there. He strode purposefully, yet gracefully, to his desk and sat down. Lacing his fingers together before him, he leveled a curious gaze on both me and my mystical companion. After a few moments of contemplation, he turned his cold, dark eyes to me alone. "So, you killed the shape shifter." It was a statement of fact, not a question.

"Yes," I replied simply. Until that moment, I hadn't really allowed myself to think about that. I'd killed someone. Not now. Now was not the time. I'd think about that later. Ugh, what I time to think of Scarlett O'Hara! "That is," I decided to add, "I believe I did. I'm not certain if she was dead when Angel arrived, but I feel she would have died even if he hadn't shown up."

Darius nodded slowly. "You stabbed her in the throat." Another statement.

"Yes, with a letter opener."

More nodding. "You seem to have suffered no serious injuries."

I suppose they weren't really, but I ached so badly that I had sort of shut down. I knew I'd pay for it later, but for now, my mind had refused to allow me to contemplate the effects of the beating I had taken, even if my head was throbbing thunderously, my right eye was nearly swollen shut and I could still taste blood in my mouth. Choosing not to comment, I merely nodded in return.

"Hazel has asked to see you. Also, Kin requested you stay here under my protection until he returns."

"What?" I exclaimed, forgetting myself. Quick, Hero, back pedal! "Forgive me, I was just shocked that you would allow me to stay here." The Magistrate's expression clearly indicated that he didn't believe me, but thankfully he chose not to call me on it.

Poor Lily, who had been sitting so still and quiet spun her head around and looked at me with saucer-like eyes. She watched Darius out of the corner of her eye and was visibly relieved when he spoke again.

"Of course," he agreed with a wave of his perfectly manicured hand. "You've had a traumatic evening. Obediah will take you to Hazel now." He reclined into his chair, seemingly relaxed, but his sharp eyes as alert as ever.

We stood to leave, and as is only natural for me, I forgot myself again. "But why do I need to be here for my protection? Leontine is dead. It was self-defense. Does this mean others are going to come after me now?" Oh, dear God, no! How much more could I take?

Lily clutched my arm and tried to shush me quietly. Too late. Even Obediah looked at me with concern. Darius, his eyes narrowed, leaned forward again. "Clearly, you are not used to our ways, human. I will overlook it this once, but in the future, you will not speak unless spoken to when you are in my presence." He reclined again, but continued. "For the time being, yes, you are still in danger. However, I, undoubtedly, will be able to work this out with Leontine's Master. It was wrong of him to allow her to break our agreement for such a foolish reason." A slight nod to Obediah signaled it was time to leave. This time, I kept my mouth shut and followed the sallow complected vampire out the door.

CHAPTER 20

Obediah left us without a word after leading us to where Hazel was resting from the battle that took place outside her home, which was ok with me. Personally, he gave me the creeps.

Hazel was lying in large bed with an ornate headboard. Apparently, nothing in Darius' residence was simple. Even against the crisp, snow-white sheets, she looked pale. She smiled when she saw us come in, but it didn't ease the guilt I felt. There was no doubt she'd been in a terrible fight. There were scratches and bandages all over. Bruises were already tingeing various parts of her face and arms numerous shades of purple, blue and red. I even thought I detected a small patch of hair missing. But the worst was the large bandage which covered most of the left side of her neck and the top of her left shoulder.

My eyes filled with tears as I reached to take her hand. "Oh, Hazel, I…"

"Shh," she said. "None of that. I'll be right as rain by this time tomorrow. Faes have remarkable healing powers." She squeezed my hand and smiled broadly. "What about you? I heard you took care of Leontine all by yourself!" All I could do is nod. "Oh, Hero, please don't cry."

"I'm sorry, I can't help it. Your neck," I chocked, gesturing toward the immense bandage.

Hazel chuckled. "Nigel. The fool. Most vampires know better than to come in such close quarters to a Sidhe." Lily shared her chuckle. I wasn't in on the joke.

When they noticed my curious expression Lily explained. "You've seen my stones," she began, holding up her velvet bag. "Each of the stones has different properties which assist us in different types of magic. Ironically, vampires are adversely affected by bloodstone. Normally, bloodstone increases physical strength, but if you press a bloodstone against a vampire's skin, it will weaken them temporarily. Not for long, but a few seconds is enough to turn the tide."

I knew that well from my experience with Leontine. "Do a lot of people know that?"

"No," said Hazel. "We do our best to keep that a secret. Vampires know that they should not come in close contact with us, but few know why. And even those that know about our stones don't know which does what, so they don't know we use bloodstone against them."

"Oh. Wow. Is it just the Sidhe that use the stones or do other types of faeries use them?"

The pair looked at each other, communicating silently before answering. "Some do," said Lily. "There is a great deal of shared magic between faes, but each tribe has their own particular methods which they prefer."

"Hero, you won't repeat this information to Kin, will you?" asked Hazel, as it dawned on her that she had shared their secret with a vampire's girlfriend.

"No! Of course I wouldn't do that. I would never betray a friend." I squeezed her hand again and reached and took Lily's hand too.

Our girlie BFF moment was cut short by the arrival of a tall, slender man with deeply tanned skin. His silver-gray ponytail oddly at contrast with his navy blue Brooks Brothers suit, Italian loafers and red power tie. "Hello ladies," he said with a thick accent as he entered the room. "I have your serum for you, Miss Greenleaf."

The healer walked around to the other side of the bed, placed his black bag on the nightstand and pulled it open. He pulled out a long crystal vial containing vibrant emerald liquid. After removing the stopper, he held the vial in front of Hazel and with his other hand he reached for a black cord which hung around her neck. At the end of the cord was a large piece of turquoise in the shape of a pyramid. He raised the stone and clicked it three times against the lip of the crystal container, then he handed the serum to Hazel and she drank it all in one swallow.

"There now. You should start feeling much better in a few minutes." He wiped the vial on a cloth, replaced the stopper and put it back in his bag. As he closed the bag he added, "I'll be back in the morning to remove your dressings. Good evening ladies." The healer smiled at each of us in turn before leaving the room.

"So, how do you feel?" I asked.

"I'm doing fine."

"Hazel, you have a huge bandage on your neck and you're covered in cuts and bruises! You are not doing fine."

"Don't worry so much, Hero," Lily said. "We don't feel things physically the same as humans. Truly, her wounds are not bad at all."

"What was that he gave you?"

"It was a serum to counteract the vampire's bite and to help speed my healing."

"Why did he touch it to that stone?" I figured since she didn't seem to mind my nosiness I'd satisfy my curiosity.

Hazel picked up the bright blue stone. "This is turquoise. Among other things, it is a powerful healing stone. I keep it against my skin to help my healing, and since the stone knows me, he used its energy to complete the serum."

"The stone 'knows' you?" I probably shouldn't have asked that. In my head it sounded rude, but it was out before I realized it.

The faeries chuckled. "Each faerie has his or her own stones. The more we use a stone, the more familiar it becomes to us and us to them. That's why we keep our stones on us at all times. A faerie would never use someone else's stones, and if we lose a stone it is a difficult task to find new ones and build a new relationship."

A relationship? With a stone? Ok, I had the presence of mind not to question that one. "Oh, I see. Thank you for explaining."

"Can I get you anything?" I asked, changing the subject.

"Oh, no. Thank you." As I looked at her, I saw her bruises were beginning to fade and her cuts were healing. Note to self: Get myself a hunk of turquoise.

"We'll let you get some rest now," Lily told her.

"Ok. I'll see you tomorrow?" We assured her we'd be back to see her in the morning.

Out in the hall, I saw Angel coming out of a room on the opposite side. "Angel," I called in a stage whisper, waving when he turned to look at me.

The vampire came toward Lily and me and something vaguely resembling a smile played on his lips. "Hello, Hero, Lily."

"Thank you for helping me, again," I said.

"No need. You seemed to have had the situation under control. Nice kill."

Ew! I knew he meant that as a compliment, so I tried to smile back at him. "Thanks. Got lucky."

"I'm sure Mike would like to see you. He was very worried when we realized Leontine had slipped through."

"Were you just visiting him?" I asked.

"Yes. Come." Angel strode back to the door, clearly assuming Lily and I would follow him. Since I would like to see Mike, especially after hearing he'd been worried about me, I followed and Lily came right behind me.

"Someone to see you," Angel said as he walked through the door.

"Hey!" Mike exclaimed as he saw me.

"Hi Mike. How are you doing?" I asked, genuinely concerned.

"Aw, I'm fine. I don't really even need to be in bed, but Dr. Galeno said I should rest."

"What happened to you?"

"Nothing really. I got my shoulder dislocated, but it's been popped back into place and I feel fine now."

Ugh! The thought of popping a shoulder back into place made me a bit squeamish. "Well, thank God that was all."

"Angel said you took out the shifter all by yourself. That's awesome!"

Mike was so excited and looking at me as though I were some kind of hero (lower case, you know what I mean) that I could feel myself turning crimson. "I got lucky, really. It's a miracle Angel didn't bust in the door to find me dead."

"Nah, don't be so modest. Shifters may be easier to kill than other Supes, but they are really strong."

"Yeah, I know," I interjected, pointing to my face which was badly swollen and covered in cuts and bruises.

"Oh, yeah. Has Dr. Galeno seen to you yet?"

"Oh! Uh…, no…" I stammered. Was I supposed to have seen him? Could he even treat humans? Thinking about that made me realize I didn't even know where I was supposed to go after this visit. According to Darius, I was to stay here until Kin returned, but where? I voiced this concern to my companions.

"I can find that out for you. Wait here." Angel replied. Without waiting for me to respond, he quickly went out looking for the answers.

After a moment of awkward silence, Mike asked, "Could you see the fighting from where you were?"

"No," I replied simply.

"That's too bad. It was great!"

Clearly, Mike thought fights and battles were a good time. "I'm sure it was," I said to appease him.

"You shoulda seen it though, Hero, really! First Leontine thought she was sneaking up on Jaeger, right?" He paused to chuckle. "Like anyone could sneak up on him. So, anyway, she thinks he doesn't hear her and then, WHAM!" he punctuated loudly, "he turned around and grabbed her by the throat. But the stupid shifter turned into a cat and squirmed away. Not that we were going to let her get away though. She didn't realize there were more of us in hiding there. You shoulda seen her!" He was really laughing now. "Man, her face, HA! She was so surprised she couldn't even keep her cat form. She cried out for Nigel and he came running with a coupla other shifters and whatever, and then things got way interesting. That was when Hazel came out and joined the fight. She said you were all safe and stuff."

"Yes, I was."

Mike wouldn't be detracted from his story now, though. He was on a roll and enjoying every rotation. "So then, when Hazel came, some other faeries showed up, you know, like Lily here," he explained, pointing needlessly to the tiny faerie. "And before ya knew it, there was tons of us all fighting on the lawn and everything. I don't know what Hazel's neighbors musta thought," he wondered, still laughing. "But after a bit, even though we was winning, right, well Angel noticed Leontine was gone, see, and he called out to ask where she was, but no one knew. That's when he went looking for you. But Angel, he told me you'd got her real good all on your own, so all he had left to do was finish her off like." He trailed off there, seeming to hope I would fill in some details of my own.

"It all happened so fast and I was so scared. I'm not even certain she would have died if Angel hadn't come in." I really didn't want to get a reputation as a Shifter Slayer. Mike looked a little disappointed, but he was running too high for lack of details to let any air out of his balloon.

"Well, I don't know 'bout that!" he commented, beaming at me. I could almost picture him wearing a t-shirt with my image on it, 'Here is my hero!' So not who I wanted to be. Don't get me wrong, I sure as hell didn't want be a damsel in distress, but I didn't want to be thought of along the same terms as these folk who think killing other beings was a hoot.

"We should let you get some rest now." I said gently. When he began to protest, I raised my hand and added, "Doctor's orders, Mike, remember?" I smiled at him and assured him I'd probably see him the next day, and then I ushered Lily out the door ahead of me.

"You were awfully quiet in there," I said to the faerie once we were back in the hall.

"There was no need for me to speak," she said matter-of-factly. "That vampire seems very fond of you," Lily observed.

Again I felt my face turning crimson. "I guess. He's a nice kid." I tried to avoid looking at her. "I wonder where Angel is?" I queried, hoping to change the subject.

"Perhaps we should walk back towards the anteroom. We are bound to run into him along the way," she suggested. I breathed a little sigh, glad that I had managed to move her attention away from Mike and his adulation.

It was no surprise to me to find that Lily was right. After a couple of minutes, we ran into Angel who was coming from the direction of Daruis' waiting room.

"You are to stay in the Ruhlmann Room. Follow me," Angel announced without stopping. He breezed right past us, once more expecting us to just follow along. And we did.

After a few minutes of traversing winding halls, Angel stopped in front of an oak door with an unusual angular door handle. He pushed the door open to reveal a lovely room, grandly decorated in the Art Deco style in shades of French blue and cream.

"Thank you," I said to him. "This room is amazing!" I was in awe. I had never seen such a beautiful bedroom in person.

"I am sure we will see each other again sometime," Lily said, breaking my reverie.

"Oh! You're leaving?"

"Yes, I am going to go home now," she answered with a smile. "As I said, I am sure we will see each other again some time."

"Thank you, Lily. Thank you so much, for everything. I hope to see you again soon." Her perky little smile broadened, then she waved and left. I turned to look for Angel, but he was gone too. Left without a word. Well, I knew he was a vampire of few words.

I walked over to the luxurious bed with the grand circular headboard. Sitting down upon the blue comforter, I ran my hands up and down the fabric, wondering if it was silk. My shoes were kicked off and I lay down, wiggling my toes and enjoying the feeling of sinking into the squishy comforter and down pillow. I hadn't realized just how exhausted I was. Within seconds, I was sound asleep.

You'd think after the events of the past several days I'd be used to waking up in strange places, but I wasn't. The room seemed so strange to me at first. My groggy mind took a few minutes to recall all the events of the past evening. Once I recalled how I ended up here, I shook my head at myself when I realized I had slept fully clothed on top of the covers. Silly Hero.

The sun was streaming through sheers covering the tall windows. I stretched and wandered around the room. What was expected of me? Should I stay in here until sent for? Would there be breakfast, and if so, where? Maybe I could go and visit Hazel. That is, if I could remember how to get back to where she was. After some careful thought, I decided I did not feel confident trying to find anything in this mansion.

I didn't even have my bag with me. No cell phone, no hair brush, no Chap Stick, nothing but what I was wearing.

Heaving a sigh, I plopped myself down in a chair near the window. I must have been at the back of the house because through the window I could see a perfectly manicured courtyard, filled with plants and bushes and little fruit trees. I'd tell you what kinds they were, but I'm not good at that kind of stuff. They had green leaves. That's about as technical as I can get.

There was no movement below accept for the occasional hoping or flitting of a finch. At least I think they were finches, don't hold me to it. There was no noise and it was just as still inside. The only sound I could hear was the faint grumbling of my empty stomach.

"Great," I said out loud to myself. "Vampires don't eat so there probably isn't any food here."

I was not starting off the day very well. Determined not to let me get myself into a foul mood, I decided to look for the bathroom and see what I could do about cleaning myself up.

A quick perusal showed that there was only one other door inside the room, and that led to a large closet. Smoothing my hair down and tucking my blouse back in, I eased the bedroom door open a tiny bit at a time until I was able to peer out into the hall.

There were no sounds, however, there were several doors in the large corridor. How would I know which one it was? How would I know if there even was one? I hadn't settled the question of whether or not vampires even needed such modern conveniences.

No. Darius had all kinds of guests here from the Supernatural world. Surely some of them needed to use the facilities. I crept out into the hall, closing the door behind me with a soft click. Before walking away, I took note to see if my door knob was the only one shaped like that, so I could easily identify my room. It was unique, but there were others that were slightly similar. I looked at the paintings on the wall and the floral arrangement on a nearby table, hoping they would help me find my way back. Deciding to leave nothing to chance, I pulled a couple of petals off of one of the flowers and carefully placed them on the floor so that they were just barely sticking out from under the door. Hopefully, no one would come by and notice them.

Ok. Now what? How did I determine which rooms were guest rooms and which might be a bathroom? I was dealing with vampires, who don't need to breathe. It's not like I could really count on listening at the doors for signs of life or whatever you call sounds made by the undead.

Tiptoeing carefully, I took a close look at the surrounding door handles, hoping to find a fish or a seahorse or something that might indicate a room with water. No such luck. I started pressing my ear against doors, trying to at least eliminate some of the rooms. Of course, now that I was looking, I suddenly had to go real bad!

"What are you doing?" said a deep voice behind me.

I jumped a mile and clapped a hand over my mouth to keep from screaming. Jaeger was standing there, watching me with narrowed eyes.

"I'm trying to find a bathroom," I replied defensively.

He actually cracked a smile. Well, almost a smile. A grin. Shaking his head, he said "Humans! It's at the end of the hall." Jaeger held his arm straight out and pointed, just in case I couldn't figure out what 'end of the hall' meant.

I thanked him, sort of, and turned on my heels and marched to the end of the hall. Seeing as there weren't too many humans about, I didn't bother knocking, though in retrospect I probably should have. Once inside, I was struck again by the incredible opulence of Darius' mansion. The faucets and fixtures were gold, and I don't mean plated. There was a tub that could easily have fit three or four people. Oh, how I'd love to soak in a tub like that!

Once I had taken care of business, and cleaned myself up as best as I could, given that I had no change of clothes, I ventured back out into the hall. As I turned the knob, I said a silent prayer that Jaeger would be gone.

Nope! Still there. I tried to ignore him as I walked back to my room. Barely had I got my hand over the door handle when he approached me again.

"I wanted to speak to you."

I closed my eyes and took a steadying breath. "Yes?" I asked as I turned my head toward him.

Jaeger looked uncomfortable. More than uncomfortable, awkward. "I…, I…" he stuttered, trying to force himself to say something that was obviously unpleasant for him.

"I never thanked you for looking out for me," I interjected, hoping to make it easier for him to speak and break the uncomfortable silence.

It did not have the desired effect. His eyes flashed and he ground his teeth. I unconsciously retreated a step.

"I do not need your sarcasm. Do you think,"

"Sarcasm! I meant that. I do appreciate that you were looking out for me!" I implored. He didn't seem to believe me. I had injured his pride.

"If you hadn't been there, she would have taken me completely by surprise and I'd never have had any chance to defend myself," I added.

The tall vampire seemed to be slightly mollified. "I did not fulfill my duty," he said stiffly.

"How can you think that?" I was dumbfounded. Sure, I had polished off Leontine, but they had kept her from me long enough for me to be on my guard and as prepared as I could have been. Not to mention they took care of all of her comrades.

"The shifter should never have had access to you. I allowed her to slip through." He was serious. He honestly believed he had failed.

"She was a shifter, Jaeger. And there were others to be dealt with and helped. How could you expect to keep a cat in place under those circumstances? You're being too hard on yourself. I thanked you for keeping her from me long enough for me to find a way to defend myself, and I meant it. I wouldn't be here now if it wasn't for you. And who knows what might have happened if you hadn't been there all along. She might have gotten me anywhere."

He looked at me severely with his black eyes, staring into mine to try to determine if I was being truthful. "Look, after the way you treated me when we met a couple of nights ago, if you had screwed up, believe me, I'd tell you. In fact, I'd probably enjoy it, but the fact is, you didn't. So thank you, really."

I doubt he wanted to hear that exactly, but on the other hand, it did seem to relieve him a bit. Straightening to his full height, shoulders back, head high, he gave a short bow and walked away. I guess that translates to 'you're welcome' in vampire.

Back inside the relative safety of my temporary bedroom, I went back over our conversation, such as it was. I couldn't be certain, but I think I just might have made a new friend.

CHAPTER 21

Fortunately for me, and my grumbling stomach, Lily came to fetch me later that morning. She brought a tray with tea and toast and marmalade. As soon as I scoffed that down, much to her amusement, we went to visit Hazel as promised.

Hazel was thoroughly healed. When we entered her room, she was busy combing her shocking red hair. "Hey! Good morning. Did you sleep ok, Hero?"

"Yes, fine. How are you feeling?"

"Terrific! Like it never happened."

I envied her that. My aches weren't as bad as they could have been, but I was still very battered looking and certain muscles were protesting loudly. Not to mention I had some cuts that probably could have used some attention. "I'm glad," I told her. "I can't thank you enough for what you've done for me. Both of you."

The faeries shared yet another smile. Faeries are very smiley kind of folk. "We are glad to have been of help," answered Lily.

"Well, what now?" I asked.

"I understand that Kin is expected later today. Provided The Magistrate has come to agreeable terms with Ilderim, you will most likely be going home." I wasn't sure how Lily knew that, but I was glad she did.

"Oh! Ok, that's great. And until then?"

"I'm sorry, Hero. I have to go and meet with the Queen of my clan," Hazel said apologetically. "Lily and I can't keep you company. I'm sure you can find something to occupy your time until Kin arrives," she added brightly.

I wasn't so sure, but I put on a happy face. "Oh, sure I will!"

"Thanks again," I said as I gave each of my faerie friends a big hug.

"We'll see you soon," Hazel promised as she reached into her stone pouch.

I knew they would dematerialize, or whatever it was those stones caused, in a matter of seconds, so I left to see what I could find to keep myself busy.

Only partly sure that I could find my way back to the room I had slept in, I wandered casually down the hallways of the great mansion, taking time to enjoy the various works of art that adorned the walls and table tops.

"Hey, Hero!" a voice called out cheerfully.

"Mike! How are you feeling?"

"Oh, just fine, fine. One hundred percent!" he declared as he swung his arm around to show me how well he'd healed. "What about you? Didn't the Doc take care of you?"

"Oh, uh, no. I'm not sure he deals with humans." I wasn't really sure, but I hadn't bothered to ask either.

"Aw, that's too bad. You feeling ok?" he asked, genuinely concerned. Again I thought what a sweetie Mike was. It was a real shame he was a vampire.

"I'm fine. A little achy, but nothing serious," I told him with a grin.

"Well, that's good. So, whatcha up to then?"

"Nothing really. Just wandering the halls," I admitted with a laugh.

"Do you like to play pool?" Mike asked excitedly.

"Uh, yeah. Pool's ok." How well did vampires play pool? Would their abilities give them an edge? I didn't want to sign up for a humiliating experience.

"Cool! Darius has two pool tables, so one of 'em's bound to be open this time of day. Come on!" He was grinning like a kid on Christmas morning. It occurred to me that a young vampire like Mike may not have a lot in common with some of the older vampires. He was probably thrilled to have someone to spend time with who wasn't all about the kill and other vampire things.

No longer surprised by anything in the Magistrate's mansion, I took the guilt edged pool table in stride. I'd never seen one like it, and that also did not surprise me. It was beautifully carved and even the cue sticks had gold accents. The surface was so perfect it looked as though it had never been used. I was a little nervous to even rack the balls.

Not Mike though! He was raring to go, apologizing for winning the toss and breaking first, as he chalked his cue. I decided I didn't really care if I lost.

As it turns out, vampire skills don't have too much effect on pool, especially as strength isn't always a good thing where delicate execution is required. I lost count of how many games Mike and I played, but I only won one, and I'm fairly certain he let me win that one. Despite the trouncing, I had a great time. Thank you, God for Mike! Who knows what my day would have been like otherwise?

My notorious growling stomach put an end to our games. "Oh, gee, Hero. I forgot all about you needing to eat. You must think I'm a real jerk!"

"No! I would never think that about you Mike. There's no reason to feel bad. My stomach rumbles at the tiniest sign of hunger. Don't worry about it," I pleaded, a bit embarrassed at my willful stomach.

He took me to a room with several small round tables, each with four chairs around it. At one table sat a couple, clearly vampire judging by the glasses of what appeared to be blood in front of them, along with their very pale skin.

A servant showed us to a table and Mike ordered. "I'll have a glass of A positive, please. What do you have for food?"

The servant turned his attention to me and listed a few items that each sounded delicious. After a moment of consideration I chose apple stuffed pork chops with mashed potatoes and green beans. He noted my order and asked if I'd like a drink. I asked for bottled water, if they had it. They did.

"This is like a little restaurant," I whispered across the table.

Mike chuckled. "Darius likes to make sure all his guests are taken good care of."

"Does he have humans so often that there's a menu ready for them?" I asked, curious.

"Humans aren't the only ones that eat, ya know. The Shifters eat, some of the faeries eat human food, werewolves, hags…"

"Ok, I get the picture. Thanks." I didn't need to hear of any more supernatural beings actually existing. I was still dealing with the three I'd encountered personally.

The food was exquisite. I half wished I could eat here all the time. Well, maybe a quarter wished. Mike was great company and I was shocked when I learned we were in the early hours of the evening.

"Is it that time already? It can't be!"

"Yup! Time flies when you're having fun, huh?" Mike asked happily.

The servant came over to our table and whispered something in Mike's ear. Mike became very serious and nodded to the servant. "Thanks."

"What is it?" I asked, my comfortable feeling quickly sinking away.

"I got to take you to see Darius now." he explained.

"Oh, ok." What else was there to say?

This time there was no waiting. Obediah met us in the grand waiting room and ushered me right in to the office. Darius was seated behind his desk. He rose as I came in and gestured for me to have a seat on a divan near one of the towering windows.

"Thank you for coming so quickly."

Oh, oh. I didn't like the sound of this.

"Kinley shall be here in approximately one hour. He will, naturally, be tied up with me for some time in connection with his work. However, when we are through, you may leave with him."

"Thank you." I said, waiting for the other shoe to drop.

"I have spoken to Ilderim about our little situation," he said, as though a fierce battle had not occurred less than 24 hours ago. "We agree that Leontine was perhaps too," he paused, searching for the right word.

"Out of control?" I offered.

Darius gave a slight smirk. I wasn't sure if it was my choice of words or that I spoke out of turn.

"Out of control will do. Regardless, he will be issuing an edict that her death is not to be avenged, against you or any of the party who participated last evening. It may take some time to be fully distributed, but I expect you will be safe by this time tomorrow."

Expect would have to be good enough. At least Kin would be back soon and I'd have him to protect me. "Thank you." I said again, nodding my head towards him as I'd seen others do.

He smiled at me briefly and stood. "Is there anything you need while you wait?" Darius asked.

"I don't think so," I replied. Satisfied that we were done, the Magistrate turned and walked back to his desk. Assuming that meant I had been dismissed, I walked toward the immense double doors. Obediah beat me to them and opened them for me.

Luckily, Mike was waiting for me. "Everything ok, Hero?"

"Oh, sure. Kin will be back in a little while and as soon as he is done with Darius, I can go home."

"Oh. Oh, that's great," he said, a little dejected. "So, um…"

Poor Mike. "I've got some time for a couple more games of pool. Will you let me see if I can manage to win more than one?"

"Yeah, sure, if you got time and all." That was definitely what he wanted to hear. So, back to the pool room to get my ass kicked a few more times.

I was so sick of pool. I never wanted to see a pool table again as long as I lived. Well, maybe not that long, but for quite a while anyway. My poor back and ribs were aching from all the bending and stretching. I hadn't had the benefit of one of Dr. Galeno's serums to make me all better.

"I think we're going to have to call it quits, Mike. I can't take any more." I flopped myself down in one of the arm chairs that stood at the far end of the room.

"Oh, ok. Sorry, I didn't mean to make you play so much."

"You didn't make me, I enjoyed it. But I'm worn out now," I laughed. "I don't have the same stamina as vampires do."

He chuckled back and sat himself down in a chair opposite me. He looked at a porcelain clock over the mantel. "Kin'll probably be looking for you soon."

"Mmm," I replied, enjoying the feel of the overstuffed chair.

"Should I take you back over to Darius? I mean, you know, to the waiting room?"

"Oh. I don't know." I really didn't. "Do you think they'll expect me to be there?"

Mike shrugged his shoulders and looked at me helplessly. The blind leading the blind. I sighed wearily and resigned myself that I'd have to get up and move eventually anyway. "We might as well I guess."

Back to the big chamber outside Darius' office. We sat down and prepared to wait.

"Have you been a vampire long?" I asked, without really thinking. I know - you're shocked.

"Almost three years," he replied, looking down at his shoes.

"I'm sorry, Mike, I shouldn't have asked you that." I reached over and patted his arm.

"Nah, it's ok. I don't mind, really." He looked around the room at the other vampires waiting for their own turns with and audience with the Magistrate. "It's just, well…" he paused and adjusted his position, turning to face me a bit. "I'm not so much like these other guys, ya know?"

I nodded sympathetically and he continued. "Not that I'm knocking 'em or anything. For the most part, everyone's been really cool to me. But I, I don't know." He sighed heavily. Lowering his voice, he confided, "I just miss my human life. I miss my friends and my family and the ordinary everyday things I used to do. You know what I mean?"

"I can understand that, Mike. I'm sure all of these men and women went through the same thing at first."

"Well, that's just it. 'Cause they say I should be over that by now, that it's been long enough since I was turned. But I can't help it Hero, I just can't. I try not to complain about anything and I do everything I'm told, but I'm just not into being a vampire. I want to go to the movies, and I want to go hang out at the bar where my old buddies are, but I can't hang out with them no more."

"Why not?"

"'Cause I'm supposed to be dead, right? What would they think if they see me, and what if my fangs came down?"

"Well, isn't there a chance they'll see you anyway?"

"Nah, not really. I'm from Connecticut, see. When I got made, my maker brought me here so I could start over," he sighed again, "but I don't want to start over. I want my old life back."

"Oh, Mike, I'm so sorry. I really am." My eyes filled with tears for the poor young vampire. How awful it must be for him.

He shrugged self-consciously. "Aw, don't worry about me. I'm ok. Just kinda in a funk today, that's all. It's not completely awful. I just gotta try harder to start thinking like a vampire and being more like the others."

"You and Angel seem to get along ok," I mentioned with a smile, hoping to cheer him a little.

"Oh, yeah, Angel. He's cool. He's been really good to me and stuff. We got the same maker, so when I got brought up here Angel kinda took me under his wing. He's a good guy. Don't talk too much, but he's a good guy all the same."

"I'm sure he is," I said with a smile. "Try not to worry, Mike. You're a good guy too. You'll find your place eventually."

"Thanks," he said a bit sheepishly.

We fell into a companionable silence. As I looked about the room, I considered the vampires I saw there. None of them did seem to be like Mike, though I don't know how to explain how I could tell. Perhaps it was that they all seemed so confident and sure of themselves. Maybe it was because they interacted with each other with such ease. Whatever it was, I was glad Mike wasn't like them and I felt sad for the day when he would be.

The door to the inner sanctum opened and Kin walked out into the anteroom. I stood up abruptly, startling poor Mike, but caught myself in time to keep from calling out Kin's name.

Kin saw me at once and smiled broadly. Briskly, he walked through the group of vampires in waiting. "Oh, Hero, thank goodness you're alright." He took both of my hands in his and gently kissed my bruised cheek.

Mike blushed and inched away from us. "I'm fine, really. Mike has been taking good care of me," I announced, turning both our attentions to the shy vampire.

"Thank you, Mike. For everything. I heard you distinguished yourself quite well last night."

Raising my eyebrows, I turned to Mike for an explanation. He studied his feet once more. Boy, he must have been familiar with every stitch of his Converse. "I did ok," he said modestly.

"Ok? Hero, did you know that it was Mike who staked Nigel?"

Whoa! "Mike, really! My God, why didn't you tell me?"

"Dunno," he shrugged. "It's no big deal."

"Mike, maybe you don't know this, but Nigel was nearly 120 years old. You're still a fledgling. For you to have taken him down is nothing short of amazing. You should be proud of yourself."

"Yeah? You think?" he asked, his spirits perking up. "I hardly even remember it really, 'cause it's all sorta like a blur, ya know? It just happened. I knew the only way to stop him was to stake him and I grabbed a low branch from the tree and just, just…. Well, I just did it."

I wouldn't have dared tell him that Nigel was most likely weak from Hazel's bloodstone. Not just because I had sworn never to tell the secret of the stones, but because I wouldn't dream of taking the wind out of his sails. I was willing to bet that this was the very first time that Mike felt as though he'd done something to belong to the vampire clan. No. I wouldn't take that away from him for all the money in the world.

"You're too modest, Mike. That was quick thinking and you had to be strong and fierce against someone like Nigel," I said.

"Yeah?" he asked, his scrawny chest puffing out a bit. "Well, thanks, Hero. And you too, Kin. Thanks a lot." He was truly proud of himself and I was thrilled for him.

Kin clapped him on the shoulder and thanked him again for taking such good care of me. "You ready to go home?"

"What do you think?" I said sarcastically.

He smiled at me and in a matter of minutes we were in his SUV speeding towards my home on Georgia Road.

* * * * * * * * * * * * * * * * *

"Oh! That was so good. I really needed that," I moaned as I flung myself down on my brand new bed. Kin chuckled.

"Are you laughing at me?" I teased.

"Not really. Just happy I suppose."

"Good," I replied, smiling up at him.

Kin leaned over and kissed my forehead, then my cheek, and then my lips. "Mmm, you smell nice," he murmured.

"Well, I should hope so after a fifteen minute shower," I replied against his cheek. I loved the sound of his laugh, deep in his chest as he nuzzled my ear. He scooted over so that his body was pressed against the full length of mine and drew me close to him. I moaned for a much different reason this time and my mouth sought out his. "I think I'm going to end up needing another shower," I said playfully after a long, passionate kiss.

"No doubt about it," my lover replied.

"Kin," I said, quite seriously. "Is it always going to be like this?"

"You bet," he said as he slid his hand inside my damp robe.

"No," I said with a laugh. I pretended to swat his hand away, but we both knew I didn't want him to stop. "I mean all this, well, stuff."

He lifted his head and laughed at me. "Would you care to elaborate on 'stuff'?"

Raising my arms, I buried my hands into his soft thick hair. "All this vampire stuff. Secrets and battles and other kinds of beings that I never knew were real?"

Kin nodded. "Yup, probably. That's part of dating a vampire."

"Isn't that just my luck? To be the first in my crowd to become an expert on dating vampires?" I asked, dripping with sarcasm.

"An expert? Mmmm? Not quite yet. I still have some secrets you don't know."

"Really? Like what?" Kin was on top of me now and I had my arms around him and one leg crooked over his.

"Oh, lots," he crooned as he nipped my neck gently.

"Will you share your secrets with me?" I asked, my voice husky with passion.

"Do you want me to?" he asked in response.

"I want to share everything with you," I declared quite honestly, arching my back to press myself against him.

"Then I will," he said after another passionate kiss. "I'll share everything with you if you'll let me."

"Yes," I said breathlessly.

Kin pulled my robe fully open, then changed position so he could finish undressing himself, raining kisses in my face and body as he did. Then he pulled me back to him, holding me so tightly it was almost too much.

"Hero, can I tell you a secret? Something I've been wanting to tell you?"

"Of course," I said, almost delirious with desire.

He pressed his hand against my cheek and looked deeply into my eyes. "I love you, Hero. I love you with all my heart."

My eyes filled with tears. I was happier than I could ever remember. "I love you too," I said hoarsely.

"And it will always be that way," he added, before he began ravaging me. "Always."

—

About The Author

Kerry Rockwood White is a happily married mother of two who lives on the South Shore of Massachusetts. Much Ado About Russian is her first published novel, though she has been writing off and on most of her adult life. She is also a graphic artist that designs and sells under the name KRW Designs and is particularly known for her faerie and fantasy work.

You can connect with the author and fans at:

www.FairHeroSeries.com

See her artwork at:

www.Zazzle.com/KRWDesigns

Get Official Fair Hero Merchandise at:

www.Zazzle.com/FairHeroSeries

www.ingramcontent.com/pod-product-compliance
Lightning Source LLC
Chambersburg PA
CBHW030028180626
46810CB00001B/262